TIME'S CLAWS

A DINOSAUR DOMAIN THRILLER
BY EDWARD J. MCFADDEN III

SEVEREDPRESS

TIME'S CLAWS

"Death comes to all, but great achievements build a monument which shall endure until the sun grows cold." - Ralph Waldo Emerson

PROLOGUE

East of Cahokia, North America, *morning, 1019 CE, during the time of the Medieval Warm Period*

As the sun ascended, painting the horizon with hues of amber and gold, Ahanu and his companions embraced the revelry that echoed the heartbeat of their ancient traditions. Beating drums chanted through the leaf-bare trees and the scent of smoke from the ceremonial flame carried on the chill winter breeze. Faint snowflakes, like dust, swirled and eddied through the forest, the group's breathing fogging the air.

Ahanu's feet were freezing. He'd wrapped his leather moccasins in buffalo hide and fur, and his leggings and cloak were thick, but the wind found every gap in his animal skin armor. A sculpted bone fragment held back long dark hair, and Ahanu's face was painted with the ceremonial colors of his people. He wore no regalia, or beads, though some of the older teens had the beginnings of beadwork on their clothing and small feathers in their hair.

The group of younglings had snuck away from the festivities to partake in *tula-pah*, an alcoholic drink conjured by the elders and used to find spiritual enlightenment. The naturally fermented corn liquor was also a valuable source of nutrients, and its consumption was a regular rite of passage.

Mato, whose name meant bear, had supplied the gourd container of fermented spirits. The newly met group of friends had come to the powwow from *kothas* all around the territory for the ceremonial dances and feast, and it was Ahanu's first time participating in the festivities.

"How long have you been here?" asked Petaquao in Ahanu's dialect of their common tongue.

Ahanu's heart pounded. Was she asking him? Petaquao was bundled beneath her parka, and only her round face was visible, but still the heat of her beauty warmed his chest.

"Two days," said Mato as he handed Petaquao the gourd.

She smiled demurely, then brought the container to her lips and took a long pull.

Mato's eyes went wide, and a wolfish grin leaked over his face. An intricate pattern of red and blue paint covered his rough features, which included a long beak of a nose that looked like it had been broken more than once.

Ahanu's heart sank. Of course, she wasn't talking to him, but when she smiled at him the sun baked his face and his stomach churned as if beset by maggots.

Petaquao tried to hand Ahanu the gourd and Mato stopped her.

The others in the group looked at the ground, gazed at the tops of the tall trees, and studied their gloved hands.

Ahanu said nothing. Did nothing.

"He who laughs isn't very funny," Mato said.

His name meant 'he laughs' and his parents had chosen the name because as an infant Ahanu hadn't cried, but constantly laughed. That wasn't the case any longer. Mato was older, bigger, and more experienced, and if the elders were asked to settle a dispute between the two teens, Mato's age, family standing, and aggressiveness would win him the day. Ahanu said nothing.

"This little crow doesn't speak?" Mato asked. Then he shifted his attention to Petaquao and added, "A little boy without a tongue."

Rage colored Ahanu's vision red. His hand shot out and snatched the gourd from Petaquao.

Mato raised a fist, but Petaquao stepped in front of him, her face etched with... anger? Frustration? Hatred?

Ahanu brought the spout of the gourd to his lips and drank deeply. The hot liquid seared his throat, and he coughed, spitting up the elixir along with saliva and chunks of fry bread he'd eaten upon waking. The liquor sprayed out his nose, his head on fire, eyes watering as he fought to regain his composure.

Laughter echoed through the forest, Mato's guffawing rising above the crowd's rumble.

Petaquao took Ahanu's arm and asked, "Are you alright?"

Ahanu's world spun and Petaquao's face blurred as Mato and the others laughed.

The drumbeats grew faster and louder, and now a voice sang an ancient melody of the sun and the moon and the timelessness of the stars and sky.

Mato snatched away the *tula-pah*, and Ahanu made the first major mistake of his young life. With liquid courage urging him on, anger painting tiny starbursts across his field of vision, and the ghosts of his ancestors raging about honor filling his head, Ahanu punched Mato in the jaw. Pain ran up his arm and settled in his neck, and suddenly the cold breeze felt like a bone-rattling gale.

The laughter stopped and all eyes turned to Mato, whose mouth hung open, his eyes wide as walnut shells. He handed off the gourd and balled his hands into fists.

Ahanu had a moment to consider his mistake before the strike came. A colossal blow that snapped Ahanu's head back. He lost his balance, danced with his arms out as he tried to stay on his feet, then hit the cold hardpan, his face smacking a tree root.

The daylight grew brighter and faded in sharp bursts as the laughter returned. Ahanu felt the hot trickle of blood on his face as he looked up and saw Mato finishing the *tula-pah*.

Petaquao surged forward to help Ahanu, her face creased with concern. Warmth leaked through Ahanu. She cared for him. She—

A vicious kick to the head made the world spin and dissolve. The last thing Ahanu saw as the world turned dark was Mato grabbing Petaquao by the arm and pulling her away, the look of concern on her face having been replaced with one of horror.

When Ahanu regained consciousness, he was still lying on the frozen ground, a thin coating of snow covering him. He was alone, the singing had stopped, and even the drumbeats had faded to a dull throb that couldn't compete with his galloping heart. White smoke snaked through the forest, the snow nothing more than tiny ice crystals that sparkled like diamonds in the thick columns of light that angled through the woods.

He forced himself to sit up, his head ringing, corn liquor and bile creeping up his throat, his swollen cheek pulsing with sharp pain. But none of that hurt as much as the shame and dishonor that gnawed at his chest, threatening to leave him hollow.

Mato had marked him as weak. A coward. And Petaquao had seen it all.

Anger drove him to his feet, and Ahanu threaded through the forest in search of the others, but they were gone. The smoke grew thicker, and his eyes stung as ghosts danced with the shadows and voices from the past lectured about how much trouble he would be in if he missed the sun dance ceremony. His mother wouldn't speak to him, but his father... If his only son, the son he would train to someday take his place in the ceremony wasn't present, it would bring his father great shame, and him much pain.

The trees grew sparse as the land rose in elevation, and when Ahanu arrived at the standing stones the ceremonial fire was nothing but embers and the ceremony was over. Smoke poured over the hilltop, weaving through the tall upright wooden logs arranged in a circle around the triangular ruins, each log placed at an equal distance from the others.

A few stragglers milled about, most folks having moved down to the northern meadow where preparations were underway for the day's feast and the evening moon dance. Ahanu walked around the circle of wooden poles, their shadows marking the coming of the endless night.

Sunlight bled through the triangle of tall standing stones, glimmering walls of white filling many of the gaps. The monolithic rocks were so worn by the elements that most of the symbols and writing the elders preached about had been long washed away. A broken standing half-circle of pink rocks was the highlight of the eastern boundary, and around it, the tall pillars had crumbled into piles of broken stones.

A faint roar carried over the hilltop.

The remains of the fire crackled and popped, and smoke filled the air.

Another wail of anger, much louder, and angst knotted Ahanu's stomach.

The ground trembled.

Ahanu stared down at his feet and put his hand to his face. Was this real? If so, the gods were truly displeased. Terror rooted him to the ground. If this was what the corn liquor did, then—

A raccoon darted from the smoke, paused for an instant as it turned its rat-like head in Ahanu's direction, and then scampered away. The pain in his stomach eased. It was only Azeban, the trickster.

He rubbed his eyes as fingers of smoke swirled through the ruins, and dark ash and icy specks of snow glittered in the curtain of refracted light angling through the half circle of pink stones.

A gust of wind gathered the smoke like a chieftain's cape, and the ground shook as a creature straight from Ahanu's nightmares stuck its lizard-like head through the standing stones, its jaws open in a rictus of fury as the beast searched for prey.

The great beast surged through the smoke with a burst of violence, a glassy-eyed monster that was twenty paces long from the end of its tail to the tip of its elongated snout. A mangy fuzz covered the beast's back, its alligator skin covered in quill-like spikes that looked like the beginnings of feathers, and black streaks ran across the beast's torso and down its long muscular tail. The monster's stocky legs pumped, its short arms meek and absurd by comparison.

Ahanu's mouth fell open. Fear massaged his stomach, but it was awe, excitement, and exhilaration that kept him from running. Seeing something from the legends. A creature that should not be. What had they done to bring on the wrath of the gods?

An arrow whizzed through the air and hit the creature in the chest. The animal's eyes tracked the broken arrow as it fell to the ground. The stone-tipped projectile hadn't left a mark on the beast's rough exterior.

The giant lizard wailed as it swung its head, searching for the source of the arrow.

Ahanu escaped his paralysis and ran.

A severe drop in elevation and a sparse copse of trees separated the standing stones from the feasting grounds, and Ahanu saw people milling about a series of fires. He threw himself forward, his knees threatening to come unhinged, his throat burning as he half jumped, half ran down the hillside, weaving between the barren trees.

The smoke thinned and members of his tribe appeared before him. The warriors held bows, spears, and tomahawks.

Ahanu ran through the men and ignored their pleas for information. He needed to find his parents.

The ground shuddered as the massive creature trundled down the hillside, knocking over dead trees and crashing through the underbrush. Bowstrings twanged, men yelled, and the sizzle of spears knifing through the air rose above the push of the wind that carried the sweet scent of smoke and charred venison.

Retreating warriors overtook Ahanu, and as the group broke free of the trees, they were met by chieftains who wore elaborate beaded parkas and decorative headdresses filled with feathers, beads, precious stones, and animal bones.

Orders were given, arrows were notched to bowstrings, spears with sharp stone tips were readied to be thrown, and knives, clubs, and tomahawks were brandished by every adult with the ability to fight.

Ahanu faded into the crowd of onlookers, the elderly leading the younglings and the frail away from the feasting grounds to the scree pile of tumbled stones at the base of the hill where they could hide.

A long snout pushed from the trees at the edge of the glade, the creature's mouth hanging open, thick ribbons of saliva dripping through two-foot teeth. The massive monster pushed from the trees, the sound of cracking wood like miniature explosions.

With a screech from a chieftain, bows sang, spears flew, and the warriors chanted as they pressed forward, a wall of humanity filled with anger intent on defending that which they loved.

Ahanu fled with the others until he saw Petaquao watching him. Shame heated his stomach, his swollen cheek tingling with cold pain, and he stopped running. This was his chance to show his worth. To act. To speak with deeds instead of words. He would be brave and make his father proud, and Petaquao...

He let loose with a battle cry as he ran toward the beast, lost in the moment. Ahanu had no weapon, no fighting skills, and he still couldn't believe what his eyes were showing him.

The beast reached the center of the clearing and reared back, fighting off the arrows and spears that bounced off its armored skin. An arrow found one of the creature's eyes, and the monster jerked and thrashed, its massive tail taking out several warriors as they tried to get in close.

A huge man wielding an axe with a long handle ran toward the beast, screaming, axe raised. The warrior's fur cloak fluttered behind him, his chest bare, his face painted in the likeness of a wolf.

The lizard's head darted forward, and its jaws snapped, but the warrior dodged and changed direction, and the jaws caught air.

Ahanu, realizing he had no weapon, no size or experience, and courage born of *tula-pah*, skidded to a halt.

The charging warrior jumped onto a broken pillar of stone and launched into the air, a mighty leap as he brought the long axe down between the monster's eyes.

A shriek pierced the day, and the beast thrashed, but the razor-sharp stone axe head was embedded in bone and the warrior hung on, the beast swinging the man around like a children's toy.

The monster slowed, and its muscles spasmed and trembled as its rear legs gave out and the creature collapsed.

A *pop* echoed over the clearing as the warrior extracted his axe and went to work, the axe head a blur, the warrior's shouts urging the others on. Spears impaled the creature's underbelly as axes slashed and cut, blood painting the green grass of the feasting grounds crimson.

The huge corpse deflated, and a rancid cloud of air pushed across the clearing.

One by one the tribe members stopped hacking at the creature. They stood around the dead beast, their animal skins speckled with blood, the remains of the giant lizard's glassy eyes staring into the next world.

The beast's jaws flexed open, a blast of air streamed from within, and spittle covered the crowd, but it was the final command of a dying brain.

When Ahanu noticed Petaquao at his side, he took her hand and smiled.

1

Hicks Dome, Illinois, *5:19 PM CST, June 20th, 2022*

Dust and grit filled the air, and Marshall Stanton squinted as he mounted the stepladder and climbed from the shallow hole that contained the intact Tyrannosaurus fossil. Wooden frames marked sections of the find, flags set boundaries, multi-colored elevation and measurement lines crisscrossed the trench, and plywood and tall stakes shored up the sidewalls.

"Do you mind carrying that?" Fiona asked. Marshall was hauling her bag of tools which contained trowels, picks, brushes, her datapad, and a laser sight.

"What else is there for me to do?" he said. Fiona was a famous paleontologist. He was just a lowly Assistant Professor of Military History along for the ride. Marshall specialized in the Western Theater of the American Revolutionary War, and the only reason he cared about dinosaur fossils was because Fiona found the long-dead beasties fascinating. So, when the opportunity to join his wife on a dig presented itself, he conjured up a travel grant to do fieldwork on the Battle of St. Louis.

"Don't say that," she said.

Marshall edged over the lip of the hole, tossed the bag of tools, and climbed up onto terra firma. He extended a hand to help Fiona, but she didn't take it.

Tall grass whispered and sighed in the early summer breeze, canvas flapped, and the chatter of researchers carried over the field. A tent village surrounded the hole, and vehicles and excavation equipment sat silent.

A short, fat man wearing an Indiana Jones-like fedora approached and asked, "Anything new down there today, Fiona?" Greg Knapp was the lead investigator and controlled the grant that funded the dig.

"A few more Native American artifacts," she said. "Some arrowheads, pottery shards, decorated bone fragments."

Greg smiled. "More to support the dating of the Tyrannosaur finding?"

"It would appear so," she said.

The paleontologists working on the dig were as giddy as children on Christmas Eve. Marshall didn't know all the lingo, but he was married to a self-proclaimed dinosaur nerd, so he knew enough to understand that the Tyrannosaur find was an extreme anomaly. The fossil and all the newly discovered Native American artifacts were roughly a thousand years down in the geologic strata, and that was no place for an animal that disappeared from Earth eons ago.

"I've got to update the logbooks," Fiona said as she glanced at a crowd of colleagues opening the day's first bottle of wine.

Marshall picked up her bag of tools and said, "I'll drop your gear at the car, and then I'm going to check out what's happening up top. The dance this morning was cool. Then I'll be back." He needed a break from bones, the past, Fiona's colleagues, and wine.

She smiled, but he could tell it was forced.

As he dropped Fiona's bag off at the car, Marshall caught a glimpse of his disheveled reflection in the sideview mirror. His short brown hair was tousled, his face smudged with dirt, and a three-day-old salt-and-pepper beard covered his cheeks and chin. His gray eyes were bloodshot, shadowed by the exhaustion etched into his features. As he attempted to smooth his hair and wipe away the grime, a dull ache climbed up his back. He grabbed his water bottle and backpack and headed up the hillside toward the Dome, trying to recall everything Fiona had told him about the place.

At over three hundred feet above the surrounding terrain, the uplifted rocks that made-up Hicks Dome provided an awesome view. The Dome was composed of Paleozoic sedimentary rocks, including limestone, shale, and sandstone, providing a geological record dating back hundreds of millions of years. It was believed by the bigheads that the Dome resulted from the buckling of the Earth's crust due to the compression of tectonic plates, or from some other seismic change beneath the Earth's crust.

Both sides of the path were packed with undergrowth, and shadows writhed as rustling leaves argued with the spirits of those who had called the area home for thousands of years. A bright gleam caught Marshall's eye, and he paused, sipping water as he peered into the perpetual dusk beneath the deep green tree canopy.

Marshall left the path, the scent of smoke tickling his nose, the smell of earthen moisture fighting for prominence. Kudzu and pricker vines with two-inch stiletto-like barbs filled the gaps between tree trunks, but Marshall zigzagged through the forest, avoiding thickets, but always working his way toward the light that sparkled like a diamond in the grayness.

The thump of drums leaked through the woods like a beating heart.

A wall of kudzu blocked his way, and he swept it aside so he could make his way through the vines.

The face of a stone monster stared at Marshall, and he fell back as his breath caught in his throat. He chuckled and cleared away the greenery.

An ancient six-foot statue covered in kudzu, its finer features long gone, loomed over Marshall. Chiseled from a chunk of gray stone that stuck from the ground like a rotten tooth, the figure appeared to be that of an animal standing on its hind legs. The creature had no forward arms, and its legs had lost all definition. Its visage was an eyeless, mouthless, blank slate of rock that had broken off at the halfway point, but it was the crown that caught the light. Embedded in the ancient stone atop the statuette's head were chunks of quartz that caught the rays of the setting sun.

From behind Marshall came a chilly male voice. "The local tribal councils didn't renovate the Shokra because they didn't want conspiracy theorists churning up the Dome."

Marshall spun around, all the warning lights on his mental dashboard flashing red.

An old man dressed in the traditional Native American garb of deer skins stepped from the shadows, the multicolored beads covering his headdress and collar standing out against the wall of green foliage. Hazel eyes studied Marshall like he was going to climb up the statue and pry the quartz stones out with the knife clipped to his belt.

"Excuse me?" was all Marshall could force out.

The man said nothing as a smile leaked over his face.

"Why would conspiracy theorists find an old, unrecognizable statue of interest?"

"That is the question, isn't it? My name is Iruno. Welcome, though greeting guests is no longer my responsibility."

"Marshall." He took a sip of water and looked around. He and Iruno were alone in the woods, with the sounds of drumming and singing echoing through the trees.

"You ask why those seeking purpose and knowledge of the unknown would come here? Have you heard of Monks Mound? Woodhenge?"

"Sure," Marshall said.

"Then you know there are a series of... the remains of exceptional structures and cities in the area," Iruno said.

Marshall nodded. He knew that Monks Mound, a Native American earthworks pyramid north of St. Louis, was approximately the same size at its base as the Great Pyramid of Giza, which was why Marshall remembered the name. He didn't know much else, so to be polite he asked, "What's Woodhenge? A Stonehenge made of wood?"

Iruno's eyes widened as he licked his lips. "Closer to the mark than you may know. Like the replica surrounding the Chaka Stones, the Cahokia Woodhenge was a series of large timber circles located next to Monks Mound constructed over a thousand years ago. The site was discovered in the early 1960s when the interstate came through." Iruno sighed. "The ceremonial Woodhenge atop the Dome has been used to investigate archeoastronomy, and that's why the annual equinox and solstice events are held at the site."

Marshall glanced at the statue covered in kudzu.

"Things at the Dome are usually very... subdued, and rarely is there a stir about the site outside the local population. I assume you know why so few of my people are still here?"

The wind gusted, and smoke snaked through the trees.

Marshall's gaze shifted to the ground. After the U.S. government implemented its Indian Removal policy in the early 19th century, the descendants of most tribes were forcefully relocated to new territory.

"Nobody cared about this place except a few rockhounds, and that's how the locals liked it. All that changed when the demon was discovered," Iruno said.

"That's a Tyrannosaur fossil, not a demon."

"Summer squash or winter squash."

At first, Marshall didn't understand what the man meant, but then said, "Ah, tomato, tomahto."

Iruno smiled. "A legend of my people tells of a great demon summoned by the gods and made of smoke and the ashes of the dead. It's said that after a fierce battle, the beast was slain, but my people left its bones in the ceremonial field as a reminder to not anger the gods."

Marshall held back a chuckle. Insulting folk's spiritual beliefs was a nonstarter. "Is there any proof of this?"

"You white men and your proof. Do you believe in nothing you cannot sense?" Iruno's question sounded like an accusation. "You may find the proof you seek above where those like you have scrubbed the stone clean of time."

Those like me? He said, "Each to his own."

With that, the conversation died a natural death, and Iruno said, "Be well, and perhaps we will meet again in the clearing at the end of the path."

Marshall thought the man meant the actual path, but as a smirk leaked over Iruno's face he realized the man was making a metaphysical reference.

Crows cawed as Marshall headed back to the trail, and he was panting after climbing the last hundred feet to the crest of the Dome where he paused to catch his breath. The view of the surrounding area was dramatic, and the field where the demon's fossil was being excavated could be seen below. He snickered. Demon. Smoke filtered through the standing stones, and the music and dancing drew Marshall on.

The wind murmured and a hushed reverence settled over the assembled crowd. Marshall stood on the outskirts and thought of Fiona. She had no interest in this, but still…

A fire raged at the center of the Chaka Stones, and the moon dance was about to begin. The ritual was a sacred ceremony that connected the tribe with the cosmos, an ancient tradition that had been passed down through generations and went hand in hand with the sun dance.

Drums beat in a chaotic rhythm that mimicked the pulse of the Earth. The dancers, adorned in vibrant regalia, gyrated in harmony with the drumming, their movements a living prayer.

As Marshall watched, he was filled with a deep sense of connection to something greater than himself. Like an approaching thunderstorm, an energy crackled in the air, a tangible force separating the earthly realm from the ethereal. The sun, now a fiery orb sinking below the lip of the Dome, cast long shadows that danced alongside the performers.

A shaman, adorned in intricate beadwork and feathers, took center stage. His weathered face was scarred with wisdom, and his eyes gleamed with *tula-pah*. He raised his hands to the sky, an invocation to the spirits. The drumbeats fell silent, and a collective breath was held.

As the dancers circled the fire, the flames flickered and leaped, painting intricate patterns on the Chaka Stones. The scent of burning sage wafted through the air, cleansing the site, and inviting the presence of benevolent spirits.

In his mind's eye Marshall saw visions of a time long past—warriors on horseback, the land untouched by progress. In that moment he understood. The sun dance was not just a performance; it was a way for the tribe to commune with their long-gone ancestors and honor the spirits that guided them.

As the ceremony reached its climax, the dancers moved with increasing intensity. The beating of drums resumed, growing faster and louder, the sun a sliver on the horizon.

Then the shaman raised his arms one final time. Gasps swept through the crowd as the drums fell silent and the chanting stopped.

As the last echoes of the drums faded, Marshall remained rooted to the ground like one of the ancient standing stones. The dance ended, but its afterimages lingered.

The chatter of spectators stirred Marshall from his reverie as the crowd broke up. He sensed someone watching him, and he turned to find a tall slender man dressed in Bermuda shorts and wearing an obnoxious multi-colored shirt giving him the hairy eyeball. The guy looked away when Marshall locked in on him.

Others milled about, but most folks headed for the path and their cars and would go on to cookouts and tribal gatherings. A woman with long red hair consoled a bored teenager, and several people sat cross-legged before the dying fire, eyes closed.

The triangle of standing stones grew dim as the sun inched toward its disappearance. He walked through the Chaka Stones, examining their worn surfaces. An old man wearing a cowboy hat nodded to him as he meandered through the standing half-circle of pink rocks that marked the eastern boundary of the ruins.

A law officer answered questions, her short blonde hair pulled back, her sunglasses dangling from the pocket of her uniform shirt below her gold badge. A couple kissed, their matching red t-shirts identifying them as part of the fossil hunter group. Marshall thought their names were Terry and Ann, but they didn't acknowledge him as he passed.

One of the tallest standing stones had a ribbon of yellow tape surrounding a section that was much lighter in color than the stele's main shade. Iruno's words came rushing back. "You may find the proof you seek above where those like you have scrubbed the stone clean of time." Marshall dropped to a knee and looked around like he was about to steal something, then used his cellphone light to illuminate the highlighted section.

The area had been treated, perhaps with a laser or chemical, which had removed all the surface dirt without causing further wear to the bas-relief. The cellphone light highlighted the contours and high points, and it appeared that a protective coating had been applied to shield the restored section from the elements.

To Marshall's untrained eye, the series of curved lines, oblong circles, and dashes resembled a standing lizard drawn by a kindergartener. It looked like Barney, but it was hard to see, and many pieces were missing. It was like a cloud resembling a shape your mind wanted to see. Was he looking at a Rorschach test? Was his imagination playing tricks on him? He blinked, and when he stared at the spot again, all he saw were curved lines, a circle, and triangles.

He rose and wandered through the Chaka Stones, the standing half-circle of pinkish blocks looming before him.

As the final glare of the dying day drained from the Dome, a spark of light, like a tiny dying flame, appeared within the broken circle of stones.

The sun sank below the horizon, leaving a bruised sky, and the first stars appeared, pinpricks on a vast gray canvas. Marshall felt a profound sense of gratitude, humility, and relief.

A shriek, like paper tearing, carried on the breeze, and Marshall went in search of its source.

2

Overwhelming dizziness, a mind-numbing throbbing that shook his innards, and a flash of white that winked out to blackness.

Marshall jerked to a stop and stood transfixed, his heart hammering in his chest, his head ringing so loud it hurt. The tips of his fingers and toes tingled and his mouth was dry as cotton. He lifted his water bottle and drank.

Darkness pressed in on the Chaka Stones, and backlit clouds hid the stars and moon. Dusk had drained from the world in a heartbeat. A tremor of fear and worry ran through him, then drained away as a cool evening breeze laden with the scent of woodsmoke pushed over the Dome.

Voices carried up the hillside.

The embers of the ceremonial fire glowed orange at the center of the standing stones, but the ring of tall wooden poles surrounding the ruins was hidden by darkness. He saw no others, and not even a bird or squirrel revealed themselves. The air was heavy with humidity, and the unfamiliar calls of animals echoed over the hilltop.

He tracked the voices as he threaded through the standing stones, and he noticed several smaller rock formations that he hadn't seen before. The piles of stones were arranged within the ruins and formed a secondary triangle.

Marshall's skin itched, and the intense sensation of being watched washed over him. He stared down the northern slope, searching for the headlights that should have illuminated the dig site, and listening for the cackle and murmur of partying researchers, but all was dark and quiet. There were no signs of campfires and the voices he'd heard only moments before had gone silent.

It was then he realized there were no lights on the horizon in any direction. The Dome overlooked the surrounding land and as Marshall turned three hundred and sixty degrees, he didn't see a single light in the stygian darkness surrounding the Chaka Stones.

He pulled his cellphone and swiped until the light app came on. As he did, he checked for service, and there was nothing in the upper left corner but dashes. Marshall frowned. Not even the fraudulent letters of an intermittent Internet signal?

The night symphony was going full tilt, but when he listened hard, he heard no planes rumbling overhead, no hum of vehicles on the interstate, nothing but the night world.

His cell light illuminated an enormous cluster of tropical foliage that spilled over several of the standing stones, and a spray of small birds erupted from within. How hadn't he noticed the plants before? It had huge round leaves two feet in diameter with a tall stigma surrounded by tiny white flowers that glowed in the darkness. Under the cellphone light's unflinching gaze, he saw that more odd plant life had encroached into the standing stones as if five years of neglect had befallen the Chaka Stones with the falling of the sun.

A primordial screech tore through the night.

The ground trembled, and a low growl reverberated through the standing stones.

Another roar and the night creatures fell silent. There was shouting, but Marshall couldn't make out the words. The rhythmic thud of footsteps grew louder, the ground shaking.

Panic gripped Marshall as a gigantic creature emerged from the thick foliage, the likes of which he had only seen in the many documentaries he'd watched with Fiona.

It was the Tyrant Lizard King, a colossal monstrosity of nature, its massive form framed against the Chaka Stones. The beast's scale-like skin was black in the murky moonlight that filtered through the cloud cover, and its massive tail swung in a lazy arc that stirred up dust and grit. Angular jaws lined with dagger-like teeth smiled, the monster's enormous head held high as the beast surveyed its surroundings with shining softball-sized eyes.

He felt like a spider creeping across the carpet when the lights came on, and he shut down his phone light and slipped the device into a pocket. Despite Marshall's instincts screaming at him to push forward, to find some hidden reserve of strength, he remained motionless, hoping the creature wouldn't see him. Suddenly Marshall wished he'd paid more attention when Fiona rambled on about the prehistoric beasties. Did they have good eyesight? Smell? How could they know? Surely the bigheads had guesses, but what they were he didn't know.

The Tyrannosaur's bright eyes locked on Marshall, its nostrils flared, and the monster's massive legs propelled it forward with a speed that defied its size.

Primitive instincts stabbed Marshall's stomach and he darted through the standing stones, the crack of snapping jaws driving him onward as he launched himself over the lip of the Dome. The hillside fell away before him as he landed, and the canopy above cast shifting shadows that played tricks on his frayed nerves.

Trees snapped, rocks tumbled, and the heavy breathing of the beast overcame Marshall like a wave. The terrain grew treacherous as he worked his way down the hillside, the ground slick with moisture from the tropical undergrowth, the hillside trembling with each of the massive beast's footfalls.

Marshall spared a glance over his shoulder and saw the beast's head thrust through two tall trees, the Tyrannosaur's primary weapon, its mouth, lowered to the ground as it prepared to strike.

Dense tropical greenery created a chaotic labyrinth around him, and leaves slapped his face and palm fronds slashed at his arms as Marshall navigated through the towering ferns and palm-like trees. His breaths came in ragged gasps, adrenaline fueling his desperate attempt to escape as he leaped over logs and jagged rocks. He sensed the fury of the creature behind him, its hunger driving it closer, but Marshall refused to be devoured by the jaws of fate.

Fate. The realization that he wasn't lost in a dream or playing a virtual reality game crashed home with a finality that weakened his resolve. The past was no longer a distant concept confined to history books and research papers; it was a tangible, perilous reality.

Marshall's legs burned with the effort of maintaining his breakneck pace on the uneven obstacle-ridden slope. Vines and roots conspired against him, attempting to trip him up at every turn. He dodged between stumpy trees with Hosta-like leaves, each step depleting his insignificant energy reserve.

He stumbled, his foot catching on a root hidden beneath a patch of moss. Marshall tumbled forward, his heart lurching in his chest as the forest floor rushed up to meet him. He hit the ground with a bone-jarring impact, pain momentarily crippling him. But he refused to surrender, and he pushed himself to his feet, his muscles screaming in protest as he fought to regain his footing.

The Tyrannosaurus loomed ever closer, its massive jaws poised to claim its prize.

Marshall ran into a grove of odd plants that looked like giant clusters of white broccoli. Beams of moonlight pierced the clouds like spotlights, and he caught a glimpse of a cluster of boulders.

He veered in the direction of the stones, the beast struggling through the dense jungle behind him, the world shaking like a minor earthquake was in progress. As Marshall approached the boulders, a plan formed in his mind—a desperate gamble that might be his only chance.

The hillside grew steeper. Thick clouds obscured the moon, and the gloom was replaced with blackness.

Marshall reached the boulders and climbed the steep pile. The jagged rocks shifted underfoot, but he pressed on, muscles straining until he reached the top.

Unable to make the climb, the Tyrannosaurus snarled in frustration and skidded to a halt.

Marshall took a moment to catch his breath, his chest heaving.

The dinosaur screamed as it lurched back into motion and strode along the base of the rock pile, its blazing eyes searching for a path to its prey.

Marshall spotted a narrow opening in the rocks, a crevice wide enough for him to slip into. He jumped from boulder to boulder, maneuvering towards the hiding spot while the Tyrannosaurus roared.

A shrill squawk made Marshall stop halfway to his goal.

The dinosaur paused in its pacing.

A creature standing three feet tall and measuring roughly ten feet in length crawled from between two large stones. Its body was covered in brown and gray feathers, and a long, wide, beaver-like tail was planted to the ground like a third leg. The beast looked like a huge bird, and its forelimbs were equipped with three-fingered hands, each bearing six-inch sickle-shaped talons. A riot of colored feathers of all lengths jutted from the animal's head at random angles, and some were frayed and broken. Its head bobbed and darted like a chicken as a purple tongue snaked out from between rows of needle-like teeth.

Marshall backed away, arms outstretched, palms out in the universal sign of 'calm down'. The animal didn't have wings, but the way its muscles rippled beneath its feathers and the graceful way with which it moved told Marshall that, unlike the Tyrannosaurs who were limited due to their size and the densely packed forest, he wouldn't be able to outrun this creature.

The Tyrannosaurus watched the spectacle with eager eyes.

As the newcomer inched forward, tongue edging through glowing teeth, it hissed.

Marshall saw a stone the size of a baseball, and he lowered himself to the ground and snatched it up.

With a violent squeal and a toss of its head, the creature came forward. Marshall thought the monster was a Deinonychus, a carnivorous dinosaur believed to have lived during the Cretaceous period. Fiona had an artist's rendition of one of the creatures on her office wall back at the university.

The rock in Marshall's hand went cold, and invisible spiders crawled all over his skin. His mind crashed under an overload of conflicting and unbelievable information, and he sucked on his lips, uncertainty and indecision holding him in place.

Two more Deinonychus moved in, one from the right, the other left. He looked over his shoulder and all he saw was boulders and darkness.

The three dinosaurs came together like side roads merging onto a single thoroughfare. Tongues licked the air, saliva dripped to the hardpan, and as the creatures came on Marshall heaved his stone.

With a *pop*, the rock connected with the skull of the alpha leading the trio.

A cackle that sounded too much like a laugh to Marshall floated up from where the Tyrannosaurus had worked its way halfway up the pile of stones.

The two new arrivals paused for an instant as the alpha reared back and released an earsplitting wail.

Marshall turned tail and ran, his legs pistoning as he sprang from stone to stone.

All three monsters lunged after him.

Marshall jumped atop a large boulder, and ran across it, the three Deinonychus in his wake climbing and bounding over one another like a horde of rats competing for the last chunk of cheese.

To his right, a steep slope packed with basketball-sized stones tumbled down into the jungle, and to his left, the huge stone cracked boulder rose like a cliff face. There was nowhere to go but forward, and there was no time left anyway.

Talons scraped on stone, and a roaring chorus of growling and hissing and clicking surged over Marshall like a gust of wind.

Darkness loomed ahead as he reached the edge of the massive boulder and leaped into the void, the cold air rushing past him as the abyss swallowed him.

Three sets of jaws snapped at Marshall's heels.

But he was already airborne, his body hurtling off the boulder into the unknown.

Time stood still as Marshall plummeted, wind rushing through his hair, his eyes watering.

He crashed through a canopy of evergreen trees, branches snapping like brittle bones as he grasped for handholds and tried to stop his fall. Tiny sharp leaves bit his face, and he landed atop a broad evergreen branch. It snapped from the trunk, and Marshall was falling again, but he'd slowed significantly.

Twisting and turning like a cat that's been dropped upside-down, Marshall grasped at branches, sharp leaves tearing his palms. He crashed to a halt in a lush patch of underbrush, his head smacking a stone.

Screaming and yelling... unknown voices...

Marshall lay there, his breaths coming in ragged gasps. But then, as the echoes of the Tyrannosaurus faded, he realized he was alive. That he knew for sure because there was no way a dead person could feel so much pain.

More yelling and the beasts of the night bitched and argued, but the ground stopped shaking. Reality's colors ran black and white, and the chime in Marshall's head reached a crescendo. His vision flickered, then retreated into blackness, and his eyes saw no more.

3

The sound of muffled voices and a calamity of cackles, bleats, and titters brought Marshall awake. Pink filled his field of vision, warmth heating his face, his head throbbing with a frenzied yet steady beat. He realized his eyes were closed and Marshall kept them squeezed shut. To open them would require accepting what he saw, and as the memories came flooding back, he wasn't sure he wanted that. Not yet, anyway.

Shuffling feet, a curse of pain, and the surface on which he lay shifted and swayed, and he felt his body roll as ropes bit into his arms and legs. More murmuring and worried chatter.

A bloodthirsty howl zapped the synopsis of his nerves, and Marshall's eyes unwillingly snapped open.

Blue sky, clouds, then a tanned and dirty face. Brown eyes stared at Marshall as a smile swept across the careworn visage.

"He's awake," the face said as if from underwater.

Then Marshall felt himself falling as his stretcher was placed on the ground.

But he didn't stop falling, the sensation rolling through him and making him nauseous. The world blinked... Black... Complete heavenly whiteness. White, black, white...

Black.

Marshall stood on the outskirts of a dense forest, the air thick with the acrid scent of gunpowder. His surroundings warped and blurred, as if he had stepped into a living painting of the Battle of St. Louis, a pivotal moment in the struggle for American independence.

Smoke billowed on the horizon, the distant rumble of cannons echoing like thunder across the fields. Soldiers, their muddy faces etched with determination, clashed in a skirmish of chaos and courage. The bravery of the patriots, the cries of the wounded—Marshall's eyes widened with disbelief as he realized he wasn't merely an observer, he was a part of the scene, dressed in a uniform reminiscent of the Continental Army.

Cannon blasts and a storm of musket fire as soldiers clad in red and blue fought for their futures. He moved among the troops, and an eerie sense of detachment settled over him as the fantasy unfolded like a vivid reenactment, each detail meticulously etched in his mind.

A deafening roar of anger overcame the music of battle. The ground quivered, and a collective gasp swept through the soldiers as they turned their attention away from their human adversaries.

Amidst the chaos, a creature of primeval terror emerged from the dense foliage surrounding the battlefield—a Spinosaurus, towering and monstrous, its serrated teeth gleaming. Tent-like scales ran down its back, supported by elongated neural spines, resembling a large dorsal fin. At a length of sixty feet, the Spinosaurus was equipped for life on land and in water. Its elongated snout, lined with conical teeth, and its muscular limbs and sharp, curved claws, highlighted its predatory prowess. The beast was cloaked in reptilian armor, its coloration blending into the darkness like camouflage.

Marshall's mind reeled in disbelief as the prehistoric predator prowled the blood-soaked field, a relic of a time long past colliding with the crucible of revolution.

Panic swept through the ranks of both armies as men turned their weapons toward the ancient menace, their muskets, and bayonets feeble against the might of nature's fury.

Swords slashed, muskets fired, and cannons were hastily turned toward the intruder, but musket balls bounced off the monster's thick, armored hide. Marshall watched in horror as the Spinosaurus unleashed its wrath upon the battlefield, tearing through lines of soldiers with ruthless efficiency. The air was thick with the stench of blood and fear and the cries of the wounded and dying.

The Spinosaurus, undeterred, charged through the chaos, its tail sweeping soldiers aside like insects.

Marshall spotted a general atop a hill, rallying his troops against this unexpected foe. There were deerskin-clad Native Americans in those ranks, and they fought with an intensity that rivaled the fiercest warriors.

The Spinosaurus seemed impervious to the tactics that had proven effective against human adversaries. It tore through both armies, its roars drowning out the sounds of musket fire. The chaos became a frenzied battle of survival, with soldiers adapting to the sudden shift in threat, their muskets and bayonets exchanged for desperate attempts to outmaneuver the predator.

In an unbelievable display that warmed Marshall's chest, the two armies became one, the red, white, and blue running together as they would so many times in the future. Primitive weapons were no match for the giant beast when taken alone, but the combination of cannon balls, gunfire, flaming brands, pikes, and swords was too much for the dinosaur to handle.

The great beast disappeared under a swarming mound of churning soldiers that transformed into ants as the world dissolved into a tornado of blood, bone, and cries of pain.

Faint screeching, fearful yells, dripping water, and the pounding of mighty wings.

Marshall came awake slowly, his eyes pressed closed as a jolt of pain jetted to his extremities and settled in the tips of his fingers and toes. The remnants of the fantasy clung to him, the sights and sounds lingering like echoes of a distant alternate reality. He had the chills, and his entire body shook.

The sensation of motion no longer churned his stomach, and he was lying on something comfortable that wasn't the unforgiving stretcher. A gentle breeze that brought the scent of cooking meat made his eyes flutter open.

As the world slowly came into focus Marshall saw he was in a cave of a kind, more of a notch in a cliff face than a true cave, but it provided protection on all sides except the entry. He could barely see his hand in front of his face, but faint moonlight angled through the cave mouth.

There were figures huddled there, and he heard the mumble of their talking.

He was thirsty, so thirsty, and his stomach cramped with ravenous hunger. When Marshall tried to ask for help, no words came, and only a short squeak escaped his lips.

One of the figures in the opening stood and strode toward him.

Marshall wanted to move, run, and hide. Who were these people? What did they want from him?

"Hey, you awake?" came a gentle voice from the gloom.

Squawking, the pounding of wings, and a cloud of dark beasts flew past the cave mouth, and the moonlight faded to black.

Fragments of memory coalesced—Fiona's dig, the Dome, the Chaka Stones, then...

Faces appeared out of the darkness above him. The person he'd seen... yesterday? How long had it been since he'd been knocked ass-over-teakettle? A woman appeared from the blackness, her police badge shining, her short blonde hair tied back. He recognized her... The other faces were blurred and amorphous, and he struggled to speak as a water bottle was tipped to his lips. He slurped, and the cool water was like cleansing medicine.

Marshall felt the water flow into his stomach, and he was overcome with nausea. As the world faded, he felt himself slipping, and he reached out, his hand disappearing as he retreated into dreams.

Marshall was trapped in a vast abyss, its surreal landscape bathed in hues that defied the earthly spectrum, a realm where the laws of physics and reason had surrendered to the whims of a cosmic puppeteer. His journey began with an unsettling blow to the head, the origins of which were obscured in the murky mists of fragmented memories.

The air itself seemed to hum, a piping melody that set his nerves on edge, his senses awash with unnatural sensations. Marshall stumbled through a shifting terrain, where the ground beneath his feet morphed between textures—soft, gelatinous surfaces that yielded beneath his weight, only to transform into jagged shards of stone.

He felt pursued by a nebulous force, an enigma woven into the fabric of the cosmos. The troubles of time and space danced, and clocks with no hands stood idle, their faces marked by arcane symbols. Fragments of his past, present, and future, the boundaries between them blurred into a chaotic montage of disjointed and fraudulent memories.

Phosphorescent wisps fluttered around him, casting eerie shadows that whispered taunts and secrets. Light, once a source of solace, had become a trickster.

Amidst the phantasmagoria, ethereal figures came together, forming the outlines of dinosaurs, like constellations. A river of liquid dreams flowed through the ghostly beasts, its currents carrying forgotten desires and shattered aspirations.

The world oscillated between oppressive silence and severe noise. Ephemeral echoes of laughter and weeping reverberated through the void, the emotional residue of the lost.

In the distance, beyond the Merlin Stones, a colossal doorway materialized, its boundaries marked by swirling constellations that pulsed with an otherworldly glow. The unseen dread that had haunted Marshall emanated from beyond this cosmic portal, and it beckoned him with an irresistible allure.

A chorus of celestial whispers enveloped him, revealing threads of fate that intertwined and diverged, weaving a tapestry of interconnected destinies. A cyclical sequence of creation and destruction danced in the sky, galaxies being born and collapsing into cosmic dust.

The face of a hideous dinosaur pushed through the curtain of reality, its jaws hanging open, Marshall's fear-ravaged face reflected in the monster's wet eyes.

Marshall climbed from dreamland into chaos. The group was on the move again, and sunlight fought through the thin clouds that fleeted across a bright blue sky. He was on his back, secured to a crude stretcher, the vines holding him in place digging into his chest and legs. He lifted his head in an attempt to see what was happening, but pain, like a nail being driven into his forehead, drove him down.

The men carrying the stretcher struggled over uneven terrain, the constant squawking and the flapping of huge wings drowning out all other sounds.

A flock of… Marshall blinked, trying to push away the haze of his delirium as his vision cleared.

A cloud of huge buzzard-like flying creatures bitched and screeched as they blotted out the sun. Marshall stared at the flock of Pterosaurs, which were commonly referred to as Pterodactyls, as they soared overhead. The air reverberated with the rhythmic beating of their membranous wings that cast enormous shadows that frolicked over the group as they ran.

The Pterodactyls wheeled and turned in unison, their plumage transforming into a kaleidoscope of colors as the iridescence of their crests and the vibrant hues of their wings caught the sunlight. Each creature had a sinuous body and elongated graceful necks, and the beating of their wings harmonized with the distant calls of their comrades.

A deep green tree canopy replaced the beasts as the party entered a grove of tall cylindrical conifer trees that rose like protective soldiers on both sides of a narrow path. The yammering of the Pterodactyls faded and was replaced by the gentle hum of forest creatures, an occasional frantic bleat or shrill call breaking the steady rhythm.

Marshall slipped in and out of consciousness, his head hammering, his stomach a snarling knot. In daylight, the faces around him became more defined, and more than once he found his rescuers staring at him as they trudged through the forest. He didn't know how many times he faded in and out, but as the sun started its fall to the horizon, shards of yellow light knifing into the woods, he started to feel like himself again.

When the group stopped for the night, to everyone's surprise, Marshall sat up.

Five people stared back at him, all of them frozen mid-tasks as if time had been paused. The cop had been working with a man who had long brown hair and wore priestly-like robes, except they were yellow, not black or white. Marshall chuckled, what about religion was black and white? The man he remembered from his first waking was there, and two more people, one black as night, and the other white as flour, stood guard at the door. Both held spears with large, sharpened stone arrowheads.

The group was inside a lean-to of a kind with a floor of pebbles. Thick tree trunk beams angled from the top of a dirt berm to the ground, and the supports were crisscrossed with thinner poles of wood. The entire frame was covered in the tight branches of conifers, and there were no windows and only one door. A small fire crackled in an earthen fireplace, its thick chimney dominating the dirt wall, and there were mounds of dead grass-like vegetation that looked to be sleeping cushions. He clinched his fist and felt the soft grass between his fingers.

Marshall trembled as hollow fear threatened to take root and his mind questioned its sensory minions. He rubbed his eyes, and when his vision cleared all was as it had been.

"You didn't click your heels," one of the shadows said, and a gentle chuckle rolled through the chamber.

"Welcome back," said the police officer.

4

The police officer, still wearing her uniform, a Glock on her hip, crouched next to Marshall, and her leather belt shrieked. She gave him a bottle of water and half a power bar, and said, "Eat something. Sorry it couldn't be more, but food…" Her eyes strayed to the multicolored pebbles covering the floor.

Marshall accepted the bottle and the chunk of chocolate-covered protein. The water was like wine after he'd crossed a desert, but whatever had happened he traveled farther than that.

"Kylie Robe," the cop said.

"Marshall Stanton."

The others crowded in, and shadows writhed on the sides of the lean-to, the fire crackling and popping.

"I know you," Marshall said. She was one of the officers working the Chaka Stones moon dance crowd. "How did you…" He was going to ask how she'd gotten to this strange new world, but he knew damn well she couldn't know any more than he did.

Kylie's chin bounced as she licked her lips, and Marshall interpreted the expression as understanding. They had been there, and now they were here, which wasn't there or here, and…

A stocky man with long brown hair wearing yellow robes stepped from the nebulous gloom. He said, "I'm sure you have many questions. As do I."

"We all do," came a voice from the shadows. The same voice that had made The Wizard of Oz joke.

"Yes," said the robed man.

"You can start with your name," Marshall said.

"He claims it's Stavero," Kylie said.

"Claims?"

"Based on what you've seen so far, can we believe everything we're told?" she said.

"And I for one don't remember seeing anyone in yellow robes at the moon dance." A tall slender man dressed in Bermuda shorts and wearing a Hawaiian shirt eased into the cloud of firelight.

"Nor, I," said Kylie.

Marshall licked his lips. He didn't recall seeing yellow robes, but he was sure there were plenty of things he didn't recall seeing. He did remember the guy with the loud shirt watching him. "I remember you," Marshall said as he pointed at the newcomer.

"I remember you too, and her." He tossed a thumb at Kylie. "Not him."

"Why would I lie, Lester?" Stavero said. He'd been standing back, his cool eyes shifting from person to person as they spoke.

That question sucked the air from the room, and outside beasts shouted, hooted, and screeched.

Stavero cleared his throat and said, "Judging by the knot on your head, I believe you've suffered a mild traumatic brain injury. You were unconscious when we found you. Do you remember what happened? How you got hurt?"

"It's foggy, but I remember falling and my head smacking a stone," Marshall said. He left out the reason he'd been falling, but he figured given what the others had already seen, the fact that he was getting attacked by dinosaurs was irrelevant.

"How's your vision?"

"Better," Marshall said as he rubbed his eyes.

"That's good news," Stavero said. "You may have some lingering effects like difficulty concentrating, dizziness, or balance issues."

"I cleaned the wound the best I could with a hand wipe I had stashed in a pocket," Kylie said.

Marshall smiled at her and said, "Thank you."

"The two watching the door are Rib and Bone. They haven't spoken a word since I... arrived," Kylie said.

"Arrived?"

She shrugged. "Stavero, Rib, and Bone found me wandering in the woods next to the Chaka Stones."

Marshall had so many follow-up questions that he had none.

"Same as me," Lester said.

"What about you, Stavero? How the hell did we get... wherever the hell we are?" Marshall's thoughts strayed to the Chaka Stones, the broken circle of pink stones, and the moon dance to celebrate the solstice. It was too much to think it was all a coincidence, but he wasn't thinking rationally, and somehow, he understood logic no longer applied.

"You are in the dinosaur domain, my boy," Stavero said. "Caught in time's claws."

"Are you a priest? Because you talk like one," Lester said.

"I am a holy man, but I am no priest," Stavero said.

Kylie shot back, "Stop speaking in riddles."

"As I told you all many times on the road," Stavero said. "I believe we now reside in the Cretaceous."

Judging by the creatures he'd seen so far, Marshall had to agree, yet the idea was so fantastic, so impossible, that he just couldn't wrap his noodle around it. That, along with the irony of him being here and not Fiona or one of the many dinosaur experts in the area where he'd... crossed over? He said, "Let's put a pin in that. Why are we on the road?"

One of the guards at the lean-to's entrance grunted, and Stavero's gaze tracked the sound. "Yes, Bone, I hear it." Then back to the group, "We've got company outside."

Marshall tried to get to his feet but didn't get far before falling back onto his butt.

"Easy," Stavero said. "We're in no immediate danger."

"Immediate?" Lester shook his head. "That was the reason we hit the road," he continued. "Stavero here says R&B know a place where there's protection and a supply of food and water. And there are others like us there."

"Didn't you just say you don't believe him?" Marshall said.

"Yeah," Lester said. "But the swarm of prehistoric dragons, the herd of raptors, and two T-rexes hastened our decision."

Marshall looked at Kylie, and she nodded in confirmation. He asked, "Stavero, how do you know of this sanctuary?"

"Know? I know little, and what I believe is about to be tested," Stavero said, but the tone of his voice and the way he tried to stare into Marshall's eyes gave him the feeling Stavero was lying. He knew more than a little, or at least he thought he did. "How? Why? These questions are beyond me. And a sanctuary isn't exactly what I called it. As to how I know of its existence?" He jerked his head toward Rib and Bone, who were only shadows standing before the gray rectangle of moonlight that marked the doorway.

"And they don't speak," Kylie said.

"Convenient, isn't it?" Lester said.

"What were they doing hanging around the standing stones?" Marshall asked.

Stavero said, "They claim their leader, Tek ri Odom, sent them to 'the sacred place' to receive any new prophets that may appear. They waited ten days before they found us."

"If they don't speak, how did they tell you this?" Marshall asked.

Lester and Kylie chuckled.

If Stavero's eyes were guns, Lester and Kylie would've been dead. He said, "They use hand gestures, and they understand basic English. They have a map, and there's a primitive... connection, which I can't explain. We just... Are you married, Marshall?"

He nodded.

"Was there ever a time when you could read your wife's mind?" Stavero asked.

Marshall knew what he meant, but it wasn't mind-reading. It was mind-numbing familiarity. "That's because I know her so well, and she knows me."

"True, but it's like that," Stavero said.

Marshall sighed.

"And R&B's map is basically useless," Kylie said.

Stavero held forth a piece of deer skin marked up with stone chalk. Rough half circles that he believed to be hills indicated how to orient the map. The left side, west, was covered in blue, like an ocean, and a red clay line meandered east through rolling hills, forests, several patches of dashes and dots and ended at a circle with an X at its center. There was no starting point, no landmarks, and not a single label.

Marshall licked his lips. "How long was I out?" His memories were basically intact, but his estimation of time was lost in the sea of unconsciousness.

"Two days," Stavero said.

"Any idea how far we've got to go?" Marshall asked.

Bone grunted twice.

"That meant two more days," Lester said. "We're moving slowly. We've come maybe… six miles."

"More like ten or fifteen," Kylie said.

"And this place?" he asked.

"Rib and Bone led us here," Stavero said.

Marshall's disorientation and shock had faded, but his head ached, and he felt tired, so very tired. He tried to get to his feet again, and this time with the help of Kylie and Lester, he succeeded. He was still dressed in his familiar clothes: a long-sleeved blue work shirt with chest pockets, sturdy cargo pants secured by a leather belt, his knife still clipped to it, and a pair of brown leather boots. As he patted himself down, and he found his phone tucked in a pocket.

It was then he remembered his pack. He asked, "My backpack? Water bottle?"

Kylie lifted his bag. "No water bottle, and… That water and half a power bar you ate was yours. Sorry."

"I've got a cooler in my car filled with beers and you're welcome to a few," Lester said.

Nobody laughed.

Marshall's gaze fell on Kylie's service weapon.

She noticed and said, "Apparently, the universe isn't as averse to inanimate objects as fiction would allow us to believe, or we'd all be naked."

That got a round of soft laughter.

"Are we staying here for the night?" Marshall asked. Thoughts of getting home and escaping the prehistoric nightmare he found himself in would have to wait.

"That's the plan," Kylie said. "Going out at night is... risky. Many of the creatures seem to thrive after sundown, and the number of creatures on the hunt doubles."

"At least," Lester added.

Marshall shuffled across the lean-to toward the entrance, and when he arrived Rib and Bone stepped aside. "Which one of you is Rib?" he asked.

The woman raised her hand. Her dark face and hair were hidden in blackness, and only the whites of her eyes could be seen. The man, Bone, was stumpy, and his skin was so white it glowed in the gloom. His eyes were distant and unfocused, and a black scar ran down his right cheek. Both wore animal skin tunics and leather sandals.

Outside the night world was alive with violence. Deep cloud cover blocked most of the starlight and moonlight, but the sounds of tearing meat, splintering bones, and the smack and growl as jaws chewed flesh left little to the imagination. No light filtered through the black carpet below, the tree canopy lost in a morass of darkness.

He felt Rib and Bone's eyes on him as he made his way back to the fire. The guards made no move to join him, and Marshall figured the pair would take turns sleeping. He hadn't been asked to keep watch, and with his head still rolling at a low boil he didn't volunteer.

Stavero, Lester, and Kylie lay on the floor, Stavero already ripping snores. Marshall didn't feel like laying back down so soon, so he sat along a wall with his knees pulled to his chest.

The fire was getting low, its glow only driving back the darkness a few feet. He felt Lester watching him, but he couldn't see the man. The dying flames flickered as if jostled by a gust of wind, but there was no breeze.

Marshall pulled out his phone and thumbed through security. The cell was on, and though there was no service, there were two unread texts from Fiona. The first was dated June 20th, at 5:44 PM. It read, "Where are you? Gary just told the funniest story, and if you don't hurry all the wine will be gone." Then at 5:48 PM, "???"

The phone's battery was at 82%. Panic flowed through him like bad clams. He didn't have his charger. What would he do when the battery went dead? He almost laughed. Almost, because it wasn't funny.

Sleep tugged at his eyelids as the lean-to filled with a chorus of snoring, whistles, grunts, and the occasional fart. Marshall didn't know these people, but he felt indelibly connected to them. It was like being on the subway when the power failed, and the lights went out with a screech of metal on metal. At that moment everyone on the train is together, one, everybody in the same boat. When the lights came back on, well, then people went back to being nasty.

Marshall and his gang of prehistoric travelers were still in the dark, barreling onward with no light in sight. The calendar app on his phone caught his eye. Perhaps they weren't completely in the dark. He'd never seen a doorway that only went one way.

Cell service was flatlined, but the calendar didn't need a signal to work. He scrolled until he hit June 2022, and he marked the 20th. Then he created a file on his note app called COUNT. He typed in the number 2 and closed the app.

An eruption of anger pressed into the lean-to, and he heard Rib or Bone grumble. A great braying and roaring and growling thundered over the sound of cracking trees and smacking stones. He nestled into himself, but it wasn't cold. Thank someone for that, because if he'd blinked into a winter storm he'd be frozen to death by now.

His head stopped ringing, and the warmth of impending sleep leaked through him. Marshall pressed a tiny button on the side of his phone, swiped off, and the device that held the last communication from his wife went dark.

5

The next morning the party drank the last of the water and ate what was left of their meager supply of food. Disposable water bottles, thin as paper, were saved and handled with reverence, as were power bar wrappers, Ziploc bags, and other trash. It wasn't conservation that drove Marshall, but the knowledge that he had no idea what he might need in the coming days in his quest for survival. With this in mind, he packed all the garbage in a Ziploc Kylie had used to hold trail mix and stuffed it in his pack.

His head still ached with a dull throb, his stomach raged, and his skin crawled with grime and dirt, but otherwise, Marshall suffered no lingering effects from his thump on the head. He no longer felt like he was going to fall, though he had many scrapes and bruises that constantly reminded him of his recent tumbles. A white halo still encroached at the edges of his vision, but bright light no longer hurt his head, his muscles had settled down, and cramping was minimal.

Outside Marshall saw that the lean-to was well concealed, its face covered by a spray of tropical vegetation with huge oval leaves. Animal trails, big enough for small vehicles, crisscrossed the jungle, each buzzing and hooting with morning life.

Before the party set out, Rib pointed to a spot on the crude map, and Marshall was able to discern that was the group's location. It was roughly at the halfway point, and there were many half circles on the map between their current position, and their destination, the circle with the X at its center. This meant the companions would be traveling through hills and mountains, which was slow going under the best of circumstances.

Constant violence and chaos surrounded the party as they traveled. Often the group was forced to leave the path and struggle through the jungle to avoid alphas squaring off in a clearing, or to circumnavigate a flock of beasts lounging on the trail. Sounds of battle and fear filled the forest, and Marshall tried to lose himself in the march as he stared at the ground, watching one foot move before the other.

It was surprising how many of the creatures Marshall didn't recognize. Feathers and different skin colors, so far as he knew from the conversations he'd had with Fiona, were a relatively new concept in the study of prehistoric animals brought about mainly by computer rendering. Traditionally, dinosaurs were depicted with dull gray skin. Evidence suggesting the beginnings of feathers on many dinosaurs that lived during the Cretaceous had sent shockwaves through academia, and many running point for the old guard still rejected such theories. All this made identifying species even more difficult for a layperson like Marshall.

The party had been hiking for a couple of hours when Bone led the team off the main thoroughfare, yet there were no beasties in sight. The short man was on point, Rib running rearguard, the rest of the group bunched in between.

Marshall had given up questioning the route R&B was taking. He'd lost all sense of direction long ago, which was perhaps the point. The newcomers might be welcome wherever they were being taken, but that didn't mean that the people who lived there wanted their location known. Tall trees and tropical undergrowth hid the horizon in all directions, and the party made many turns. The trails themselves twisted and bent in a chaotic mess that could be expected given they'd been shaped by prehistoric beasts.

Kylie inched up beside Marshall and whispered, "Do you see any other option except go along to get along?"

Marshall glanced at her, pursed his lips, and shifted his gaze to Bone, who gave no sign he'd heard the question. "A bit late to be asking that, no?"

"It's your first day on your feet," Kylie said, a slight flourish of exasperation in her tone. "And..." she looked over her shoulder at Lester and Stavero. "Going it alone didn't seem smart."

"Still isn't," Marshall said. "What the hell do you and I know about surviving in an environment like this? Can you hunt?"

Kylie said nothing.

Marshall saw no wedding ring, no jewelry at all, but that wasn't odd. Police officers, he believed, were prohibited from wearing jewelry while on duty, but he thought exceptions were made for wedding bands.

Noticing him looking at her bare hand and possessing a level of marital precognition that wasn't justified given the length of time the two had known each other, she said, "I'm divorced. You?"

He almost blurted out, "Married" but something held him back. His stomach grew as hot, and as his insides baked, he said nothing. Why? He was married, for sure, and he loved Fiona, but... Some little voice in the back of his head said that traveling back in time might be a loophole for the "until death do you part" commitment. Add to that the stirring in his groin he felt whenever Kylie was within ten feet of him, and his tongue was suitably tied.

"Is that a difficult question?" Kylie pushed.

Marshall smiled. "Married."

She looked at him askance.

Whatever happened, he needed this woman. She had a Glock on her hip and spare magazines in leather holders on her utility belt that he was sure were loaded with 9 MM rounds. A gun in this world would not only be the ultimate protector, but the ultimate tool of power. Still, that couldn't be the reason, nor could the cloud of his attraction, so he made up a lie and he made it up quick.

"It's just... I feel like we've left our old lives behind, you know?" Marshall said.

"What about if... when we get home? What then?" she said.

The path made a sharp turn, and the party entered a grove of trees that looked like large black celery stalks. Marshall had never seen anything like it. The entire forest looked like it had been burnt, except for the undergrowth which was mostly vibrant green dappled with splashes of color.

Marshall asked, "Did you ever see that movie with Tom Hanks? The one where he's stranded on the tropical island?"

"Castaway," she said.

"Yeah, that one," he said. "Do you remember when he escaped the island and found his way home?"

Kylie said nothing, and when Marshall looked over at her to gauge her reaction her gaze shifted to the path.

"The world, his old life, everything, had moved on and he hadn't." As he spoke questions bloomed in his head like weeds in a vegetable garden. Did time flow at the same rate here? Marshall didn't see how it wouldn't, then again, he knew the laws of physics precluded time travel other than of the time dilation variety, yet he had traveled in time.

"I see your point, but—"

Bone screamed and disappeared into the foliage.

The trees at the edge of the path swayed, and leaves rattled as the ground vibrated. Ahead a massive beast pushed from the greenery. It was twice the size of a hippopotamus, and it looked similar, except three times as nasty.

Triceratops was a magnificent beast. Standing on sturdy legs, the creature moved with surprising agility, its massive body covered in rough, pebbly skin reminiscent of armor plating.

Marshall knew the dinosaur was a herbivore, but the thing looked angry. The beast was at least twenty-five feet long, and its gigantic body rose ten feet above the path, the creature's long shadow disappearing into the jungle. Triceratops's most distinctive feature was its formidable shield-like head frill adorned with bony spikes that extended from the back of its head. Three thick facial horns, each measuring several feet in length, curved menacingly forward. Their tips were stained black with what Marshall could only assume was dried blood. Per Fiona, Tyrannosaurs regularly hunted the creatures, and the blood was most likely from defending itself against attack.

Rib ran into the trees and took cover beneath the thick boughs of a conifer tree, and the others followed, leaving Kylie and Marshall alone on the path.

The Triceratops charged, the ground trembling, muscles rippling beneath its hide as it galloped forward, the beast's long, muscular tail swaying in rhythm with its movements and providing balance and stability as it barreled forward.

Marshall stood rooted with horror, unable to move. Tension and fear set the palms of his hands aflame.

The beast let loose with a bark that sounded like a pig getting punched in the gut.

"Back up!" Kylie yelled. She drew the Glock and chambered a round.

Marshall wanted to call out. To offer help and guidance, you know, to mansplain, but no words escaped his lips. That was for the best because he had no doubts that Kylie knew what she was doing.

The cop adjusted her stance, her badge gleaming as she gripped the gun in a two-handed grip and sighted the weapon on the charging monster.

A wail of anger carried down the path as the beast dropped its head low to the ground, its parrot-like beak bobbing up and down. Small, black eyes, like burning nuggets of coal, locked in on Kylie, who didn't waver under the beast's stare.

The dinosaur was forty yards away when Kylie fired. Three fast shots that silenced the frenzied buzz of insects and the bleats and burps of the smaller creatures.

At first, Marshall thought Kylie had missed, but when she didn't fire again, he figured he was wrong, and he was.

The dinosaur slowed, its right rear leg stopped working, and the beast stumbled as it veered right.

"Bullseye," Kylie yelled and pumped the air with her fist.

With a cry, the Triceratops fell forward, its beak digging into the path like a garden hoe, the back of its body lifting from the ground as the beast tumbled face-first onto the trail.

It was then Marshall realized Kylie had put three bullets into the monster's brainpan via its eyes or mouth.

The corpse skidded to a stop, the monster let loose one last breath, then deflated like a popped balloon. The corpse was twenty yards away, and Marshall said, "Thanks. Nice shooting. Mouth or eye?"

"You're welcome. Mouth."

Rib and Bone reappeared, and Bone patted Kylie on the back, then worked his way around the fallen creature and continued down the path. Lester and Stavero reappeared and sheepishly joined the line like reprimanded school children at recess.

As Marshall passed the dead beast, he wondered if its meat was edible. His stomach grumbled at the thought, but none of the others said anything, so he stayed quiet.

The commotion had stirred the jungle, but in a good way. When the big boys tangled the little guys hid. As the party left the dead dinosaur behind an explosion of braying and screeching and fighting followed them down the path.

Flying carpets divebombed the Triceratops corpse, and beasts took turns biting through the dead creature's tough hide. The sight made Marshall sick to his stomach. Kylie had no choice—there was no debate there, but to kill a beast so rare, so unusual, so stunning, he almost felt bad.

The companions hadn't gone far before the sound of cackling water overcame the jungle's band. Bone led the group off the path to a thin stream where they stopped to drink and rest. Rib and Bone cupped water into their mouths, and most of Marshall's concerns about dangerous microbes in the water fell away. It wasn't that they still couldn't get sick, but they had no vessel to boil the water in, so it was take the risk or… He could only live for a couple more days without water, so he drank.

All water bottles were filled, and Rib harvested a bunch of white mushrooms from a dead log for food. It wasn't much, but it kept Marshall's stomach from bitching. He had no reservations about eating the shrooms, not only because R&B had eaten them first, but because he'd seen the local gazelle-like creatures eating them.

Back on the trail, the party came to a thick copse of conifer trees, an opening leading to a dark path at its center.

"We can't go through there," Marshall said. "That's an ambush waiting to happen."

"You want to go around?" Kylie said. She made a show of turning her head left, then right as she examined the edge of the forest that extended in both directions as far as the eye could see.

Bone pulled the map, and everyone crowded around him. First, he pointed at himself, then at a spot on the red chalk line indicating their current location. Then he pointed at a spot below the path where it met a section of forest and shook his head. He moved his finger above the line and repeated the process.

"Can't go around," Lester said.

Rib and Bone nodded in unison.

As it turned out Marshall's concerns were for naught. The woods were free of large beasts. The trees were packed too tight together, and the game was too small and agile for the bigger dinos to bother with. As the tall evergreens receded and rolling hills emerged before them, the sun passed its zenith and began its descent toward the horizon.

The companions marched the rest of the day, steadily working their way upwards, the climb subtle, yet substantial. They were constantly delayed by having to hide or change course to avoid the natural fauna, and as the sun kissed the western horizon, Marshall suggested they stop for the night beneath an overhang of stone that created a natural lean-to. Despite their elevated position, nothing could be seen on the horizon in any direction except a never-ending sea of thickening blackness.

Nobody protested Marshall's suggestion. He was the new guy in town by all measures, and yet more and more he felt the group bending to his leadership. Not something he wanted, but not something he could control. This wasn't Survivor, it was survival.

6

Marshall woke to the gut-churning smell of charring meat. Rib and Bone had gone hunting in the predawn hours and were roasting three small creatures that looked like skinned squirrels over an open flame. Smoke filled the notch in the rockface and spilled out over the jungle. If anyone had been watching, the smoke signal would have been visible for hundreds of miles. It made him think about how many others were out there. Humans didn't exist during the time of the dinosaurs, at least that was the commonly accepted belief. But what if there were other… doorways? Did they all come here? To this time and place?

He shook off the questions as he finished his water and chewed on a bone that he'd picked clean of its meager meat.

The view from atop the hill was expansive, and though Marshall was amazed at what he saw, he wasn't all that surprised. He pulled his field binoculars from his backpack and scanned the horizon in every direction.

Orienting based on the rising of the sun, which everyone agreed was still in the east, he faced north and slowly turned three-hundred and sixty degrees.

The north was a chaotic tangle of hills, and shards of mountains that looked out of place, black spires of stone that rose from the jungle like monuments, and at first that was what Marshall thought they were. The forest canopy to the west gave way to a hazy, jagged line of blue that marked the beginnings of a large body of water. To the south, the water was much closer, and it encroached into the land like giant fingers that transitioned to rivers that disappeared into the greenery. The party's path east was hidden by a sprawling jungle that faded into the mists of morning.

Marshall handed the binoculars off to Kylie, and as she examined the surrounding area, he said, "The Earth looked much different during the Cretaceous."

"That Pangea thing?" she said.

"Yes. At one time all the land on Earth was one giant landmass, and it will be again someday in the distant future. If my memory serves, Pangea had fully separated by the end of the Cretaceous."

She looked away from the binoculars and met his eye. "I heard somewhere that the continental drift is like two feet per year?"

"That I don't know, but..." He pointed west. "If we are in the Cretaceous, that body of water to the west there is most likely the vast inland sea that split what would become the United States in half."

"And that?" She pointed south toward the body of water that looked so close they could touch it.

"Most of Louisiana, those southern states, are on the bottom of the sea," he said.

Rivers snaked through the surrounding rolling jungle, and lakes and open fields dotted the landscape in all directions. Trails of dust crisscrossed the open plains as beasts of all sizes frolicked and fought.

Rib and Bone were resting from their early morning efforts, and Lester and Stavero showed no signs of wanting to leave, yet an urgency bit at Marshall's stomach, and it wasn't just anger. He said, "Kylie, are you ready to roll?"

"A journey not started is never finished," she said.

Marshall chuckled. They sure were starting a journey they might never finish. He raised his voice slightly and said, "Everyone ready to go?"

No answers, but Lester got to his feet and Stavero began packing his things. For whatever reason he was now somehow the de facto leader, and though he didn't like it, he did see the advantages.

Marshall noticed a white, flat stone at his feet and an idea sparked a series of questions. He needed to keep track of the days, that was basically all he knew, but he didn't want to kill his cellphone battery, so he planned to limit its use as much as possible. But as he picked up the stone, intending to mark it each day to keep a count, and then update the note on his phone periodically, the date February 29th flashed before his eyes.

Leap year. Without it, the calendar the inhabitants of Earth used to run their lives would be thrown askew. He did some mental calculations. It had been June 20th when he'd... arrived, and this was his fourth day here, which meant back home it would be June 24th. But here? He doubted the calendar that was created millions of years hence played a role, and days were days, thanks to the Earth's rotation and its trip around the sun. This all meant he was fairly confident that, if he applied the Gregorian Calendar to his current time, it wouldn't be close to June. The only saving grace was he didn't think it mattered.

Marshall filed this all away as he marked his stone with a darker rock and slipped his counter stone in a pocket. Then he dusted himself off, put away the binoculars, and pulled on his pack. He'd asked himself the question of how time flowed here, and even if it flowed at the same rate, if… when he got home, the calendar and its relation to him in time would most likely be askew. A problem for another day, if ever.

Rib led, her spear in hand, her dark skin slick with sweat. She was followed by Lester, who had lost much of his luster over the last couple of days. He was no longer loud, and his jokes had become few and far between. Stavero tried to hide his discomfort, but they were all hungry, tired, scared, and confused. There was no playbook for what they were experiencing, and when the unknown came calling, and the pressure increased, some people turned to diamonds, others to dust.

Kylie was trudging on before Marshall, her head down, and Marshall heard the grunts and heavy breathing of Bone behind him. The party threaded through an evergreen forest, and wide animal trails formed a maze within the towering green conifers.

Rib came to a halt so suddenly Lester bumped into her, followed by Stavero. She grunted and pushed Lester, and the man spun, arms out, and hit the hardpan in a whirlwind of dust and grit.

In her first display of humanity, Rib's face went slack as she licked her lips, embarrassment darkening her brown cheeks. She hurriedly helped Lester up, and to Marshall's surprise, the man didn't struggle, bitch, or complain. She dusted him off, nodded, and then turned her attention back to the reason she'd stopped.

Vines, which looked like kudzu to Marshall, trailed over the path, and something gleamed within its tangled embrace. It was a crushed and broken plastic water bottle. It had a faded green label, and the letters P, r, and er were readable.

"Perrier?" Kylie said.

Marshall was never good at word games, and he sucked at Wheel of Fortune, but now even he could see it. "I think so, but don't they use glass bottles?" The crunched bottle was aged black and brown with time, and though it was cracked, its basic composition was still intact.

"They switched a ways back," Lester said.

Stavero stared at the trash with a look of disgust on his face, as if the bottle was a symbol representing everything that was wrong with humanity.

The broken bottle had no use in its current condition, so the group left the garbage where it was and moved on.

But Marshall couldn't get the bottle out of his mind as he trekked. Who brought it here and when? Was the person still here?

Kylie sidled up to Marshall and pointed at Stavero's back. "He knows more than he's letting on," she mouthed.

Marshall nodded, then hiked his shoulders. She was the cop with the gun.

She mouthed, "Follow my lead." Then she picked up her pace until she was walking stride for stride with Stavero.

Marshall fell in behind the pair, close enough so he could hear the conversation.

"What sect are you with?" Kylie asked. "The only folks who wear yellow robes, that I know of, are Buddhist Monks."

Stavero laughed. "Thank you, but I'm not that disciplined."

She waited, and when Stavero didn't continue, Kylie asked, "So what's with the robes, then? If you're not a priest, why do you wear them?"

"I am a potentate of Destinies Shrine, a group of similar-minded individuals who believe there is more to this existence than what we see."

"God?"

"No, no," he said. "Think bigger."

Kylie said nothing, and Marshall could almost feel the heat of her frustration. She said, "What does that mean, exactly?"

Stavero sighed. "We believe there are other worlds, alternate realities if you will."

"Ah, like a metaverse? You're a new-ager?" she said.

"Not exactly," Stavero said. "I'd like to thi—" He tripped and almost fell, and he said, "Shit!"

"I guess there are no rules about using foul language?" Kylie said.

Stavero sniffed, and continued, "What we believe is more… scientific. Our beliefs are based on evidence."

"Sure." Kylie's tone couldn't have been more condescending. "So, you're saying…" She paused. "You're not surprised we're here?"

He laughed. "I am but a humble servant of the cosmos."

Dust filtered down the path as two huge beasts fought, and Rib led the party off the path into the thick jungle. It was slow going and bushwhacking with sticks was beyond difficult. The ground was uneven and filled with holes, pricker vines, and an assortment of flora and fauna that threatened to tangle up the party at every turn.

An hour dripped away, and Rib was leading the party back to the path when she screeched, and the group came to a halt.

Within the overgrown jungle stood the remains of a colossal stone octopus statue. A testament to some unknown civilization's artistic prowess, the sculpture rose from the lush greenery, the centuries revealed in its weathered surface.

The immense creature, crafted from a coarse, grayish stone, dominated the landscape with its eight sinuous arms sprawling in every direction. Each arm, meticulously sculpted, possessed a powerful sense of movement frozen in time that appeared restrained by the vines that gripped the twisting appendages. The limbs undulated gracefully, evoking a sense of fluidity as if the beast was swimming hard to break free of the vegetation. Carved into the stony surface there were intricate details that captured the essence of an octopus's majestic form, with suckers and texture carefully etched into the stone to give the statue a lifelike quality.

Nature hadn't forgotten the sculpture. The entire monument was streaked black and weatherworn. A tapestry of overgrowth covered it, and moss clung to the rough bare patches. Tiny ferns found homes in crevices, imbuing the structure with an organic quality.

The head of the enormous octopus was conspicuously absent. Where once a commanding visage might have surveyed the jungle, now only a mysterious void remained.

Sunlight filtered through the forest, dappling what remained of the octopus in a dance of shadows and light, and the statue came alive in the symbiotic fusion of nature and artistry.

The silent guardian was surrounded by the vibrant energy of thriving flora, but though the party searched the entire area, moving out in a circle almost half a mile, the head of the giant stone beast was nowhere to be found. Marshall and the others were perplexed by this. Who, how, and why would anyone go through the trouble of hauling the massive head away?

There were signs of past tending around the statue; stumpy trees that had been cut, oddly shaped vines that had been trimmed, and the ground around the statue had less weeds, as if the area was occasionally cleared.

Marshall approached Rib and Bone, who stood staring at the giant wonder. He asked, "Have you ever seen this before?"

Rib and Bone shook their heads no.

"What about the head? Have you seen that?" Kylie added.

More shaking heads.

A low gurgle emanated from the jungle to the south.

Blue sky filled the gap in the tree canopy above the monument, a gentle breeze whispered and sighed, and the scent of moisture and earth pushed through the jungle. Leaves rattled, small creatures tittered and clicked, and birds hummed and chirped.

The familiar feeling of being watched leaked over Marshall, and Kylie gripped his arm.

Two wet, baseball-sized eyes peered at the party from their hiding spot within the foliage.

7

Sunlight filtered through the lush tree canopy, creating a dappled melee across the vine-covered headless octopus sculpture. Marshall eased back behind a partially buried stone tentacle that stuck from the ground like a leafless tree created by a twisted mind.

The eyes peering from the cover of the forest shifted, appraising each member of the company.

Kylie slowly drew her gun, the sound of metal rubbing on leather carrying over the titter of the jungle and the gentle push of the breeze. Marshall judged that the cop had seldom, if ever, drawn her gun, so the holster was likely unused, which explained the sound.

Stavero and Lester stood frozen, and Rib and Bone were sitting on the ground at the base of the monument. Nobody moved.

Huge ferns swayed gently, their cackling fronds broad and painted vibrant green. A raptor-like head emerged from the foliage and ranged right to left as it surveyed its prey. Its head was adorned with iridescent scales, and sunlight caught the serrated edges of its crest, casting ghostly shadows over the writhing stone tentacles.

Large fronds cradled the raptor's head like a crown as the beast tilted its head, revealing the intricate patterns etched into its scales. Feathered plumes adorned the sides of its face, and the beast's snout was elongated and bore the scars of battle.

"I've never tangled with a dinosaur before, but I'm thinking they're like bears? No sudden movements and we try to scare it off?" Kylie said. "I can't shoot and kill everything that crosses our path. The sound will draw every creature for a hundred miles."

It occurred to Marshall that perhaps the group should have had a safety briefing of a kind. He was no expert, but there had to be a better plan of attack or retreat than hair on fire. He said, "The no movement thing sounds right, scaring it off I'm not…"

The raptor-like creature inched from the jungle, and it was obvious the dinosaur wasn't a Velociraptor. It stood eight feet tall and had no feathers. Built like a baby Tyrannosaur, it occurred to Marshall that could be what the creature was, but he didn't think so because it was age-worn and scarred. The dinosaur powered forward using its two hind muscular legs, its tiny forearms hanging like afterthoughts. Railroad spike teeth filled the beast's open jaws, and its nostrils flared as it reared back and let loose with a shriek that might have broken glass had there been any within earshot.

Kylie aimed her service pistol at the creature's head and said, "Should I—"

Two more raptor-like beasts appeared out of the greenery, one on either side of Marshall.

He didn't know how many hours he'd spent listening to Fiona and her friends talk about the inaccuracies of the Jurassic Park franchise. How the dinosaurs weren't depicted correctly, their color, size, and especially their identification. Dinosaur nerds aside, if the thing looked like a raptor, and acted like a raptor, he'd consider any of these mini-T-rexes a raptor.

Kylie fired.

The shot thumped into the lead raptor's mouth, and the bullet bounced around inside the creature's skull before exiting out one of its eyes and plunking into the hardpan. Muscles flexed and the beast's jaws closed as it took a hesitant step forward, its eyes straying in different directions. With a snort, the raptor fell on its side and deflated.

This development gave the dead creature's two mates pause.

Kylie shifted her aim between the two raptors but didn't fire.

As if the beasts understood on some primal level that permeated every living creature's will to survive, both beasts squawked, spittle flying as they disappeared back into the jungle, fronds rattling and tree branches snapping as they fled.

Kylie holstered her gun, wiped the sweat from her forehead with the back of her hand, and said, "I have to conserve ammo."

Marshall nodded, but he'd barely heard her. His ears rang and his heart hammered, so he sat on the end of a stone tentacle to catch his breath.

Time healed and cajoled, and Marshall and the others shook off their concerns, drank water, gathered themselves, and set out on the final leg of their journey.

Bone led with Rib following up the rear and the rest of the party stuffed in between. They walked tight together, nobody wanting to stand out from the herd for fear of being singled out for attack by one of the many creatures that roared, growled, and hooted in the perpetual dimness beneath the tree canopy.

The hike was arduous, but the remainder of the day was uneventful. Water bottles were replenished, mushrooms eaten, and other than having to take cover a few times to avoid the big boys wandering around looking for snacks, there were no major issues. The companions walked in silence, and if everyone's mind was churning with the same questions and uncertainties Marshall's was, the group was in for a long night when they reached their destination.

As the jungle thinned and the party emerged atop a tall cliff the sun caressed the western horizon. An expansive jungle blanketed the land to the east, and at the center of the greenery, which was fading quickly to black as the sun said au revoir for the night, pinpricks of flickering firelight formed a circle.

Marshall pulled his binoculars hoping the firelight would allow the field glasses to work, but he had no luck.

"Is that the spot?" Stavero and Lester said at the same time.

Rib and Bone nodded in the affirmative. With the two guides unable, or unwilling, or under orders not to speak, the party had no idea what the fortification's name was.

Marshall wasn't excited about the prospect of hiking in the dark. Nor did he like the idea of another night sleeping in the woods, tree roots digging into his back, flies and gnat-like insects constantly buzzing his nose, mouth, and ears, as if the little buggers were intent on spelunking in all Marshall's exposed orifices.

"Are we staying here for the night?" Lester asked. The tiny man had retreated into himself, his loud shirt dulled with dirt and speckled with blood.

Without thought for the ongoing ramifications of taking a leadership role, his mouth surged into action without orders from central command. "I think we should push through," Marshall said.

All eyes shifted to Marshall.

Dusk crept over the land as the sun disappeared, and there was a brief lull in nature's concerto as the creatures of the day scuttled off to their holes and dens for the night and the creatures of the night took center stage.

He added, "If what Stavero told us is true, there's food and a safe place to lay our heads until we can figure out our next move." What went unsaid was the idea that had been slowly working its way to the forefront of his mind: what if there is no next move? "Doesn't that sound good?"

"Do we make torches?" Lester asked.

It was a good question. Rib and Bone knew how to make fire from nothing, but that wouldn't be necessary. Marshall had a lighter in his pack, and Stavero also had a Bic, though he'd been unable to explain why he was carrying it. He said, "We could use sticks, some cloth from our clothes, but what of a propellant to keep them going?" He was sure there was sap or other natural catalysts they could use, but how he'd identify them, and where he'd find them and how quickly made the option less than ideal.

"Then there's the issue of do we want to be seen?" Kylie said. "It's going to be pitch-black soon, and we'll stand out like a cockroach on a birthday cake. Look how much brighter those fires have gotten in the last few minutes." Then she reared back like she'd been pushed. "Shit, I just remembered." She massaged her utility belt and the snap of a button coming undone echoed over the clearing. "I've got this." In the growing darkness, Kylie displayed a small Maglite in her hand.

"Still, you've got a point," Marshall said. The village in the jungle looked much closer, and as dusk faded to black the torches in the jungle got brighter.

"No lights, then," Marshall said.

With that decided, the companions got themselves together and girded themselves for what Marshall hoped would be the final push—at least for the day.

Rib led the party along the lip of the cliff until she came to a wide natural staircase of uneven stones that led down to a path that threaded into the blackness of the jungle.

Here Bone took point, and as the companions entered the forest the buzz of the night symphony was so loud it pushed out all other sounds except for random barks, squeals, bleats, and roars that temporarily silenced the smaller beasts. It was as if, like bosses of all time periods and breeds, the alphas had to remind those beneath them on the food chain who was in charge.

The party trudged on, and the path gave way to an open field filled with an ocean of blackness, thousands of glowing eyes visible in the darkness. There wasn't much farther to go, but their forward progress was stalled. Rib and Bone didn't appear to want anything to do with the beasts, and both guides stepped back as if a decision to proceed was beyond them, or at a minimum, not permitted.

Marshall had an idea for dealing with the prehistoric cockroaches. Although the creatures were probably more formidable than the typical household pests, he still thought that if Kylie lit them up, they would scatter. Or they might attack, or…

"Kylie, give them a blast of light," Marshall said.

A snap came undone, and then harsh LED light drove away the blackness.

Shifting and swaying and bouncing around within the undergrowth was a pack of creatures that looked like huge roosters on speed, except the beasts had no feathers, and brown and yellow and pink skin was pulled tight over knotted muscles. Neck frills flared, the beasts shrieked and argued, but the roiling knot of muscles, teeth, claws, and bones didn't move out of the way.

Then Kylie did something Marshall could never have predicted. She bolted by Bone and charged the beasts.

Lester called out, but his voice fell dead as the rest of the party watched her run forward, flashlight out before her like a lance, the fierceness of her cry giving the beasts pause.

The lead alphas jumped and bounced around like puppies vying for a single bone, but when Kylie got within twenty yards of the things all the creatures scattered like flies in a strong wind.

Heart pounding, Marshall and the others formed up on the trail and continued. As the glow of firelight leaked through the forest, Marshall said, "What the hell was that?"

She gaslighted him and hiked her shoulders.

"You could have bit the donut," he said. "Huge risk. For what?"

Kylie nodded and looked at her feet.

"You can't leave me here with…" Marshall rolled his head around to indicate everyone in the party.

She chuckled softly and it was like gentle music.

Marshall said, "That flashlight might seem like a magic wand to these folks. Best to keep it hidden."

"And what about this?" She casually motioned toward her gun in its holster.

Marshall nodded and bit his lip. The gun was valuable beyond belief, and surely whoever ruled the community they were traveling to would want it. "I think you have to conceal it. At least until you're comfortable. Plus… I hate thinking this way, but it never hurts to have the element of surprise on your side." He was a student of the Revolutionary War, after all, where freedom fighters had used terrorist-like tactics to confound one of the world's strongest militaries.

He saw her nod almost imperceptibly in the gloom as she unholstered her weapon and notched it in the small of her back. If any of the others had noticed, they didn't let on. "Holster?" she whispered.

"Ideally, but you're in uniform and wearing a badge. I'm betting someone will know what that means."

"And if I'm asked?" she said.

"Say you lost it in a fall while getting chased," he said.

Kylie pointed at Stavero. There was no way to know what the man might do, and the same went for Lester. Then there was R&B who had seen Kylie gun down a raptor.

Marshall hiked his shoulders. It was what it was.

There was yelling and movement in the trees.

Rib called out, a strange animal-like bark that was answered by a similar call. Marshall figured it was some type of code so the party didn't end up with arrows in their backs.

The village emerged from the bosom of nature, a seamless fusion of organic splendor and rustic craftsmanship. Fires in earthen basins sat atop crude battlements, the town's walls a conglomeration of stone, earth, and wood.

At the center of a crude arch large gates stood closed. Odd chunks of metal, remnants of another era, protruded from the structure, the juxtaposition of metal against wood and stone creating an odd harmony as if the town had emerged from the dreams of a visionary craftsman who worked both wood and metal. The face of the gates told tales of storms and claws, and lichen clung tenaciously to the walls like graffiti.

Mortared stones, worn by the weight of countless seasons, formed the foundation of the town's wall and its entrance. Many of the stones, like a chapter in an ancient tome, bore the imprints of history etched by wind, rain, the gentle touch of time, and the tap and chip of a mason's hammer and chisel.

Rib and Bone stopped before the normal-sized door at the base of the left gate. A bolt slid back, a tiny window opened, and a face appeared within. The person chirped and grunted to Rib and Bone as if speaking a language perfected by pelicans.

"Everyone stay calm. Let me go get the boss," said a high-pitched male voice. The window slid closed.

8

Torchlight drove away the darkness that pressed in on the party as they shifted on their feet and rubbed nervously at their dirty faces. Marshall and Kylie exchanged glances, and Marshall thought of something he hadn't thought of before.

What if the powers controlling the gate required newcomers to be searched? Surely, they would, and the gun would be found and taken. That being said, to give it up, even to hide it, would be a big risk. A risk he wasn't sure Kylie would take.

Marshall looked over his shoulder at the spattering of sparse jungle that worked its way into the thick tangle that enveloped the path. He leaned toward Kylie, and said, "Say you have to go to the bathroom. While you're gone hide the gun."

She turned to face him, her eyes wide white orbs in the gloom, doubt etched into her features. But then she squinted, her lips narrowed, and her hand went to the small of her back where the gun was hidden as if confirming its existence.

"I have to go to the bathroom," she said to nobody in particular. Then she turned and marched toward the trees.

Rib and Bone said nothing, and the people atop the walls let her go. Two guards standing at the edge of the jungle stepped in her path and Kylie explained she had to pee as she did that crossed-legged bent-over thing little kids did when they'd held it in as long as possible because they didn't want to leave the playground.

The men called out, warning the watchers in the woods, and no sooner had Kylie disappeared into the jungle than the order came from beyond the wall. "Hands in the air, everyone."

Rib and Bone stepped back, hands up. Their spears were leaning against the gates that towered over the scene.

No orders from Marshall were necessary. The group complied.

"Now get on your knees."

Uncertainty crept under the veneer of Marshall's resolve. But the companions had come too far to back down now. They needed help, that was obvious, and where could they go? Until that question was answered, he saw no choice. If the inhabitants of Rib and Bone's village wanted them dead, they'd already be buried to stop the stink.

Marshall nodded to the others, and the companions dropped to their knees.

A screech, then pounding feet, and two men emerged from the jungle with Kylie between them. She looked worried, but when she arrived at Marshall's side, she knelt next to him and whispered, "All good."

Marshall just hoped she remembered where she'd buried the gun, because if she didn't...

An oval piece of shiny metal was mounted on the regular-sized door set in the gates. There looked to be the depiction of a tree at the center of the emblem, and below it the words New Holland were etched into the metal, and below that in smaller type, Machine Company. Anyone who lived in the Midwest United States knew that New Holland Machine Company had been an early manufacturer of farm equipment, though the company was acquired by Ford ages ago. The insignia looked to be from the grill of a tractor.

With a crash, six people spilled through the small door as it opened. The advance team carried crude wooden shields and long, pike-like spears with metal-shard heads, and they wore helmets and masks made of tightly knit straw.

The advance team surrounded the party and pointed their spears, bunching the group into a tight knot. Nobody moved. The breeze whispered and sang, Marshall's heart providing the rhythm.

A huge man wearing a black motorcycle helmet with its face shield pulled down and threadbare overalls and no shirt folded himself through the door and approached Marshall and company. Rib and Bone fell in behind the person, who Marshall assumed was a man based on the thick cords of muscle that twisted down both the person's arms.

A memory fart pushed through his disbelief and a chuckle almost escaped Marshall's lips. The newcomer reminded him of Darth Vader, and when the guy spoke the hollow echo created by the helmet and face shield gave the man's voice a deep mechanical tone.

Vader asked, "Do you consent to a search?"

Marshall looked at the others, and when he saw no objections, he nodded consent.

The soldiers didn't move as more people spilled through the doorway and clustered around the companions. Marshall felt hands on him; his neck, on his shoulders, all along his body, and someone grabbed his balls. When the frenzied inspection was over the searchers retreated like ants back into their hill. They took both lighters, Marshall's knife, and all the cellphones. They even took Marshall's counting rock, which now had three marks on it. Those, plus the note on his phone, made five days since he'd entered the domain of the dinosaurs.

Marshall breathed a sigh of relief when he saw Kylie had hidden all her valuable possessions, not just the gun. She'd buried her light, and both spare magazines filled with 9 MM rounds, but they did take her useless radio.

"We will bind your wrists until she says otherwise," Vader said.

It worried him that all their valuable possessions had been taken, because the currency of the realm was most likely items, and all their stuff had just been stolen. But they'd passed the point of no return, and stuff can be retrieved and returned. Marshall stood and held out his hands, and as he did so much of the anger drained from him. How could these people trust him? The others? He had a good idea that in these parts there'd been enough pain and loss to go around, and when people are desperate and hurting, betrayal hides just around the corner. Marshall would have put the same precautions in place if he were in charge.

The others followed, and the group was forced through the open door by the tips of spears. Firelight danced on the walls, and smoke swirled in the air. The settlement was smaller than Marshall had envisioned given the height, thickness, and complexity of the barrier wall. Then again, they did have to ward off forty-foot T-Rexes.

Huts were sporadically strewn about, and dirt lanes ran in between, torches on wooden poles creating puddles of light along the way. It was like a campground that had never progressed beyond its original spattering of locations, which was based on where people dropped their stuff when they'd arrived.

A wide road that might be called Main Street led to a log cabin the size of a small house. It was the largest structure in town and the only one that looked like it wouldn't get blown away in a strong wind. Cookfires filled the lane with swirling smoke, and the ring of metal rose above the murmur of voices as the group threaded through town. Most of the people Marshall saw gaped at the newcomers like they were exotic animals. There were young and old folks, and Marshall saw a child hiding behind a pile of firewood. Everyone looked like peasants; their clothes ratty, their faces dejected and careworn.

Two guards flanked the entrance to the log house. Neither man glanced at the party as the guard on the right opened the door, and the group was ushered into an audience chamber of a kind.

Moonlight angled into the room through two windows, and torches notched in the walls cast flickering firelight that pushed away the darkness. The scent of woodsmoke clogged his nostrils, and Marshall coughed gently as he was politely driven forward.

Vader took up position with his men at the rear of the chamber.

Rib and Bone peeled off and disappeared into the shadows as if they weren't permitted at the meeting.

Unlike the kings of old, there was no jester, no grandstand of adoring subjects hanging on their king's every word. An old woman sat on a throne carved from a giant log, and she seemed to blend into the chair as if she too was made of wood. She wore no special robes, no crown, but her clothing was a mismatch of time; purple bellbottoms, white sneakers, and a leather jerkin, all of it representing at least a hundred years of fashion. Her dark skin looked wet in the firelight, and her gray hair, which was one notch above a crew cut, seemed to glow.

The man who stood next to the throne could only be described as weasel-like. Long, greasy hair fell about his shoulders, and a hooked nose cast a shadow over his Asian features, which were white as powdered snow. Eyes like onyx pebbles stared out from blackened sockets, and he wore a cloak that appeared to be dyed deerskin. But it was the sheriff's star pinned to his chest that made the worry worms in Marshall's stomach jiggle and complain.

"Welcome to New Holland," said weasel-man, but the voice held no warmth, and was filled with arrogance and suspicion.

Marshall recognized the voice as the one that had instructed the party to wait outside the gates while the boss was consulted.

"This is Tek ri Odom. She is the ruler of this place," Weasel said.

"Oh, Leeri, stop it. I am no more ruler of this place than you are." She rose and called out to the guards, "Are they unarmed?"

"Yes," came the echo of Vader's voice.

"Remove their bonds."

Guards came forward and unbound the party's wrists.

Tek ri Odom rose and said, "Take no offense from the precautions. Call me Ida. Please sit." She motioned toward a table where a gourd pitcher held brown water, and a variety of smoked meats and vegetables were laid out on cutting boards. There were cups made from bamboo, and Ida filled enough glasses for everyone.

Kylie took a seat next to Marshall, and Lester and Stavero flanked them on both sides.

Ida sat on a log stool and sipped her water as Marshall and his team dug in like animals, Ida watching the entire time, a slight smirk playing over her face. "I'll want to hear each of your stories, of course, but we've got plenty of time for that. As you eat, I'll state the obvious," Ida said. "You're in Wonderland, or Oz, or whatever mind-bending place you associate with the impossible. This place, New Holland, has been here longer than any living person. There are foundation stones etched with dates that go back thousands of years. From our relative time, I mean."

Marshall looked up from his eating but said nothing.

"Me, and others like me, arrived here in much the same way as you," Ida said. "We're a diverse community spanning several time periods. I have been here for eight years, and I'm only the leader of this place because everyone else stepped back, and because the prior fool gave me this." She pulled back her jerkin, revealing an old revolver in an ancient leather holster on her hip.

Marshall looked at Leeri, who was examining the hardpan floor. Were there bullets in the gun? There was no way to know for sure until someone pulled the trigger or kicked out the cylinder.

Ida said, "I know you all have many questions, but I have few answers."

"People from other time periods are here? How…? Are there other… portals?" Stavero asked.

"This I do have an answer for, though it won't help you," Ida said. "I don't know if there are other portals, or if they all lead to one place or different locations. But what I do know, is regardless of when you enter the standing stones, all roads lead to the Cretaceous. Here. Now. Why? How? Who created the doorway or doorways and for what purpose?" She threw up her hands and stuffed what looked like a flat green potato into her mouth.

Marshall took a pull of water and said, "Are we prisoners?"

"No."

"Why did you take our stuff?" Lester asked.

Ida snapped her fingers and all the possessions taken from the party at the gate were returned.

Leeri grunted, but Ida waved a hand at him. "Not everyone agrees with every decision I make, there are factions that… Well, that's for another time."

"Did you send Rib and Bone to the Chaka Stones?" Kylie asked. She'd downed three glasses of water, eaten four slabs of jerky, and was gnawing on a chunk of squash that looked to have been grilled over an open flame.

"I did," Ida said.

"Why?" Stavero asked.

Ida laughed. "You need to ask? To see if anyone crossed over, of course."

"And what exactly does that mean?" Kylie asked. "How did you know someone might be… coming through?"

"Because it was the longest day of the year," Ida said.

Marshall and the others had already surmised that the solstices had something to do with the phenomenon that brought them to this place, but to hear it spoken so casually, sent the imaginary maggots marching up his spine.

"Is that how the stones work?" Marshall asked.

"Like you, all I know are coincidences," she said.

"Why are you here?" Kylie asked. Realizing her tone and the conviction with which she'd spoken her question, she added, "I mean, haven't you tried to go home?"

Ida's face tightened. "The answer to your question requires more time than we have today."

"So, it's true we're in an alternate universe," Stavero said. "The great one said it would be so."

Ida looked Stavero up and down like he was a bug she was about to step on as she shook her head. "What's your deal? Why the robes? Are you a man of God?"

"Not exactly."

"Not exactly?" Ida shook her head. "Who told you there were alternate universes?"

"There aren't?" Stavero said.

"How the hell should I know? We're here, not there, and as long as we're here, it's our reality, regardless of whatever theoretical physics bullshit you want to apply to the situation."

"Bullshit physics?" Marshall asked.

"Theories upon theories upon theories, none of which has ever been proven," Ida said.

"Look, I don't mean to be impatient, and I appreciate the food, but can I ask if anyone has ever gotten home?" said Marshall.

"How would I know?" Ida said. "We lose people here all the time. In case you haven't noticed, there are creatures here that don't appreciate our presence, and if they don't find us tasty, they at least think humans are palatable."

"That's not an answer," Kylie said.

Ida's eyes softened and she nodded. "I believe, there is a way, but I don't know the way to the clearing at the end of the path."

Something about those words... "The clearing at the end of the path." Where had he heard that phrase? Marshall searched his memory but found nothing.

"You need to start thinking about the here and now," Leeri said. "Home, at best, is a long time off. I'm interested to know how you plan to contribute to our community. There are many chores and tasks that must be completed so we can survive in this harsh environment."

A feeling of complete hopelessness crept through Marshall, and suddenly he felt very old. Even if he could figure out how the Chaka

Stones worked, how would he tune them to the moment he left? It seemed impossible, but he didn't care.

"Is there anyone who does know how to get to the clearing at the end of the path?" Marshall said. "Because if there's any chance of getting home, I'm taking it."

9

"Perhaps we should start with the rules," Leeri said. The guy's face was as cold as a dead fish.

Ida sighed. "Yes, I suppose that's a must. You've met my lead man, Ringo? The one in the helmet? We call him Ringo because behind that face shield is the face of Ringo Starr." She reared back and put her bamboo cup down on the wooden table. "You do know who that is?"

Marshall and the others nodded.

"Good, well, Ringo isn't like that Ringo," she said. "If I must send him to find you, here in New Holland, or without, that means things aren't going to end well for you. But… follow the rules and the closest you'll come to him is on a stool at Kerny's Pub."

"You've got a pub?" Kylie said. The tone of her voice gave the impression that she was going to reach for her radio and call the Illinois Liquor Control Commission.

"If you can call a hut, with log tables, and log stools, where they serve a thin, bitter, headless brew, then yeah, we've got a pub."

Lester opened his mouth to speak but closed it.

"Would you like a brew?" Leeri said. The man's voice was exceptionally deep for a person of Asian ancestry.

Lester nodded eagerly.

Marshall wasn't surprised by Leeri's offer. He looked like the kind of guy who would use alcohol to break down a person's inhibitions.

"Bring them beer," Ida ordered. "Now hold your questions… Back to the rules. The penalty for theft of any kind—a slice of bread, a cup of water, anything, and the punishment is expulsion from New Holland… at a minimum."

Marshall made a mental note: scorned people were running around outside the town's wall.

"Minimum?" asked Kylie.

"It depends on what you steal, but know I have the power to, well, impose stricter punishments that include the ultimate penalty," Ida said. She paused to let that sink in. Hurt the community badly, and the sentence was death.

"We are a welcome wagon, but that only goes so far," she continued. "There are those who believe you and your friends already owe a great debt to New Holland because we expended resources to retrieve you and bring you safely here."

Marshall started to protest, but she put up a hand.

"I am not one of these people," Ida said. "If you decide to leave, nobody will impede you. But if you want to stay you must agree to a job, which must be performed to your clan head's satisfaction. This entitles you to basic rations and chits for other items, but trading is the main source of commerce."

Marshall nodded. Not a utopia, but far from a dystopia.

"Personal space rules are the same, basically, as back... home, for lack of a better term. Touch no one without their consent, hurt another in any way and you'll be subject to my justice." She smiled and leaned across the table, and Marshall and the others eased away from her. Her gums peeled back revealing clean teeth. "I've commanded three men to death, and one woman. Do not make it a nice even five."

The wind whistled through the log cabin, a gentle melody filling the silence.

"Questions?"

Marshall eyed his friends, but they gave no sign.

Stavero started to say something, thought better of it, and coughed. Wouldn't want any truths to spill out.

Marshall's transformation to group leader was complete. Even Kylie looked at him expectantly. He said, "Not at the moment. We're exhausted."

"Fair enough. We're almost done for now. Thing is, this has been a one-way conversation, more of an interrogation, really," Ida said. "Let's start with you, Marshall. Let's hear your tale of woe."

Marshall saw no reason to lie, or exaggerate, so he told it true, starting with the moon dance, wandering into the stones, how he'd somehow ended up back in the Cretaceous, and suffered a concussion that he'd recovered from.

Ida nodded, smiled, but didn't interrupt.

When Marshall was done, she had no questions, and she moved on to Kylie. "I see you're an Illinois police officer."

Kylie said nothing.

"Anything different than Marshall here?" Ida asked.

"Not really," Kylie said. She told of her assignment to Hicks Dome for the day. How she'd watched the morning celebration, had a nice lunch provided by the folks excavating a fossil, and finished her day at the Chaka Stones. "I remember seeing Marshall there, but not Stavero."

Stavero said nothing.

"What about Lester?" Ida pushed.

"I saw him," Kylie said. "How could you miss him?"

"Yes, surprising he made it through the jungle pass looking like a peacock with all its feathers displayed," Leeri said.

"Lester?" said Ida.

"I was at the solstice ceremony for the St. Louis Gazette. I'm a reporter," Lester said.

Marshall knew the man was lying.

"And what about you? You've been too quiet," Ida said, nodding at Stavero.

"I prefer to observe. Words are so overrated."

"You seem calm and unflustered to be here," she said.

"I believed, yes, but things change when those beliefs become tangible and quantifiable," Stavero said.

Leeri chuckled. "But you're not a priest?"

"No. My people believe we live on a vast plane between all other planes. There are infinite worlds and within are limitless possibilities," Stavero preached.

"You were hoping to come here?" Kylie asked.

Stavero licked his lips and said nothing.

"O.K.," Ida said. "We've got nothing but time, but you need rest, and I still haven't answered Marshall's question."

A gust of wind shrieked through the room, and somewhere a woman screamed.

"You asked before if there's anyone who might know a way to get home," Ida said. "It is said Coeus is a man of many worlds."

"Can we speak with him?" Marshall asked.

"I have never met him, and I'm told he doesn't mingle with the… common folk. It is said he dwells in an elaborate cave that serves as a doorway in time."

"Like the Chaka Stones?" Lester asked, his voice two octaves above normal.

"No, not like that at all," Ida said. "I questioned a man, who knew a man who met Coeus and had seen his home. People have sought out Coeus, but none have returned, at least during my time here. Whether they made it home, died on the quest to find him, or perished by one of the infinite dangers that press on the wall of this town every day, I do not know.

"But I learned that the cave he lives in, and the surrounding area is a kind of hall of records. A repository of history. Cave drawings, artifacts, and such."

"Are there any pictures of the place?" Marshall asked. It was an odd question given where he was, but as long as there were cellphones in the Cretaceous, there could be pictures.

"No," Leeri said, a smirk spreading over his angular face.

Marshall was going to explain himself but then realized perhaps Leeri had come from a time before cellphones. It wasn't that long ago.

"Do you have an idea where Coeus can be found?" Marshall asked.

"As I told you," Ida said, patience dripping from her voice like honey. This wasn't the first time she'd answered these same questions from confused and scared strangers. "I do not know for sure. I have never traveled there, nor has any living person in New Holland."

Marshall felt all his energy drain from his body.

"That said, we have clues, a crude map, and there are landmarks I and others here can help you identify." She looked hard at each of them. "If that is what you decide. Otherwise..." Ida pushed to her feet. They were being dismissed. "You can report to Leeri here, tomorrow... actually later today, it's just past midnight."

Stavero broke his verbal fast and asked, "How would you know what time it is?"

Ida strolled across the chamber to where a flat board sat on an easel of a kind. She turned the display around, and torchlight cast flickering shadows across a painting of a celestial clock. "I know this all has been more than most folks can handle, and after the few days you've had..." Ida wrung her hands as she rejoined the group at the table. "Every day here is a struggle to survive. Each moment is new and unpredictable. The only folks around here who get lost in the doldrums of daily life are the farmers, and even they see plenty of action."

Marshall nodded but said nothing. He didn't know about the others, but he was no farmer.

"I know what you're thinking. I thought the same things when I got here, but home is more than a place where you're born," Ida said. "And what passes as home means something different for all."

The party was ushered through the dark town to a hut where they were allowed to rest. Dawn would bring a meeting with Leeri, and from there...

Marshall was exhausted and was asleep five minutes after his head hit straw.

The companions woke to find food waiting for them, water, and a guard casually loitering outside their door. It was day six, but it felt like day sixty. Marshall rolled his shoulders as he ate and drank. He needed to go to the bathroom, and his imagination conjured up a pit toilet facility that stank like a dairy's dumpster in hell.

The guard, who said his name was Palan, claimed he wasn't a guard and had been sent by Ida to assist them with their morning necessities. He carried no weapon that Marshall could see. Orders had been issued by Leeri, who was unavailable, and when the party was refreshed, they were to be brought to Palan's clan chief, Dingman, who would put them to work in the fields.

Palan answered no questions, other than to say the party's work assignments were temporary and could be changed if they decided to stay and agreed to an evaluation of their skills. It all sounded very communist to Marshall.

Bladders drained, stomachs full as they could be, Palan informed the group they'd be heading out to meet Dingman shortly, and then he retreated, leaving Marshall and his companions alone in their hut to wait and ponder their impossible situation.

"What are we all thinking?" Lester said. "They can talk all kinds of crap about how home is where the heart is, but I want out. Marshall, are you going to find Coeus?"

"That's the direction I'm leaning," Marshall said. "But we need to be patient. Take our time. Ask questions and do our own investigation before we trek off into the unknown with one gun and a load of desperation." That was if Ida and her clan hadn't found the gun.

Lester nodded and turned to Kylie. "Will you be going with Marshall?"

"Sorry. I should have asked you before I opened my pie-hole," Marshall said. "I won't be going anywhere without you and your gun... or at least the gun, and I don't see you giving it up." It occurred to Marshall then that Kylie hadn't shared the location of the hidden weapon with anyone.

"Not an issue," Kylie said. "I agree with everything you said. When the time is right, we try and find this seer guy, so we can get home. I agree we've got a bit of time, especially if getting home is tied to the solstice in some way, which it seems clear it is."

Dingman was a barrel of a man who had been in the dinosaur domain for over ten years. He'd come the same way as Marshall and the others and had no desire to go back to "a world that was going to hell in a handbasket. And things are interesting here."

New Holland's fields weren't extensive, but they were well-maintained and fertile. The field reeked from the dinosaur dung fertilizer, and the guards who walked the sides of the fields wielded bows, primitive wooden clubs, and spears, and they carried shields and had quivers of arrows on their backs.

The party spent the next five days picking corn and peppers and asking questions. By all accounts, there were about ninety people who called New Holland home, and they came from various periods, and some were the descendants of travelers. Almost everyone spoke English, having come via America, where the Chaka Stones were.

A calm wrapped the town that Marshall thought the world back home could learn from. There were Caucasians, African Americans, gay folk, straight folk, and yet their society ran with few hiccups, and little drama.

Still, as each day passed, he longed for home and the more he missed Fiona. Back home had he been declared missing? What would Fiona do? He didn't want to think about it, because he knew the answer. If he didn't get back to her, soon, doubt would creep in and the woman he'd find if he ever made it back to her wouldn't be the person he loved.

Six days after the party arrived in New Holland, Marshall and Kylie were picking corn in one of the fields on the outskirts of New Holland, the midday sun beating down on them, when a discord of screaming voices carried over the fields.

Marshall and Kylie paused in their work as a grim-voiced woman ran through the swaying cornstalks screaming, "A dragon. A dragon is coming!"

Kylie sprinted after the woman, and Marshall followed.

When the trio broke free of the corn field, they found a small group of people staring at the western horizon. The screaming woman continued yelling as she ran toward town, but Marshall and Kylie pulled up short and gazed west with the others.

A dark blotch, like a huge smudge falling from the heavens, grew bigger as it approached.

Horns blared, and the sound of metal being beaten and men yelling echoed over the field as the town sounded the alarm.

The crowd jerked into motion as one, as if controlled by one mind.

A shrill cry pierced the day as a massive Pterosaur streaked toward New Holland, its sail-like wings pounding the air.

Marshall and Kylie sprinted with the crowd, the looming hulk of the town's wall rising from the jungle that separated the village from the fields. Five hundred yards to go before they reached the cover of those walls, and as Marshall looked over his shoulder, he realized he and Kylie weren't going to reach safety in time.

"Here!" Marshall grabbed Kylie's arm and jerked her along with him as he dove beneath the spreading boughs of a huge conifer tree that stuck from the stubby tropical vegetation that lined the path.

"What are you—" Kylie's words caught in her throat as understanding bloomed.

The crowd ran on, and as the fleeing farmers shrieked and wailed the dragon swept over them, its wings moving up and down in slow, graceful strokes as its long beak opened, its white teeth tinged crimson.

If the creature had indeed been a dragon and was able to breathe fire as the legends foretold, the folks running full tilt for the village would've been ash in the wind. As it was, the Pterosaur shrieked as it flew overhead, and the flying carpet didn't slow, its narrow head pointed like an arrow at New Holland.

10

Marshall and Kylie slipped out from under the evergreen and joined the crowd, which was now jogging, not running, toward New Holland.

The giant Pterosaur shrieked as it came in low, its shadow racing over the jungle and reaching out for the wall.

As the crowd's leader veered left, in the direction of the town's entrance, several people peeled off and took up defensive positions. Vader stood next to the opening, helmet gleaming as he urged people on as they passed through the door in the great gates.

Wood screeched on stone, and atop the wall, a massive crossbow was pushed into view. A ten-foot arrow with a shard of sharpened bone as its tip and large multicolored feathers adorning its tail sat in the weapon's cradle.

The crowd bunched up at the entryway, and everything came to a slow crawl as people passed through single file.

With a roar, the dragon wheeled as it glided over the town, slowly banking left as it circled. Now the crossbow was pointed in the wrong direction.

As he waited Marshall stared at the giant crossbow in awe. How had such a weapon been created without forging metal? But the answers came immediately. He had extensive experience with the weapons used by Native Americans during the Revolutionary War, and though the crossbow was big, its basic design had been used throughout the ages, and everything needed to make the giant weapon could be found in nature.

The weapon's frame looked to be made of ash, or hickory, and its bow was black and slick with some type of grease, most likely rendered animal fat. Braided animal tendons likely made-up the bowstring, and the entire thing was held together by vines. Large drips of what looked to be solidified tree sap oozed from many of the joints.

A gust of wind brought the scent of rot as the Pterosaur's mouth fell open in a vicious smile. It dipped low, disappearing from view as the beast attempted to pluck something, or someone, from the ground. Yelling, the crack of jaws snapping, and the zing and twang of bows being loosed carried over the wall.

The giant flying carpet stroked its wings harder, faster, as the creature wheeled.

Marshall and Kylie were nearly at the door when the beast soared overhead.

The men working the crossbow yelled and readied the weapon to fire. One man stood next to a simple wooden trigger mechanism that held the bowstring in place until released. A second man turned a wheel, which added tension as it pulled back the bow string. The gunner stood behind the wooden war machine using the arrow as a sight.

A great shadow fell over the gates and the gunner screamed, "Fire!"

The thwap of the trigger releasing, the twang of the bowstring, the sound of air tearing, and the whistle of the arrow as it streaked like a missile toward the dragon carried over the chaos.

With a cry, the beast dipped its right wing, and the flying tent listed downward, its wings vertical. The bolt missed the creature and slowly lost velocity as it streaked into the jungle.

The Pterosaur flew overhead in a crazed kilter as Kylie slipped through the doorway followed by Marshall.

As the duo entered the safety of New Holland, Vader said, "Get to the bunker. Fast!"

The crowd flowed left, and Marshall and Kylie let the river of humanity carry them along.

Wings stretched wide, the intricate patterns of their membranes catching the intense sunlight and painting them a ghostly pink and black as the monster circled. The creature's skin, smooth and leathery, rippled with every powerful stroke of its wings. Dark hues of charcoal and midnight blue adorned its body, and Marshall wondered if he'd be able to see the creature when it was wrapped in darkness.

The membrane between the creature's claws stretched as the beast thrust its talons forward in attack position. Its body was slender, and its long, tapered tail trailed behind and served as a rudder that helped the animal navigate the air currents. The creature's neck extended gracefully, supporting a head adorned with a sharp, curved beak.

As the beast banked and turned, the air whistled through the openings in its crest, producing an eerie melody.

The men above on the wall were struggling to reload the crossbow. One was trying to fit another arrow into the cradle while the other two did their best to pull back the bowstring and notch it onto the trigger mechanism.

An opening to an underground shelter loomed ahead. Again, the entryway was limited by the crowd size and the group came to a shuddering halt as folks squeezed into the shelter one by one.

Marshall wished for Kylie's gun. If he'd had it, or she did, all this could be over with a bullet or two... or three. But the weapon was hidden, and guilt leaked through him. If someone died on this day, he and Kylie would have blood on their hands. He shook his head, fighting back the thought.

Sunlight returned as the flying carpet passed over the wall and out of view, the nasty wind of its wake pushing over the town and stirring dust, grit, and anger. The clicking of the crossbow's tension wheel carried over the chaos, but when it stopped Marshall was filled with renewed hope.

Though he couldn't see the beast, he knew it was circling back, because the gunner had his head low, his gaze running along the shaft of the newly notched arrow.

The gunner screamed fire, and two seconds slipped away before a loud thump echoed over the wall, followed by a shrill death wail, and the ground trembled as the Pterosaur crashed to the hardpan.

Yelling, screaming, and bows sang, arrows zipped through the air, and spears thumped into flesh. Then the unmistakable sound of cheering rumbled over the wall.

New Holland cleaned up well. There was a town square of a kind, more of a mud pit that never dried, but the place looked good with the torches set, ornamental vines decorated with cut flowers strewn about, and the scent of roasting Pterodactyl wafting over the celebration. With a nasty beer in his hand, Marshall almost felt relaxed.

The great beast had been butchered out on the field, and its carcass was left to be picked clean by the smaller animals that were drawn to the blood and meat like iron to a magnet. A buzz of excitement ran through the town, and even Vader, A.K.A. Ringo, had his mask off.

Ringo never took his eyes off Marshall, and when he wandered over, Marshall felt his gut tighten a little. The guy's huge, muscled arms and legs were twice the size of Marshall's. If the guy meant him ill, there would be no fighting with this man, it would be a beatdown.

"How are you feeling?" Ringo asked as he approached. "Name's Ringo, though I gather you know that."

"I do," Marshall said. "And I'm fine."

Kylie stood next to him sipping beer, and Marshall saw Lester in his obnoxious shirt working the crowd. He didn't see Stavero.

"Good. Good. I figured I'd touch base because the rumor is you're leaving soon," he said.

Music floated over the celebration as someone took up some type of stringed instrument. People laughed and talked. There was no fighting. No discussion about politics, budgets, or cancer.

Ringo said, "You can see why some people don't want to leave here."

Kylie harrumphed. "That's a stretch. I like to go camping, but that doesn't mean I want to live in a tent."

"And how often does something like today happen?" Marshall pushed.

"The odds of you getting killed here aren't much worse than back home if you take appropriate precautions," Ringo said.

"So, you're from modern times?" Kylie asked.

He nodded. "But I've been here twelve years."

"You said 'some people'," Marshall said.

Ringo's eyes narrowed and he sipped his brew.

"You said 'you can see why some people don't want to leave here.'"

"I would think it was obvious," Ringo said.

A song broke out, and to Marshall's disappointment, it was A Hundred Bottles of Beer on a Wall.

When Marshall and Kylie said nothing, Ringo said, "There are basically two factions. One that thinks all the community's efforts beyond basic survival should be focused on getting home. The other two-thirds are... well, happy might be too strong a word... Most folks are content to make life here as good as we can."

"What about what you left behind?" Kylie asked. She had left behind an ex-husband—basically nothing. Marshall had left behind Fiona.

"Fair enough," Ringo said. "Those in my boat do have a conviction that their lives are better here, and one component of that is we, I, have no real reason to get back to a world I wasn't too proud of, or very happy living in. Here..." He spread his arms expansively and drained the last of his beer. "Come on. There's someone I want you to meet."

Marshall hiked his shoulders and he and Kylie followed Ringo a short distance to where a group of women were playing a game with wooden dice.

"Mary Pat?" called Ringo.

One of the women looked up, her dirty blonde hair obscuring her features. Mary Pat brushed hair away from her face, her expression morphing from frustration to happiness. She excused herself from the game and pressed to her feet.

"Mary Pat wants to join your expedition," Ringo said.

"Thank ye, kindly," Mary Pat said.

Introductions were performed and life stories were shared.

"I was on vacation from Ireland when it happened," said Mary Pat, her blue eyes aglow with vigor. "I study... studied Native American traditions, and I always wanted to see the moon dance up close."

"And I take it you got your wish?" Marshall said.

66

She nodded. "I've been here eight years, and I can't take it anymore. I want to come with you."

"You didn't tell them that you're a great arrow maker and you have extensive knowledge of the surrounding area," Ringo said.

"That would be helpful," Kylie said.

"I can come with you?" Mary Pat said.

Marshall hiked his shoulders. "Can't see how it's my call, but the more the merrier."

"I'd keep that sentiment to yourself," Ringo said. "Not everyone who might want to join you is as... qualified as Mary Pat."

"What sentiment?" It was Ida, and she'd appeared as if out of thin air wearing her gun on her hip.

Ringo said nothing.

"Ringo was just introducing us to Mary Pat. She'll be joining us in our search," Marshall said.

"You've decided then?" She glanced at Kylie as she said this.

"Yes," Marshall and Kylie said as one.

"When do you plan to leave?"

"Soon," Marshall said. Based on what Ringo had told him, he decided to keep his cards close to the vest.

"Will you and Kylie join me for... a more refined beverage back at my place? I'd like to propose something... someone, actually, and I made a map for you."

Marshall looked at Kylie, who shrugged. He said, "Lead on."

"Here I take my leave," Ringo said, taking the hint. The invitation was offered to Marshall and Kylie, not him, or Mary Pat.

"Why don't you take Mary Pat with you," Ida said.

Mary Pat's mouth opened to protest, but she said nothing. And with that one interaction, the pecking order of the company was permanently set.

Ida led Marshall and Kylie through the revelers to her hut. Marshall was surprised to see that the structure looked no different than all the others. There was no preferential treatment here, not even for the town's mayor.

Leeri waited outside Ida's home, and he held the door open for the group as they passed inside.

The place was sparsely furnished with hand-hewn wooden seats, a cot, and a table. Ida motioned for them to take seats, as she retrieved a green bottle filled with crimson liquid. "This is the only glass bottle I've ever seen here. It's old. Real old, and I use it to ferment berry wine." She laid out bamboo cups and poured everyone a couple of fingers of wine.

Marshall sipped and the sting of the alcohol, the burn, the warmth heating his stomach, it all made him think of home.

Leeri produced a rolled-up deerskin and placed it on the table.

Ida undid the knot securing the rawhide string keeping the thick map rolled, and it sprang flat when released from its bonds. "I took the liberty of reproducing my own map." She pointed at a large drawing of New Holland and the surrounding areas painted on a wall. There were vast areas marked uncharted between Mount Sight, where Coeus was alleged to live, and New Holland.

"It's said Mount Sight provides a good view of the surrounding area—hence the name, not unlike Hicks Dome. Most accounts label Mount Sight as a dormant volcano, and it's possible it was left behind as the supercontinent broke up. As you can see, New Holland is east of the Chaka Stones," Ida said. "The distance is approximately twenty-five miles as the crow flies. I know that doesn't sound far, but you made the trip and…"

What else was there to say? Marshall and the others had barely made it to New Holland.

"Though it's a guess, we believe Mount Sight is closer to the standing stones than New Holland, but it's to the north of the stones."

"So we're looking at about thirty miles to Mount Sight," Kylie said.

"Give or take," Leeri said. "Our maps are imprecise, but I believe the trip will take six to eight days, assuming there are no delays. What isn't imprecise are the various landmarks and distances in and around New Holland. Also, the bamboo forest, the canyons, the desert waste… Most of these locations I have seen at least part of. But again, the map is an estimate. What would be best is if someone in the party has actually seen some of these places."

"Like Mary Pat?" Marshall asked.

"No," Leeri said. "Like me."

11

The sun rose and fell four more times before the fellowship set out.

Preparing for an expedition without the Internet was a bitch. Marshall was the only one with a backpack, so the first order of business was figuring out how everybody else was going to help carry the supplies. Marshall was confident food and water could be found on the way in the early stages of the journey and watering holes were marked on the map. Dried meat and other foodstuffs needed to be brought, as well as weapons, primitive cooking implements, straw-woven bed rolls, and a tarp made from a dried Pterodactyl wing, the creature's delicate wing bones serving as umbrella-like supports.

It was more than just gathering supplies and making plans. Everyone in town had to give the team advice. "Don't stray from the path" was the most common refrain, and after that gem had been thrown at him five times, Marshall stopped saying, "Yeah, but the path ends a quarter of the way to Mount Sight."

The agreed-upon public plan was, regardless of what information was obtained via the quest, an attempt was not to be made at the Chaka Stones without returning to New Holland first. At that time, if necessary, a case would be made so those who wanted to attempt to go home could join the expedition to the standing stones.

That led to a general sense of support, the people of New Holland having nothing to lose.

Marshall and Kylie decided to keep the secret of the gun between them until they were outside the walls and on their way. Then Marshall would call a halt, Kylie would circle back, and then the fellowship would be on their way. While Kylie was gone, Marshall would tell Leeri and Mary Pat about the weapon, and explain why they'd chosen to hide the pistol and Kylie's other items.

With all preparations done, a layer of excitement and angst settled on New Holland. Marshall was eager to get going, but the comfort of New Holland was hard to leave. He knew it was time, however, and when he announced at the pub that the party would be leaving the next morning, Ida requested an audience.

The six travelers stood before Ida like they were being judged for a heinous crime. Outside a crowd was building. Everyone had been permitted to delay their chores until after the departure, and a party was already brewing outside with a bit of beer for breakfast.

"I wanted to wish you luck," Ida said. "I hope if we meet again, that you have found that which you seek. One piece of advice. That thing you seek, your purpose, may change and shift during your journey. Don't forget where you are. One lapse, one daydream, one ill-advised moment of hesitation could mean the end of the road."

She appraised the group and then addressed them each in turn.

"Marshall, you have your knife, but I'm told you're skilled with the long pike."

A guard stepped forward and handed Marshall a beautiful six-foot pike that could also serve as a hiking staff. Its shaft had been carved with designs and initials as if everyone in the community had put their mark on the weapon like friends signed casts on broken arms. The pike was tipped with a shred of polished metal that Marshall couldn't identify, but it was clearly a piece of something that had come through at some point and had been dissected.

Ida's attention slid to Kylie. "You, I do not believe need my assistance." The two women locked eyes, and Kylie, a trained police officer, knew to keep her piehole shut. When the brass was chewing you out, and knew you were lying about something, the best course of action was to bite your tongue and hold on tight. "Regardless," Ida continued. "You have shown great proficiency with the bow and arrow, and the people of New Holland present you with this."

The bow was as long as Kylie was tall. It had been meticulously worked, and the bowstring was slick with oil. A quiver of arrows held twelve bolts, each adorned with multicolored feathers.

Mary Pat said, "I made those." She pointed at the arrows.

"Lester," Ida said. "You never stopped for weapons training, therefore we've constructed a staff."

Lester was handed a stick that had been stripped of its bark and sharpened to a point on both ends. It was about six feet long and had no carvings along its length.

"And lastly, Stavero our man of... mystery? You took it upon yourself to learn how to make weapons and so have made a spear and bow for yourself."

Stavero dipped his head.

"And Mary Pat, you made Stavero's arrows?" Ida questioned.

"I did, ma'am."

Ida bared her teeth as if some custom or rule had been violated.

"He's my teammate, ma'am."

"I see," Ida said as she nodded. "You have your weapons... your blade, spear, and sling, but I would like to offer you this for your bravery."

Mary Pat was given three pieces of thin metal that had been hammered and shaped into crude throwing stars.

"May their aim be true."

Mary Pat bowed her head.

Cheering outside, and someone was chanting Mary Pat's name. She'd become a local hero, Leeri not so much. Ida's right hand man had been given no gift, and Ida hadn't even glanced in the man's direction. Something was up, that was for certain.

"And finally, I offer this to the party in hopes it will lead you when all else fails." Ida produced an old brass compass that looked the worse for wear.

Marshall accepted the gift, and he didn't have the heart to tell her his cellphone had a compass app that didn't need a signal to work. But that was stupid. He needed to conserve the phone's battery at all costs, so he was happy to see the device's needle still floated, and as he turned the compass it pointed north.

"A recent traveler lost that at dice," Leeri said.

Marshall nodded.

Ida's voice was a wet whisper when next she spoke. "If fate wills it thusly, you will return and tell what you've found, plead your case, and perhaps, just perhaps, it might mean the end of New Holland as we know it," Ida said.

And with that, there was nothing left to say, and the party gathered their belongings, said their farewells, and went out to meet the crowd, which was now comprised of most of the citizens of New Holland.

Vader nodded at the party as he watched over the festivities, helmet gleaming in the sunlight.

Marshall and his companions marched down the broad way waving like they were going off to war. In a way, they were. Marshall recognized many faces. Rib and Bone were in the crowd, as was the woman from the early nineteen hundreds who spoke little and walked around like she couldn't believe where she was. There was Dime Bag Donny, who had flashed out of the sixties, and Stumpy who had been a soldier home on leave from World War I. They all watched with eager eyes, but Marshall felt their pity bubbling just below the surface. None of these people expected to see any members of the party again.

The group exited via the doorway in the great gates, and once they were in the jungle Marshall called for a break.

Kylie scampered off to retrieve her Glock.

"I figured as much," Leeri said when Marshall was done explaining the situation. "Ida suspected as well—we saw her empty utility belt. Plus, we knew about her little bathroom break before you all entered

New Holland. Still, it's understandable. I would have done the same thing. You had no idea what you were walking into."

Marshall nodded. He still didn't.

The first three days of the quest were easy-peasy. There were premade hiding spots to get through open areas and there were lean-tos like the one he'd woken in when he'd first arrived. The trails were narrow and walled by thick vegetation, which made hiding from the larger beasts easier, but limited visibility and flexibility.

On the fourth day, the end of the line on the map marking the trail looming like a life-altering decision, Stavero inched up to Marshall and said, "May I have a word."

Marshall made a show of looking around. "No secrets in this group."

"It's not that," Stavero said as he glanced over his shoulder. "Don't look, but I think we're being followed."

Marshall nodded ever so slightly.

The party was trekking through a thick forest of evergreens, the spiked leaves casting sharp shadows on the bronze needle-covered ground. The scent of pine filled the air, and cones of various sizes hung from branches and littered the hardpan.

Marshall called a halt, and the companions ate mushrooms and drank water. The party missed the steady support of Rib and Bone. Lester and Leeri weren't much help, but Mary Pat was a good hunter, and as it turned out, so was Kylie, so food wasn't an issue. There was plenty of material for fires, and everything was dry and gave off little smoke.

Searching for their tail, Marshall peered back the way they'd come, but the only movement he saw were shadows fighting amidst shifting leaves, clouds of insects, wren-like birds, and an occasional small mammal that looked like a groundhog but had long fangs. He said, "Stavero, I don't see anything."

"Whoever, whatever it is, keeps itself hidden," Stavero said. "But I can feel it. Can't you?"

Marshall couldn't, but he hadn't been hiding from apex predators for very long.

The party moved on, and the forest gave way to an open field where three species of plant-eating dinosaurs languidly feasted on tall grass and the leaves of trees at the edge of the clearing.

The grassland stretched to a thick jungle in all directions, and the lush vegetation swayed gently in the warm breeze.

None of the magnificent dinosaurs looked up from their eating.

A massive and imposing Triceratops with a distinctive frill and three intimidating horns adorning its massive head stood proudly on sturdy legs at the center of the clearing. Its body was covered in a mosaic of bony plates and thick, armored skin that offered protection from predators. The beast's frill bore intricate patterns and vivid colors, a striking display that Fiona and her colleagues believed might be used for communication or to establish dominance within the herd.

In addition to the Triceratops, a slender and agile Hadrosaurid moved gracefully through the high grass, its elongated neck reaching up to pluck succulent leaves from the higher branches of the prehistoric trees that lined the edge of the glade. Known for its elaborate crests, this Hadrosaurid displayed stunning cranial ornamentation reminiscent of a delicate multicolored fan. Its body was covered in smooth, overlapping scales, giving it a streamlined appearance that facilitated swift movement through the dense vegetation. The Hadrosaurid's tail, a counterbalance to its long neck, swayed gently as it ate.

Completing the trio was a gentle giant, a mighty Sauropod, its long neck extending high above the surrounding trees as it reached for the most delectable foliage. This colossal herbivore's movements were slow and deliberate, its massive body supported by four tree-trunk legs. The huge beast's tail swung like a pendulum, creating a rhythmic motion that echoed its unhurried pace, and its skin was adorned with irregular patterns that provided camouflage amidst the vegetation.

As the sun cast a warm glow over the dinosaurs, the field came alive with the harmonious sounds of munching and the occasional low rumble of potential communication. The air carried the scent of ancient flora, a fragrance that made Marshall think of happier times.

An earsplitting shriek shattered the peace, and the dinosaurs and the party looked to the sky as one.

A Pterosaur streaked overhead, its shadow falling over the beasts as they grazed. Everyone, including the trio of dinosaurs, watched the flying carpet circle and wheel away.

Marshall breathed a sigh of relief.

An intense clicking leaked from the jungle, and an angular head with flexing jaws pushed through the foliage and surveyed the field.

12

The Triceratops was the first of the grazers to notice the newcomer and the tank-like monster threw back its head and screamed, but it sounded less like the battle cry of a T-rex, and more like a pig crying because it hadn't been fed. Its bony frills framed the beast's weathered face, and its thick, armored hide bore the marks of countless battles.

Beyond the Triceratops the Sauropod's long neck bent gracefully as its head turned, huge, wet eyes scanning its surroundings, the gigantic creature ever vigilant for signs of danger despite its overwhelming size. The irony of it hit Marshall; the dinosaur was one of the largest beasts to walk the Earth, yet it appeared constantly afraid.

Unease rippled through the air like a gathering storm as the Sauropod's skin undulated as it stepped back, its neck swaying as the massive teddy bear's eyes found the new arrival.

A magnificent beast strode from the jungle. Standing ten feet tall and stretching to a length of twenty-five feet, the apex predator's body was streamlined for efficiency and adorned with scales that glistened in hues of earthly browns and mossy greens. The colors acted as natural camouflage, and the creature almost disappeared against the backdrop of the jungle.

"*Baryonyx*," Leeri said.

"Yes," whispered Marshall. Baryonyx fossils were rare, and Fiona and her colleagues didn't speak of them much, but he'd seen several computer renderings in documentaries and in Fiona's research papers.

The Baryonyx's crocodilian snout dominated its facial features. Its jaws were lined with a series of conical teeth for grasping and tearing prey, and its eyes gleamed with intelligence. A distinctive crest adorned the top of the beast's head, and powerful muscles rippled beneath the skin of its hind limbs. Its forelimbs were shorter, but they were equipped with formidable claws.

Those claws left deep imprints in the soft jungle loam as the Baryonyx inched across the clearing.

The herbivores watched with wet eyes, still as stone.

With a huff and a snort, the Baryonyx threw back its head and wailed. Its torso shook, and a series of bony scutes that acted as natural armor shifted and dipped. The beast's hind legs churned, and its tail, which served as a counterbalance and weapon, swung back and forth, sweeping across the vegetation.

Without warning the Baryonyx turned away from the herbivores and charged at Marshall and the others.

Kylie drew down and two shots rang over the clearing.

Both bullets hit their mark. One punched through the dinosaur's armored breastplate and the second pierced the monster's head below its eye and tore off the side of the beast's snout. The Baryonyx took several staggering steps as it slowed, and then collapsed. Marshall dry-heaved, spittle hanging from his mouth as the rancid scent of feces leaked over the clearing as the dying beast emptied its bowels.

Unseen birds and smaller beasts exploded from the vegetation like a swarm of disturbed bats. The Triceratops squealed and bolted into the jungle, but the two other beasts went back to pulling leaves from trees like nothing had happened.

All eyes shifted to Kylie, then to the bloodied corpse of the Baryonyx, a dark puddle of sludge leaking into the ground all around the corpse, the creature's eyes already staring into the next world.

"We are a scourge," Mary Pat said.

"It's kill or be killed," Stavero said. "Thank you, Kylie."

Being complimented by Stavero made the woman's face scrunch, but Kylie nodded as she holstered the Glock.

Hoots and roars carried from the forest and the ground shook.

"Looks like the commotion has attracted some unwanted attention," Marshall said. "Let's get a move on."

Leeri took the lead, and the party picked up their pace, the forest thinned, and the undergrowth grew less tangled. When the group came over a rise, the path dipping into dense jungle, Leeri called a halt and said, "Let me see the map."

Marshall tossed the rolled piece of deer skin to Leeri, and the group bunched in as he opened it.

"This is it," Leeri said.

"This is what?" asked Kylie.

"The farthest from New Holland I've ever been." Leeri handed the map to Kylie and she and Mary Pat studied it.

Lester had no interest, and he shifted on his feet, staring at a cloud of tiny black specks circling way above in the tree canopy.

Stavero watched but said nothing.

The line on the map ended at a marked section of jungle, an occasional rolling hill represented by a half circle rising above the triangular trees. Beyond that was a section labeled the canyons, beyond that the wastelands, and finally Mount Sight.

Marshall broke out the compass, took a reading, and found due north. Then he angled his body northwest in the direction that, according to the map, was where Mount Sight would be found.

With the fourth day of their quest winding down, the companions had only traveled a quarter of the distance to Mount Sight.

Despite the overall dejectedness of the party at seeing how little progress had been made, it was alleviated by the fact that they made excellent progress the rest of the day. The jungle beneath the thick tree canopy was sparse, the undergrowth almost nonexistent. There were huge patches of evergreens filling vast areas where the only things on the forest floor were bronze pine needles, and this allowed Leeri to lead quickly and stealthily, and with great confidence.

The end of the fourth day found the fellowship sitting atop a tall hill covered in devil grass and pricker bushes that offered excellent protection from the smaller and mid-sized beasts that might feel the newcomers were ripe for the taking.

Lester and Stavero made a fire within the sheltered notch of a giant stone that provided cover on three sides.

Marshall set a watch schedule and agreed to take the first shift.

When the team was finished eating and drinking, they shuffled off to sleep atop their bedrolls of woven straw. There was no chatter, no questions, and no complaints. Everyone was weary to the bone.

Marshall sat in the stygian blackness, the faint glow from the embers of the dead fire glowing like nuclear waste in the darkness. Clouds streamed west to east—some things never change, and the moon and stars provided little light on this night. The buzz of the jungle below carried up the hillside, a riot of busted bassoons, out-of-tune fiddles, and the occasional tap, gurgle, and crack of an out-of-rhythm percussion section. All of it would periodically go still after an alpha asserted itself with a roar that left no doubts it was time to quiet down.

When the sun dawned on day five of the expedition the clouds had cleared, and the view of the northwestern horizon from atop the hill was clear.

Leeri and Marshall studied the map as Marshall worked the compass. The jungle to the northwest was dotted with hills that broke through the lush green carpet, but beyond that, as verified by the map, was the region called the Canyons.

Marshall pulled free his binoculars and pressed them to his eyes.

The Canyons, carved by the caress of water and the harsh persuasion of wind as the landmasses of Earth split apart and reformed, stretched out to the west and north, cutting through the vibrant jungle. Towering cliffs of weathered sandstone and limestone danced with intricate shadows, their surfaces etched with the severe imprint of time. The gaps in the earth stretched for miles and formed a labyrinth of deep crevices and narrow gorges that showcased the intricate layers of sediment deposited over millennia, each colorful stratum a chapter in the Earth's history.

Waterfalls spit from steep walls, and natural rock formations, sculpted by the elements, formed fantastical shapes, some of which look like severely worn statues of people. The landscape was painted in rich and varied colors, but earthy tones dominated, with the Canyons sporting hues of rust, ochre, and brown.

The six companions stared at the horizon and Marshall could almost feel the energy and determination drain from the party because his drained as well. They were tired, hungry, bruised, and mentally battered, and Mount Sight wasn't even...

Thoughts of turning back cajoled, pictures of food and bamboo mugs of beer dancing in his head like a fantasy. Marshall was about to hand off the binoculars when a bright sparkle of light caught his eye.

There was a small clearing to the northwest that looked like it had been burned to the hardpan. Whatever had caused the fire occurred some time ago because vines already covered the charred ground and clung to the blackened spires of tree trunks. The flash of light had come from the clearing.

"What is it?" asked Kylie.

"Not sure." He handed her the binoculars and shifted his attention to the map. "Leeri, that clearing... it would be about here?" He pointed at the map indicating a spot just beyond their current location.

Leeri nodded.

"It's kind of on our way," Marshall said.

"What did you see?" Lester pushed. The guy hadn't spoken in two hours and suddenly he'd found his tongue.

Marshall licked his lips and didn't dignify the question with a response. If he knew what the hell he'd seen he would have told the group. He rolled his shoulders and cracked his neck. They were already getting on each other's nerves, and they were only five days out.

Kylie took point because she had the gun, and nobody had the stones to ask if she'd let others use the weapon. Leeri came next, though as a guide he could only make educated guesses like the rest of them.

Marshall followed, the compass always in his hand now, his pike in the other.

The party was forced to change direction several times as they approached the Canyons to avoid obstacles both of flesh and blood, as well as stone and wood. Larger creatures had difficulty moving in the forest, and the rolling hills and uneven terrain were less than ideal for the bigger beasts, who often looked awkward in their movements, despite their agile and muscular frames.

Herbivores plucked leaves around every turn, and though they paid little attention to the fellowship, still the group didn't get too close to the beasts for fear of unintentionally getting trampled should the massive creatures get spooked.

Marshall smelled the clearing before he saw it, the stale scent of smoke permeating the jungle like paint fumes.

The jungle thinned, the black stain materializing out of the green gloom. Something mounted to the tallest burnt tree trunk sparkled like a huge diamond.

Marshall jerked to a stop and tugged on the back of Kylie's shirt.

She wheeled on him.

He put a finger to his lips as the fellowship huddled up. Marshall's stomach was partying. Something didn't feel right. It was almost as if whatever was mounted on the tree was deliberately put there to attract attention. He said, "I think it might be a trap."

Kylie's eyes grew wide.

"A trap?" Lester and Stavero said as one, and their tones left no doubts that they thought the idea preposterous.

"Could be," Leeri said. "There have been reports of attacks by wild men and…" Leeri looked at the ground. "And a few of our own."

Marshall recalled what Ida had said about the punishment for almost every crime. He pulled his binoculars and examined the item attached to the blackened tree trunk. It was hard to get a bead on the thing with it reflecting light into the binoculars, but after a few minutes, he was able to identify the object.

"It's a mirror," he said. The piece looked to have once been part of a makeup compact, but the bottom half containing the rouge had been torn away leaving only a round mirror with a diameter of two inches.

To that, nobody had anything to say. The wind gusted, and evergreen leaves whispered, palm fronds argued, and the scent of earthen rot and animal waste competed for top smell with the scent of burnt wood.

Marshall scanned the edges of the blackened clearing, and his breath caught as he squeaked.

"What is it?" Leeri said.

"There's a bowman in that big evergreen at four o'clock."

All eyes shifted as Marshall lowered the binoculars. The person was impossible to see without the aid of the field glasses.

Marshall put the binoculars back to his eyes and scanned the edges of the clearing and found a second person sitting in a tree at the clearing's edge, arrow notched to a bowstring. "I've got another one. Kylie, is your weapon ready?"

She chuckled. "Way ahead of you."

Marshall glanced over his shoulder at Kylie and beyond her three dark shadows slipped through the forest.

Mary Pat, who was watching the party's back, saw the strangers but was unable to react in time.

Branches snapped as two men and a woman surged from the undergrowth, clubs in hand, and came at the party harder, faster, and with more anger than any of the prehistoric beasts they'd tangled with so far. The leader of the trio let loose with an earsplitting wail that momentarily silenced the jungle creatures and stirred the maggots in Marshall's stomach.

Mary Pat was knocked from her feet as she swung her bow and missed.

The leader continued his charge and took down Lester, a brutal tackle that made the man screech. Marshall was happy the wail wasn't followed by the sound of cracking bones. A broken arm or leg out here would mean...

Kylie aimed the Glock, but the gun discharged as the female attacker bounded into her and the bullet sliced and ripped its way through the dense tree canopy.

The third assailant made the mistake of going for Mary Pat, who had found her feet, and that cost the guy. She delivered a brutal one, two, three, four combination that knocked the guy back like he'd been hit with a series of bullets.

Stavero stood watching, eyes wide as quarters.

Marshall charged with his spear, but he pulled up short when the woman wrestling with Kylie got the upper hand. The nutter was covered in natural camouflage; branches tied to her arms and legs with vines, her face smudged black with dirt. She held the Glock in one hand and gripped a knot of Kylie's hair in the other. "Everybody freeze, or the bitch is dead."

13

People thrown into stressful situations experience a unique connection often referred to as trauma bonding. This theory states that when a group of people from diverse backgrounds, economic strata, and differing attitudes are thrown into a stressful and life-threatening situation, strong bonds are formed much faster than normal, and the sidecar of trust gets pulled along for the ride.

Kylie and Marshall exchanged a glance, and then both looked at Mary Pat. At that moment, the three companions understood what was going to happen next. In Marshall's mind Lester, who was behind him, Leeri, who he didn't trust, and Stavero, who never seemed to get involved, didn't possess the newly developed marital-level sensory perception that allowed him to communicate with them without words, so he didn't try.

Marshall flopped to the ground, and as he did so he threw back his left arm and planted his hand on the ground for support as he swept his right leg and delivered a blow that cut the attacker closest to him down to his knees. Muscles screaming, Marshall rolled, pressed to his feet, and punched the guy in the chops.

Kylie jerked her elbow back and it connected with the face of the woman holding the gun.

A loud *crack* reverberated over the clearing as the woman fell back and fired the gun, but the bullets smacked into a tree. Kylie was on the woman like a spider, clawing and raking at her eyes, tearing hair from her head, and driving her knee into the woman's midsection as Kylie pounded the woman against the hardpan. The nutter tried to raise the Glock, but Kylie chopped it from her hand and pinned the woman to the ground.

Seeing the lack of success of his two partners, the guy squared off with Mary Pat decided whatever the travelers possessed wasn't worth the effort and he bolted into the jungle.

Mary Pat sprang for the Glock and picked it up hesitantly, the weapon wavering in her hand as she shifted her shaky aim between the two attackers, who looked like their control valves had been pulled and all the air and energy had been drained from them. Mary Pat took two baby steps until she stood next to Marshall, and then she handed the gun off to him.

"Hate those things," Mary Pat said. "Never shot one in my life, so…"

Marshall trained the weapon on the man who knelt before him and said, "Hands behind your head."

The man complied, as did the woman.

"Shit, is that you Tony?" Leeri had found his voice. He, Stavero, and Lester had stood by, hands up, and done nothing, which was about what Marshall figured he could expect from the men.

"You know this gu—"

Arrows sliced through leaves and speared the ground at the edge of the burnt clearing.

Marshall dropped to the ground, followed by Kylie and Mary Pat, but the two strangers, Lester, Stavero, and Leeri stood gazing at the clearing as if they had x-ray vision and they were looking to burn the bowman to cinders.

An arrow plunked into a branch next to Lester and he and Stavero took cover behind a thick tree trunk.

"Either of you run and you're dead!" screamed Marshall, but he didn't believe it. These folks had attacked him, but he was no killer and hadn't fallen so far as to shoot a person in the back as they ran.

Whether it was fear of the threat or worry that they might get shot with a friendly fired arrow, both strangers got low, which left only Leeri standing like a weed.

Mary Pat reached up and dragged Leeri to the ground.

Kylie inched up beside Marshall and he returned the Glock to her. "Let's see what we've got," he said as he peered through the binoculars.

Vines snaked over the black ground and slowly blended into the lush greenery that boxed in the charred area. He examined the edge of the clearing, arcing the field glasses slowly, his eye sockets hurting from pressing the lenses to his eyes too hard.

"Got you," Marshall said. With the binoculars still pressed to his eyes, he asked, "Can I borrow that gun again?"

Kylie handed him the weapon.

Using the field glasses as a kind of sight, he aimed the Glock at the guy sitting in a primitive tree stand sixty yards away holding a bow with an arrow notched to its string. Marshall breathed deeply. He hadn't fired a weapon since the military, but he'd been a good shot, and it was like riding a bike.

Marshall fired twice, and the bowman fell from his stand like a bird that's had a heart attack.

Hooting and hollering exploded from the jungle as the guy hit the hardpan with a thump.

There was a blur of movement on the opposite side of the clearing and Marshall swung the Glock and the binoculars.

A woman with a long red braid trailing down her back jumped from the low branch of a tree and disappeared into the foliage.

Marshall pressed to his feet and put the tip of the Glock's barrel to the head of the man Leeri had called Tony. "Are there more?" He pressed the gun deeper into the guy's cheek.

"It was just the two," he said.

Tony and the woman who called herself Raya were dressed in rags and looked almost feral. They agreed to answer a few questions in exchange for their potential freedom, but very little was learned.

The man Leeri knew as Tony was cast out of New Holland for theft. He'd been on a hike looking for deer antlers when he came across the sun ceremony. At home, which was the 2030s, he was unemployed and divorced.

Raya, who only spoke in one to two-word sentences, was much older and she'd been in the wild for years. Leeri had never seen her, and the woman claimed to have never been to New Holland.

"People like Raya aren't common, but they do exist. Not everybody is scooped up by New Holland and there are other crossover points," Leeri said.

That nonchalant statement made the angry invisible ants march up and down Marshall's spine. Other points? It wasn't a crazy idea to think there were other rings of stones, other spots where… time and space bent? Morphed?

When the questioning was done the sun waited just above the horizon and Marshall decided the party was done for the day.

"What about them?" Kylie asked as she angled her chin toward the prisoners.

Marshall handed her the Glock and said, "They're going to have to stay with us tonight. We're keeping watch anyway, and I don't want them going back and getting their friends. Plus, it will be easier to keep two eyes on our backs in daylight."

Kylie nodded.

At the start of the sixth day out from New Holland, Marshall asked Kylie and Leeri to march the prisoners away as he, Mary Pat, Stavero, and Lester broke camp. He didn't want the prisoners to see exactly what direction the party went.

Marshall was folding the Pterosaur wing tarp when Lester asked, "Did you believe them when they said they've never come across Coeus, didn't know anything about him or Mount Sight?"

"I believe they never met him," Marshall said. "The rest?" He hiked his shoulders.

Kylie and Leeri returned sans prisoners, and Kylie said, "They took off like captured animals being returned to the wild as soon as we told them they could go. I don't think we'll have any more trouble with them."

"It's not them I'm worried about, it's their leader, whoever the hell that is," Marshall said. "Any idea who that might be, Leeri?"

"No," Leeri answered, a bit too fast and Marshall knew the guy was lying. Again.

The party spent the next two days watching their backs as they carefully avoided the Canyons that cut through the jungle. Most of the chasms were deep but traversing them proved easier than Marshall had initially believed.

Chirping insects, rustling leaves, and the distant calls of unknown creatures echoed beneath the dense foliage. The party was trailblazing now. There was no path. Marshall continually consulted the compass, but maintaining a course was difficult given the constant presence of flora and fauna.

The forest thinned and the group reached a shallow river, its crystal-clear waters meandering lazily through the dense jungle. Canteens were filled, faces washed clean, and amidst the tall ferns and cycads that ran along the river's edge, Leeri identified a Brachiosaurus. It towered over the canopy, its long neck stretching to pluck leaves from the highest branches, and with each of its hesitant movements, the ground vibrated.

Continuing along the riverbank, the party stopped at the edge of a section of grassland where a herd of Triceratops grazed. Marshall and company had seen many of the beasts, but the creature's formidable frills and three sharp horns never failed to invoke awe. Their low grunts and the occasional clash of horns carried over the area, the air thick with humidity and the scent of decaying foliage.

Marshall led his flock all day. They saw Ankylosauruses resting beneath the shade of towering conifers, and the heavily armored herbivores, with their thick bony plates and club-like tails, seemed unperturbed by the party's presence. They leisurely munched on low-lying vegetation, their armored hides protecting them from the many threats lurking in the shadows.

The ground trembled regularly as if the world was constantly being jostled. Marshall and crew were forced to hide from several Tyrannosaurs of various sizes and colors that dominated the landscape and sent all other beasts scuttling for cover.

As the day drew to a close, the fellowship exited the canyon-torn jungle and a vast marshland stretched to the northwest.

"This isn't on the map," Stavero said.

The swamp looked passable. There was no path, but the pools of stagnant water were spaced out, and the land in-between looked like a bog, but was solid in most spots.

Fog hung above the ground and Sauropods dotted the landscape. The immense herbivores waded through the shallow waters, their long necks stretched out to reach the lush vegetation that lined the banks. In the fading light, their silhouettes against the setting sun painted a majestic picture of a world untouched by time.

Dark clouds pregnant with rain marched across the western horizon chasing the fading sunrays. It occurred to Marshall that it hadn't rained once since he'd arrived in the dinosaur domain.

The next day the party tackled the swamp, and when they emerged on the opposite side, they were fly-bitten, sore, wet, and hungry. More than once the ground had grown soft and everyone in the group had been sucked into waste-high mud, only to be cleaned off by sinking in stagnant pools that appeared in the ground as if by magic.

As they left the marsh the fellowship was confronted by a wall of thick bamboo that ate the land.

"We can't catch a break, can we?" Kylie said.

The woman had a point, but he said, "We'll see."

Marshall's positivity didn't last long. There was no trail, and without a machete—even with one—hacking through the thick patch of bamboo was impossible. The stalks were two to five inches in diameter and the green notched spires rose eighty feet in the air. The stalks creaked and moaned, and there were snarls and barking from within.

Heading east made no sense, so Marshall led the party west, skirting the edge of the bamboo patch. Trailheads appeared several times, dark maws that led into thick greenery. These paths, while tempting, were bypassed. There would be no escape from the maze within the bamboo, and without a clear path through there was no sense taking the risk.

The day was fading, and Marshall was starting to despair when the bamboo stalks grew thinner and more spaced apart.

Then the rain came, cold sheets that beat the bamboo and the company. Bamboo cracked and bent as thunder boomed and lightning danced in the sky, the flashes painting long spidery shadows over the party.

There was no place to shelter from the storm, so Marshall pressed on. He led the group around the western tip of the bamboo patch where they found a thin barrier of jungle hidden in mist. With the excitement of something new driving him onward, his wet socks chafing his feet, the weight of his soaked clothing like an extra thousand pounds, he double-timed it through the thin forest.

The rain eased as the jungle ended.

Marshall slowly came to a stop and stood with his mouth hanging open. There was no way to spin this. No good side of the coin. The others came up behind him. Kylie gasped and Mary Pat let loose with a low whistle.

The map didn't do the place justice. Ahead a cloud-covered vast emptiness stretched to the north, south, and west. Nothing moved on the barren wasteland of arroyos, sharp stones, and devil grass. Marshall peered through the field glasses, expecting to see giant beasts thundering across the plain, rooster tails of grit chasing them. Where were the huge bones and carrion birds? The wastelands were quiet. Eerily quiet. There was no wind, not so much as a murmur, and no dust hovered in the air as it always did, even within the wet confines of the deep jungle.

There were no trees, which meant no shade, and the flatness of the plain distorted the distance, and he figured the expanse of nothingness was probably much larger than it looked. Marshall decided camping at the edge of the jungle and starting fresh the next day was the best way to go.

With the mountain seemingly so near, there were only a few grumbles. It appeared to be an opportunity to sprint to the finish line, but the group trusted Marshall, that trauma bonding thing again. He'd already helped the team avoid a trap, and most likely death, and that had only strengthened the group's trust in him.

So it was that the fellowship made camp under the boughs of a large conifer at the edge of the wasteland. Marshall started a fire, and Kylie and Mary Pat caught, skinned, and cooked several small furry marsupials with long ears and fat meaty bodies. Lester and Leeri stretched the Pterosaur-wing tarp between three trees to ward off the weather, but it turned out to be unnecessary. As the party ate the storm broke up, and the sky began to clear.

Before Marshall tried to catch some sleep, he examined the wastelands a final time with the binoculars, searching for threats. Tattered clouds swept over the wasteland as dusk transformed into darkness, huge wisps of white with gray gaps speckled with faint stars in between. And, like a merry-go-round going round and round, as the clouds fleeted across the sky, the black spire of Mount Sight appeared and disappeared in the rolling gaps.

14

With the mountain in view, Marshall felt an urgency to set out early, but the team was talking quietly around a fire and having a thin breakfast as dusk turned to dawn. Seeing them all together reminded him of a class that was making progress on its own. Stepping back was often the best way to build a team, and if he was going to get home, that's what his companions needed to become.

He wandered out of the glow of the firelight, but not far. Beasts screeched and argued in the grayness, the night creatures not wanting to go to bed, and the beasts of the day not wanting to crawl from their burrows, nests, and holes. It reminded him of his own species, night owls and early risers. His circadian clock had always found a happy medium.

Marshall lifted the binoculars, but without light, there wasn't much to see.

The dark outline of Mount Sight rose sharply from the barren wasteland as if placed there after the land had been formed. Even in the half-light, Marshall had to agree with the general assessment that the mountain was a long-defunct volcano. His morning explorations revealed that the wasteland was comprised of a foot of sediment covering black hardened lava, which left no doubts that Mount Sight at one point had been an active volcano and might explain the lack of life and the barrenness of the plain.

Why the dormant volcano still stood, and why it was alone, he didn't know. He had several friends who were geologists, but who listened to their buddies when they were talking shop?

What he did know was that Pangea, the supercontinent that existed more than three hundred million years ago—his time, began to break up during the Triassic period. Unlike Hollywood stars, this breakup occurred gradually over millions of years through a series of harsh geological events as the Earth's tectonic plates shifted. The supercontinent split into two major landmasses: Laurasia in the north and Gondwana in the south. As the tectonic plates moved, rift valleys formed, leading to the creation of new ocean basins that separated the continents.

Marshall also knew that the Earth's landmasses continued to drift apart, and eventually they would meet again.

And then there was the dinosaur in the room. At some point, an asteroid would plunge into what he knew as the Gulf of Mexico, and the majestic beasts that were trying to kill him would become extinct unless they could somehow be preserved. That day could be tomorrow or today. There was nothing he could do about the asteroid, or the date of its expected arrival, which had a plus or minus of something like a million years.

The clouds had fully cleared, and huge invisible waves of heat rolled over the brown hardpan as the sun rose, the wind a gentle caress that carried fine particles of grit that caught in the slightest of cracks.

Lester joined him and asked, "How far do you figure we have to go?"

Marshall hiked his shoulders and said, "Tough to tell with no large markers on the plain other than that thick patch of greenery. With no frame of reference, it's difficult to establish depth. But I'd guess we've got at least a ten-mile walk ahead of us today." Marshall had no intention of camping out in the open, so if his leadership held, the fellowship would march until they made the mountain, even if they had to proceed in the dark.

Camp was broken and as the party stood at the edge of the jungle no words were needed. Everyone wanted their journey to end, but nobody was looking forward to crossing the terrain that lay ahead.

The flat, featureless plain extended as far as the eye could see in all directions, a vast expanse of desolate wasteland that looked like a far-off lifeless planet. The somber brown hardpan resembled the aged parchment of forgotten scrolls, and it was baked dry by the relentless sun, its surface cracked and fissured and unforgiving.

Peculiar rocks of hardened black lava jutted out sporadically from the ground across the plain, their odd shapes breaking the monotony of the landscape. Some were weathered remnants of ancient formations, worn smooth by the ceaseless winds that swept across the wasteland. Others stood defiantly, their jagged edges a testament to their enduring strength.

Despite the barrenness, there was a curious anomaly at the center of this desolation—a patch of devil grass. This peculiar vegetation, so named for its resilient nature and sharp-edged leaves, formed an oasis amidst the sea of brown. The thicket's wiry stalks emerged from the cracked earth like defiant sentinels, their deep green hue contrasting starkly against the drab surroundings. Marshall thought there might be water there, but the party was carrying full bottles just in case.

The air was heavy with a silence broken only by the occasional shriek of the wind as it massaged the rock sculptures. A sense of solitude permeated the landscape as if time itself had abandoned this corner of the world.

Marshall gathered his flock and set out on the last stage of the quest, which had already taken longer than anticipated. The fellowship walked single file, avoiding holes and fissures in the ground, some of which looked to have no bottom.

Kylie led, her gun holstered, her uniform shirt gone, her tank top undershirt stained and torn. Marshall eye's strayed to her more than he wanted them to, and more than once she'd caught him. Her badge had been packed away, and though she carried the gun, the necessary arrogance needed to be a police officer in modern times had already been worn down, the sharp edges rounded, and Marshall found he liked her. A lot.

The itch of guilt tickled Marshall's balls, Fiona reminding him from the distant future that his senses were only supposed to tingle for her, or something was wrong. He didn't think that was true, but there it was.

Lester and Leeri appeared to have formed some type of alliance, because the two men walked together, Leeri telling the tale of his years in the dinosaur domain as if trying to sell Lester a condo on a golf course.

Mary Pat hung just behind Marshall and Kylie, and it didn't take much intuition to know that's where the woman was most comfortable. Earn her trust, respect, and loyalty, give her a task, and she would run through a brick wall to complete it. Had to love the Irish.

Marshall fell back and caught Stavero's attention. "Any sign of our tail?"

Stavero shook his head no. The fellowship had been followed from New Holland, the person—or beast, staying far back and out of sight.

"Do you think it was Tony and Raya's people from the start?" Marshall asked.

Stavero hiked his shoulders. "That, or we lost the tail, or... who knows. Either way, I can't see how anyone, or anything without wings could follow us across that." He pointed at the wasteland before him.

The morning wore away, and the party didn't encounter so much as an ant. Dark shapes wheeled overhead, but none of the beasts came close. Though the terrain was unforgiving and uncomfortable, Marshall felt more at ease than he had since he'd been whisked away from Hicks Dome. Perhaps that was why Coeus had chosen Mount Sight for his base. That and the commanding view and barren terrain would make approaching his home in secret very difficult.

An uncomfortable thought pushed its way to the front of the line. Coeus would see the party coming. It was unavoidable, so if Coeus wanted to hide from them he'd have more than enough time.

The patch of devil grass grew on the horizon, and odd slashes appeared in the hardpan as if carved by running water or by something heavy being dragged over the ground.

Leeri had taken point, followed by Kylie, the Glock in its holster.

Stavero appeared to be losing steam at a precipitous rate. He still wore his yellow robes, which were torn and dirty, but much of his air of superiority had blown away with the wind. His knowing eyes had faded to confusion, and whatever he'd hoped to find in the dinosaur domain, whatever his guru, or whatever the hell he called it, had told him, it was like Ida had said. Stavero's purpose appeared to have shifted from exploration and spiritual enlightenment to getting home as fast as possible. Guess the multiverse with dinosaurs was too much for him.

The land dipped into a shallow bowl and small tufts of devil grass sprouted sporadically from the hardpan. The odd slashes increased in number, and there was something else... something Marshall just couldn't put a finger on. The wind massaged the wasteland, but beneath it... a hiss... of air filtering through stones... or...

"Hold up!" Leeri shouted.

The party halted at the edge of the thicket of dense devil grass, and before them, a huge hole eight feet in diameter spiraled into the ground.

Marshall put the hissing sound, the hole, and the slashes in the hardpan together, his mind forming a surreal picture of—

From within the depths of the tangled devil grass emerged a creature of nightmares—a Titanoboa, a colossal ancient serpent. Its sleek, ebony scales glinted ominously in the sunlight, and its eyes gleamed with primal hunger. Narrow jaws slid open revealing fangs, and a red forked tongue thick as a drainpipe lashed out between sharp teeth.

The explorers froze in terror as the Titanoboa slithered towards them, its sinuous body weaving effortlessly through the devil grass. Marshall felt the earth tremble beneath its weight, and the air grew thick with the stench of decay.

At first glance, one might mistake Titanoboa for a fallen tree trunk. Typically stretching over forty feet in length and weighing upwards of a ton, the serpent's body was thicker than Marshall's waist, and it coiled and shifted with fluid power as it navigated through the tall grass. Each sinuous movement sent ripples cascading along its dark, glossy scales, the colors of which were a study in earthy tones. Rich shades of olive and beige adorned its dorsal surface, broken only by irregular bands of darker hues that striped its length.

The beast's head was perfectly suited to its role as an apex predator. Broad and wedge-shaped, it tapered to a blunt snout adorned with rows of needle-like teeth.

Panic erupted among the group as they scrambled to escape the deadly coils of the Titanoboa. The giant snake appeared to grow larger as it got closer, and its eyes blazed with primal intelligence, its forked tongue licking at the party's heels.

Entering the snake's domain of devil grass wasn't an option—not a smart one, anyway, and the party scattered as they fled. Kylie fell in on one side of Marshall, Mary Pat on the other. Marshall looked over his shoulder and saw Stavero and Lester heading south, and Leeri was hiding in the tall grass at the edge of the thicket.

Not that it would help, but more of Fiona's dinosaur knowledge leaked from his subconscious. Titanoboa was a constrictor snake, which meant it relied on constriction to capture, control, and kill its prey rather than biting it. But once the prey was subdued, it would use its powerful jaws and sharp teeth to tear into the flesh and consume its meal.

Marshall thought perhaps Leeri's strategy might work. The Titanoboa couldn't chase everyone at once, and the beast appeared locked on Marshall as he and his partners ran west at full tilt.

The Titanoboa was nearly past Leeri's hiding spot when the beast suddenly changed direction and sprang at him.

Leeri had nowhere to run, and no time anyway. As he attempted to sprint past the monster, the snake encircled him, coiling its massive body around him as he struggled to escape. The snake's body undulated and constricted as it came together in a knot, and Leeri disappeared within the mound of flesh.

Marshall slowed to a jog. They had to do something to help him.

With each breath the snake's body expanded and contracted as the Titanoboa tightened its coils, cutting off Leeri's air and blood flow.

Leeri screamed and the Titanoboa uncoiled to consume its kill.

The enormous snake used its powerful jaws and sharp teeth to tear into Leeri, who was now nothing more than a bag of skin filled with blood, cracked bones, and crushed organs.

Marshall winced as the beast ripped away chunks of meat, Leeri's lifeblood leaking into the hardpan as the massive monster prepared its kill so it could be sucked down its gullet.

Kylie had a clear shot, and she fired at the snake, the shots cracking over the wasteland.

Two of the shots hit the beast, and what was left of Leeri fell from the Titanoboa's jaws. The snake hissed with fury as the beast recoiled, its massive body thrashing wildly.

Leave no man behind was a good thought, something to strive for, but Leeri was dead, and hanging around to become the next course in the Titanoboa's meal wasn't something Marshall was interested in. He seized the break in the action and started running full speed, his heart pounding as he raced around the thick patch of devil grass, his breath coming in ragged gasps.

The others followed, and soon the remaining members of the fellowship ran across the open plain and left the snake and Leeri in their wake.

Marshall looked back as he ran, his binoculars swinging from the lanyard around his neck, his spear held uselessly in his hands. Behind him, the Titanoboa let out a deafening shriek of rage, its primal cry echoing over the whispering grass as the giant beast slithered back into its hole with half of Leeri's corpse in its jaws.

15

The husk of the once-mighty volcano stood guard over the desolate plain, a monument to the relentless march of time and the unforgiving force of nature. Mount Sight was broken and weathered and bore the scars of countless eons, but its rugged silhouette was still a testament to the tumultuous history that had shaped it.

Marshall and his companions huddled in a hollow carved into the side of a large, twisted stone that stuck from the hardpan like a broken black tooth. The scree pile leading up to Mount Sight towered over them, and the mountain's cracked and weathered cone cast a fat shadow over the wastelands.

Nobody wept for Leeri, but Marshall's heart was racing like it wanted out of his chest as a deep shame washed through him like sewage. He hadn't trusted Leeri, but to see the man killed hit Marshall hard. He'd seen death, but not like that. And to think all that separated him from the same fate was a prehistoric monster's tiny lizard brain randomly deciding to attack Leeri and not chase him down. It drove home the helpless feeling that everything they were doing—their purpose, was a fantasy that was crumbling under the hard reality of the dinosaur domain.

An eerie stillness broken only by the occasional gust of wind that whispered mournfully through the desolation and the distant shrieks of flying carpets pressed on the wasteland.

"He didn't even want to come with us," Lester said.

"What do you mean?" Kylie asked.

"Leeri. He told me Ida made him come with us and he was ordered to report back everything we saw and did."

"He was a plant," Stavero said. "That misdemeanor doesn't carry a death sentence."

"It could have been any of us," Marshall said. It wasn't a surprise that Ida wasn't the ultra-idealistic hippie-type after all.

Mount Sight was pockmarked with fissures and crevices, the remnants of ancient eruptions that had torn through its heart, and cave-like holes from secondary vents pocked the mountainside. A thick layer of windswept soot and ash coated everything, and the crater had crumbled away, leaving behind a jagged rim that offered a precarious vantage point over the surrounding desolation.

"See the flat spot up on the broken section of the rim?" Marshall said as he pointed.

"A good spot to see in all directions," Stavero said.

The slopes of the volcano were littered with nature's detritus, great boulders, and chunks of rock and baked earth strewn about.

"Let's get going," Marshall said. "There's got to be a path."

The party was trailing along the western edge of the scree pile and was halfway around the base of the volcano when Kylie saw the bone sticking from the hardpan.

Marshall called a halt.

The "it's a trap" conversation no longer needed to be had, and even Lester and Stavero seemed to realize caution was needed. Both men climbed into the rocks that littered the slope and took cover behind a large boulder without even having to be told. With Leeri's death fresh in their minds, fear had yet to run its course and both men were most likely thinking about their futures and how quickly they could have none.

Mary Pat was a different beast altogether. Marshall asked her politely to hang back, and when she told him colorfully no, she joined Marshall and Kylie as they approached the anomaly.

Kylie led, sweeping her gun around like she'd just entered a drug house. When she reached the top of a stone staircase that marched down into a dark hole she stopped and looked back at Marshall.

The steps cut through the surface layer of dirt, dust, and sand, through the dried lava, and into the virgin ground that had been there before the volcano was born and spewed its death.

Kylie gave Marshall her flashlight and he trained its beam down into the hole, and what he saw both surprised and scared him.

The bone that poked above the ground was the front spike of a massive fossil that rested almost vertically in the ground. It was as if the giant had been washed across the plain by a great tidal wave of earth that closed out on the monster, burying the creature, and protecting it from the lava flow. Marshall couldn't identify the beast. The fossil was about eighty percent exposed, and it had thus far been meticulously excavated, each bone curvature painstakingly brushed and cleaned.

Marshall sucked on his lips. The dinosaur's skeletal structure spanned an impressive length, he estimated it easily exceeded eighty feet from snout to tail. Each bone, preserved, yet weathered by the passage of millennia was clearly defined. The skull was broad and imposing, adorned with rows of menacing teeth. Its eye sockets, though hollow and empty, were dark and foreboding.

The beast's forelimbs were thick, and the hind legs, though partially fragmented and buried, still conveyed a sense of agility and speed, suggesting the unknown goliath was a predator that most likely ruled the dinosaur domain. Marshall examined the intricate details preserved in the fossilized vertebrae and thought of Fiona. The fossil could be an undiscovered species. That was a paleontologist's Super Bowl.

Kylie inched down the steps, gun up, followed by Marshall, and Mary Pat agreed to stay on the surface and keep watch.

Down in the hole, there were obvious signs of human activity. Smoke filtered through the hole driving out the scent of parched earth. Two empty gourd bottles sat in a corner, and a t-shirt that read "We CAN do better" and below in smaller type, "Vote Kennedy in '60" hung from a bone that jutted from the side of the hole. Stranger still was the thick burning candle that sat atop a log.

At the sight of the flame flickering above the candle every mistake Marshall had ever made poked and scratched at the underside of his skin. After all his speeches about traps, he'd walked right into one.

But there was nobody there. Marshall and Kylie searched the trench, Kylie leading with the gun. When they were done, Marshall pulled out his phone and fired it up. He consulted his counting stone and made a quick addition to his number of days in the dinosaur domain list, then took two pictures of the fossil before shutting the cellphone down.

Marshall hadn't turned the phone on in days, and the funny thing was he hadn't noticed, other than not getting a text here and there from Fiona. If he ever got back, he had proof, and who knew? Maybe the excavated fossil was buried still beneath Illinois?

Back up top, the party once again trudging along the edge of the scree pile at the base of Mount Sight, Mary Pat asked, "How long do you think that candle has been burning?"

Marshall said nothing, and everyone else was smart enough to say nothing as well. They all knew that little mystery only meant one thing: someone was ahead of them on the trail, or hiding and watching—but then why leave the candle lit?

The fellowship found what appeared to be a path soon after they left the dig site. They'd traveled three-quarters of the way around the base of Mount Sight and were on the southern side.

There were no markings, no signage, no footprints, no real trail, but it was the first spot Marshall had seen that allowed them to get up the slope of tumbled stones to the mountainside.

The non-trail was treacherous but it formed into a path, and here and there Marshall saw the signs of human intervention massaging the mountainside. A carefully placed stone to advance the trail up to the next ledge, a section where the side of the mountain looked to have been intentionally cleaved, and they found the remains of several large fires ringed with stones.

Halfway to the base of the cone the trail delved into a tunnel that bore into the side of the mountain. The maw of the cave entrance was dark, and Marshall saw no signs of life.

Yet, there was no way to get around. The tunnel looked to have been created when a section of the hillside was swept away onto a huge rock that angled against the foundation stone of the volcano. The walls were a slanted, uneven nightmare, and the floor angled up and down as chasms as black as the deepest night cut across the rough surface. At the center of the tunnel, another candle burned.

"I don't like this," Kylie said.

"What part?" said Marshall.

She cuffed him gently on the back of the head, and he chuckled, and the odd sound in that place echoed off the stones and brought the answer. "I don't like it either, but consider this," Marshall said. "If whoever is leaving the trail wanted us dead, don't you think we would already be dead?"

Lester harrumphed.

"That's pretty thin," Stavero said.

"Did he ask you?" Mary Pat scolded.

Stavero said nothing.

"You two can wait here if you want," Marshall said. He was losing his patience with the negativo brothers, but he drove back his frustration. Nobody was themselves. That was the point that always dominated the dinosaur domain. The logic Marshall and the others had lived their lives by was now different from their programming. Their operating systems weren't outdated, they were too advanced, but with each passing second all the members of the party were learning to let some of those instincts, which weren't really instincts but inconveniences and manipulations, go from their lives.

The party inched into the tunnel, and it turned out there was nothing to fear. A white triangle of light appeared a hundred feet away, and the companions were out the other end and back on the path in minutes.

Marshall smelled the fire before he saw it. The path meandered around a large boulder that had tumbled down the side of the cone and got caught up on a larger rock that had blocked its path. As Kylie came around the huge rock she came to a halt and raised the Glock.

Fire ran across the path as if following the line of poured gasoline, and the air was redolent with the scent of burning tar. Thick black smoke poured off the flames, and the path forward was obscured.

"This is indeed unexpected, Marshall," came a voice from beyond the smoke.

If there were bugs scuttling among the rocks, they were all watching Marshall, his back smoldering with the heat of his companions' stares.

A cloaked and hooded figure stepped from the smoke beyond the line of fire.

Kylie planted her feet, gripped the Glock in a two-handed grip, and aimed the weapon at the newcomer.

Smoke swirled as the person drew back their hood.

"Iruno?" Marshall said. The old Native American he met on his trek up Hicks Dome stood before him wrapped in a deerskin cloak. Marshall recalled those hazel eyes. It was like they could see through solid objects. Iruno's care-lined brown face looked stress-free, and he appeared unconcerned that a Glock nine was trained on his melon.

"I never expected to find you *on* the path," Iruno said.

"That's why we're here," Marshall said. "And, you know, if you would have said something about the doorway in time I wouldn't be here!"

Iruno said, "Come. Come. You've all had a long journey and I'm sure you have many questions."

"Are you Coeus?" Stavero asked.

"I am known by many names here, and in other places," Iruno said. "But yes, I've heard I am sometimes referred to as Coeus."

"Why?" Marshall couldn't help himself.

Iruno shrugged. "You can call me Iruno since that is the name I was given by my mother."

"If no one else is going to ask, I will," Kylie said. "How do you two know each other?"

"We met on the hillside right before... I crossed over," Marshall said.

"And you didn't tell us?" Lester blurted.

Marshall wheeled on the guy.

Lester took a step back.

"Tell you? What? That I met a guy while I was walking up the hillside?" He sucked in the rage and frustration again, took a breath, and put his hand on the man's shoulder. "I'm sorry. I'm thrown by all this also."

Stavero stood back throughout this entire interaction, his eyes never leaving Iruno.

Once again, tuned in on that marital band, Kylie asked, "You live here alone?"

Iruno nodded.

There were so many questions Marshall didn't know where to start, so he said nothing.

Iruno said, "I've been watching you for two days and..." He paused and looked at the ground. "I am sorry about your friend."

Marshall said nothing as he felt the cool touch of Leeri's ghost.

"Are you hungry?" Iruno asked.

Marshall's stomach growled in answer.

Iruno chuckled. "Of course you are," he said. "I assume you've come from New Holland?"

The party nodded as one.

"How are things in the domain's largest city?" Iruno asked.

Hearing New Holland called a city made Marshall think of home, and he searched his memory, combing through the interaction he'd had with Iruno, searching for red flags, but he found none.

"If you agree to stop pointing that gun at me, I have refreshments for you."

"You live out here in the middle of nowhere, but you just let people into your... home?" Mary Pat said.

Iruno chuckled again. "Trust me," he said. "If I felt any of you were a threat, I would never have shown myself to you. As you will see, finding my... home isn't easy without my help. Plus, I had a good feeling about Marshall, and I know from speaking with him that he's no ripper."

"Ripper?" Lester asked.

"What I call the lost, people who come here and return to a kind of feral state," Iruno said.

"Like Tony and Raya," Stavero said.

Iruno's face creased and his eyes narrowed.

"Two rippers who attacked us in the jungle," Kylie said.

Iruno nodded at Kylie and said, "Do you agree to lower your weapon?"

The cop glanced at Marshall but didn't wait for his approval before lowering the Glock.

"Good," Iruno said. "Let us go."

16

The trail twisted around Mount Sight and ended at the base of a sheer rock face that was part of the dormant volcano's cone. A slope of tumbled stones climbed from the path to a series of rat-like holes that looked to be secondary vents that had been created when lava pushed and branched out from the main vent before it broke through the surface. The holes pocked the entire side of the cliff face.

"Which one is mine?" Iruno said.

Marshall almost chuckled. Almost. He'd been expecting a balanced stone door, or some maze of booby traps, but in the end, like most things, it turned out to be a numbers game.

The first thing Marshall did was look for patterns between the larger stones. Even the lightest of treads left trails over time. But there were many possible paths, the wind swept across the mountains, and there were flat rock precipices that an elephant could walk across without leaving a trace. No, it truly was a numbers game and one that he couldn't win.

Within a quarter-mile radius there looked to be about a hundred cave mouths dotting the sprawling rock face. Some holes were the size of huge water mains, others dark maws that could house the land's largest creatures.

"I'll give you a hint," Iruno said. "It's not the biggest one."

White-gray sludge streaked black coated the stone in front of the largest hole. It looked like bird shit, but there was so much of it. Maybe Pterosaur guano?

Marshall did some mental gymnastics. If left to their own devices and the party worked a simple grid pattern from top to bottom, with climbing gear, and a spotter on the ground, it might take five or ten days to stick a flashlight in every hole. In the meantime, there were many ways to stop an intruder that Marshall could see, which meant there were probably many more.

Aside from the fact that there must be at least one escape route, there was a line of boulders along the crest of the thin precipice that towered over the holes. With a simple cantilever, the line of stones could be tumbled easily, and anyone climbing on the cliff face in the vicinity of the holes would be swept away. Then there was a direct assault from above with rocks, slings, arrows, and spears.

Iruno pulled Marshall aside and out of earshot of the others. He whispered, "Can these two men you've brought with you be trusted?"

Marshall almost laughed at the omission of Kylie and Mary Pat. In the few minutes they'd all been together, Iruno had come to the same conclusions he had, but it had taken him a bit longer. He considered vouching for the men, but something told him that wouldn't be smart. "I don't know," he said.

"Will they accept being blindfolded?" Iruno asked.

Marshall looked back at Lester and Stavero. Both men had softened, and though Stavero hadn't given up all the details of Destinies Shrine, the organization appeared to be nothing more than a group of lost souls searching for purpose and order in a universe run by chaos. Lester was sticking to his story. He was a reporter covering the fossil dig and the solstice events. Marshall would have bet his life the man was lying, but why—and why still? It worried him. He knew there was a point of no return when a lie has been around so long fessing up would prove useless, but this was a unique situation where character was of the upmost importance, at least to him. The person next to him could save his life. Or not.

"You in there?" Iruno asked.

"What they'll accept doesn't matter," Marshall said. "We have to ask them."

Iruno's eyebrows lifted.

Marshall nodded, dropped his pack, and drew out a shirt that had seen better days. He went to his companions and said, "Look, we have to be blindfolded until we get to his spot." The use of the word "we" wasn't an error. He ripped up the shirt that was mostly destroyed anyway, and he handed out blindfolds and took one for himself.

"If I trip and break a leg," Kylie said, the rest of the threat unnecessary.

Marshall tied his blindfold on and then lifted it a smidge so that he could see where he was walking, and yet it still made it appear as though the thin fabric completely covered his eyes.

The climb wasn't far, there were several tunnels and a solid path, but the ascent was steep, and it wasn't long before the party was instructed to take off their blindfolds.

Marshall and crew stood within the opening of one of the mid-sized holes at the center of the pack that overlooked the southern expanse of the wastelands.

Iruno's sanctuary was a warren of twisting tubes made from flowing lava that forced its way out before the main vent blew. He lived in two roundish chambers, and both had window-like openings on their sides filled with blue sky.

One wall displayed an intricate star chart made up of colored lines in various clay tones made from colorful rocks. There were odd shapes with numbers next to them and arrows. It looked like a calculus professor had gone mad after talking to a theoretical physicist who had gotten advice from an astronomer.

On the opposite wall, there was a large triangle with a numerical formula at its center.

The place was sparsely furnished: a cot of woven vines and dried grass, wooden stools, and a table. But there were many modern items as well. Marshall saw a flashlight, a rifle in the corner, a modern backpack, a fleece blanket on the bed, a stainless-steel cup, and a cooler. All the guy needed was solar panels.

The fellowship sat at a table on a grand stone terrace with a commanding view of the wasteland and ate like people for the first time in a long time. There was lettuce with tomatoes. Tomatoes! And meat that tasted so sweet it made him forget about steak. They drank wine that Iruno said was made from wild grapes that grew in abundance in the wilderness to the north, and there were spices and salt. Salt!

Iruno's tales were just as powerful. He kept the party's questions at bay with his own story, which was a tale of loss and wonder and waste. He came through the portal when he was a boy, and he survived alone for several years before he met a man who taught him about the portal. Iruno had gone back-and-forth many times since then and he was visiting for the day when he met Marshall.

Between bites, Marshall asked, "Why don't you live in New Holland?"

Iruno sat silent for a long time, sipping his wine and gazing out at the sun as it touched the horizon.

"I'm sorry if I've offended," Marshall said. He had a feeling he'd picked a scab.

"No, it's O.K. It's funny how people you don't know can do that," Iruno said.

"Do what?" Kylie asked.

"Hit me right in the heart with your first question."

The wind whispered over Mount Sight and the scent of charred meat hung in the air like perfume. Marshall sipped wine and savored its unbelievable taste.

After a time Iruno continued. "I don't live in New Holland because I enjoy the solitary life. There are those in New Holland who know me, though they may choose not to speak of it. I was known under a different name back then. People don't last in the dinosaur domain,

Marshall, if you haven't already figured that out. We're all gazelles amidst lions."

"So why not go back?" Lester asked.

"Because I have nothing there, and…"

Ida's words echoed in Marshall's head. "Your purpose, that which you hold dear, may change." Marshall looked over at Kylie, who was examining a crack in the floor. None of his companions spoke and the silence stretched on until Marshall said, "That's understandable, but wouldn't you be happier around people? So you had a little help?"

Iruno shrugged. "The more I learn, the less I know, and all those people do is fight about things I don't care about, not unlike back home. At least here they don't have nuclear weapons and armies and chemical bombs. The dinosaurs keep them behind their wall, and if you're smart and if you pay attention, this world is fertile.

"When I have regrets or homesickness, I go back to modern times, and it doesn't take much to remember why I stay here. Air filled with gas fumes, the never-ending crowd of overpopulated, overindulged morons prattling about nothing. When I see the deforestation, the garbage, the graffiti on the Chaka Stones… No, Lester, I don't think about going back."

When dinner was over, and stars blinked in the clear sky, the companions moved indoors. No torches or candles were needed because Iruno had an old-school camping lantern that burned oil.

"I've been working on that most of my life," Iruno said as he pointed at a large map drawn on one of the cave's mighty flat walls. "Drink? Water? Whiskey?"

All eyes turned in Iruno's direction as he lifted a bottle of Jack Daniels.

Everyone nodded, and the group drank from real glasses. Marshall held his up and said, "Seems you've thought of everything." He sipped and the burn of the whiskey going down his throat made him smile.

Iruno shrugged. "Not really."

"You've been in stores in… our time?" Stavero asked. The man hadn't spoken in an hour.

"Sure have," Iruno said, and his face scrunched like he'd eaten bad fish.

Marshall wanted to ask which stores. Where did you get the money? How did you get there? All these questions would have adventure-like answers and curiosity burned him like a flame, but there were more important questions at hand.

The map on the wall showed Iruno's known world. A vast inland sea marked the edge of the map to the west, and to the north, there was a vast jungle labeled "unexplored." Marshall saw the Chaka Stones to the south, New Holland in the southeast, the bamboo patch, the Canyons... It was all there in full color. Several dots were labeled Shokra, and there was a large circle with an X at its center labeled Toro ki' Temple.

When everyone was seated before the great map, sipping their drinks, Stavero asked, "Don't you worry about the big one?"

Marshall didn't know what the man was referring to, but Iruno did.

"The idea of living every day like it could be your last is particularly appropriate here in the dinosaur domain, and I'm not just talking about the beasties," Iruno said. "There is no way to know when the asteroid will come, but I fear it might be soon."

"And you keep coming back?" Kylie asked.

He shrugged. "Isn't that life? Who knows when their day will come?"

"But you said you feel that time is soon," Lester said.

"The stars say as much, and I believe there are other... portals."

"I don't understand," Kylie said.

"Nor me," Stavero said.

"I don't know who created the stones, though I believe their purpose had something to do with research or the transport and preservation of the dinosaurs before the extinction event, but that's just my theory based on evidence that's circumstantial at best."

Marshall didn't know what to say.

"And what of it anyway?" Iruno said. "Not everything will be laid waste when the meteorite hits. The fact that the Chaka Stones still stand in modern times is proof of this."

"Why the solstice?" Marshall asked. "Why not the equinox?"

Iruno shrugged again. "Whoever, or whatever created the portals didn't seem to care if light and day are equal. To travel from the dinosaur domain to an unfixed point in time the portal opens at sunup when the sun's first rays reach the Chaka Stones, sundown is the reverse. My guess is the solstice plays an integral role in the biorhythms of Earth that help drive time."

"I've been wondering about that," Stavero said. "Does time... work the same here? Pass at the same rate? If we came through to a fixed point, didn't you? But you've been here for many years."

"My fixed point and yours are different because we come from different points in the time stream relative to our position in time. You can't un-age and the years you spend here will stay with you, even if you manage to return to the exact moment in the future you left," Iruno said. "Those who have gone home after many years, and there have only been three that I know of, all suffered mental breakdowns from either keeping the dinosaur domain a secret, or cracking from no one believing their story and being called delusional, sick, and concussed."

Marshall hadn't thought about that. What would he say if he got home? The "if" stabbed at him.

Everyone sipped, and outside a beast screeched, but out on the desolate plain just below the clouds there was no answering roar of an alpha.

"And before you ask," Iruno said. "No, the flutter of a butterfly's wings here can't cause a hurricane back in your time."

Nobody spoke.

"Your contemporary, Mr. Ray Bradbury, may have written interesting tales, but there's nothing any of you can do here that will change the future."

Marshall was so confused he felt like he was on the first day of freshman algebra. "You use the portal, obviously, so you must know how it works."

"Now we get to it," Iruno said. "You are all, as of this moment at least, intent on going home?"

They all nodded.

"Fair enough," Iruno said. "But know the path is long and will have many stops."

None of the companions protested.

"The backward cycle is tied to this exact time period relative to your position in time. Why is unknown to me, but to me it's further proof that the creators of the portal were specifically interested in the dinosaurs prior to the extinction event."

Nobody spoke. Marshall's skin tingled with anticipation.

"There are three components to opening the portal at the Chaka Stones to a specific point in time, theoretically your time. Think of it as a triangulation of forces."

"Triangulation?" Lester said.

"Yes, and as it sounds, it's a method used in various fields such as geography, surveying, navigation, and social sciences to determine the location of a point by forming triangles utilizing known points. The concept is based on trigonometry, specifically the law of sines and the law of cosines.

"Triangulation relies on the principle that if you have two fixed points or baselines, and the angles formed by a third point, the target point, the baselines can be used to calculate the distance and location of the target point relative to the known points. By measuring angles and distances, it's possible to calculate unknown distances and locations. In the case of the Chaka Stones, a point in time."

"What are the points?" Marshall asked.

Iruno said, "There are many possibilities, and one error can throw the equation off. I know from my studies that many ancient civilizations like Egypt and Greece used triangulation in many of their theories, so the methods have long histories. In modern times the development of trigonometry and advanced surveying techniques during the Renaissance and Enlightenment periods made the solstice calculations easier. Celestial bodies, like stars or the sun, are used as fixed points to measure angles and determine their position on the globe... or in this case, in time."

Marshall recalled the large triangle painted on the cave wall with the formula inside.

"First you must have an anchor, and the solstice must be in perfect harmony with the Chaka Stones. But what further tunes the timeclock to the future is Woodhenge," Iruno said.

And as understanding bloomed, Marshall smiled.

17

Marshall unrolled the map and laid it flat on the table. "Do you have chalk?" he asked.

Iruno said, "I can do you one better." He disappeared into another section of the cave before returning with a pencil. "Keep it and use it well," he said as he handed the stubby and battered #2 to Marshall. The thing brought back bad memories of scantron sheets and scoldings from his parents. He hadn't always been professor material.

With the group looking on in eager anticipation, Marshall updated the map with all the new information they'd learned since leaving the marked path. He extended the trail line through the jungle, the maze of the Canyons, around the bamboo patch via the southerly route, and when he drew the line across the wastelands, he gave the devil grass thicket a wide berth and labeled the area "dangerous indigenous fauna." He added other prominent landmarks and several dots which he labeled Shokra, along with an X for the Toro ki' Temple.

Then he turned the map over, drew a triangle, and, starting at the top and moving clockwise, he labeled each point anchor, Woodhenge, solstice / Chaka Stones. "Based on what you've told us, I think I understand the basics," he said. "Portal activation requires the perfect meeting of your anchor, the pure solstice as the sun rises or sets through the Chaka Stones, and the shadows of Woodhenge set to a specific setting."

"That is correct," Iruno said. "Did you see the Woodhenge reenactment when you were atop Hicks Dome?"

Marshall nodded as he licked his lips.

Iruno stared at him as if waiting for Marshall to work something out on his own.

Then it came to him. "If the dinosaur domain end of the portal is fixed when coming from the future, what is Woodhenge needed for?" Marshall asked.

"There you go," Iruno said. "In your time Woodhenge is part of my people's rituals that go back a thousand years."

"It's purely ceremonial?" Mary Pat said.

Iruno nodded. "In modern times, yes, but I believe it wasn't always that way."

"And here?" Stavero said.

"To get home from the dinosaur domain you'll need Woodhenge calibration distances from the time wheel. The formula, which you saw in the center of the triangle is the key and was allegedly discovered and worked through by a Greek explorer long ago."

Marshall deflated. The formula he'd seen was complex and he was no mathematician. He'd ended up studying history because of a failed attempt at physics.

Iruno laughed. "You can put the formula in your fancy phone," Iruno said. "It still works, yes?"

Marshall brightened as he nodded. It was at seventy-one percent power.

Kylie said, "Back home, the Chaka Stones have a half circle at one end."

"As you've guessed, that's the porthole," Iruno said.

"I'm told it's a full circle here in the dinosaur domain, but back home half of it is gone," Lester added, his voice shaking.

"This does not matter, though I know not why," Iruno said.

"Something I've been wondering about makes sense now," said Stavero. "It was irking me that no dinosaurs happened to be in the wrong place at the wrong time and wandered forward in time, but— That fossil dig on the side of Hicks Dome?"

Marshall nodded vigorously. "It was way too high in the geological strata. Not where it was supposed to be."

"Woodhenge is a failsafe of a kind, I believe, to stop just that type of disaster from occurring," Iruno said. "But clearly someone's primitive attempts to manipulate the portal led to a beast crossing over."

"You mentioned a time wheel," Marshall said. "Can you gi—"

An earsplitting shriek tore through the cave and Iruno vaulted to his feet and killed the camp light.

It was pitch-black outside, and the faint gray moonlight leaking into the cave went dark as the thunderous flapping of giant wings resounded through the cave.

Another shriek and the air inside the mountain seemed to tinkle with energy.

"Toothless coming home," Iruno said.

Nobody spoke, and the ground vibrated and then fell still.

"What the hell is a Toothless?" Kylie asked.

"That large cave you saw? The one with all the guano coating its entrance?"

Everyone nodded except Lester, who seemed lost in a Jack Daniels haze.

"It's more than the desolation and the climb that keeps people and beasts away from Mount Sight," Iruno said. "Toothless is the king of the sky. And my nasty neighbor."

The group waited in darkness for a few more minutes, the growl of their frenzied breathing the only sound. After what felt like an hour, but was only five minutes, Iruno switched the light back on and said, "Marshall, you were saying?"

"Yeah…" His nerves were on fire, his head was spinning from the alcohol, and he felt cold despite the heat. "Can you give us the Woodhenge measurements from this time wheel? Is it here?"

Iruno's smile faded, and he drank the rest of his whiskey. "No," he said after several moments of silence. "You need what I call the time wheel, which is like a cosmic compass."

Marshall rolled his shoulders. Nothing was easy. Ever.

"The Toro ki' Temple contains what is known in this land as the Starry Stele, which is sort of a giant astrolabe. Its stone steles were quarried from an unknown ancient location that, from what I've been able to gather, was the site of a meteorite crash, or if you can stomach more of a conspiracy-driven type theory, an alien spacecraft."

"An astrolabe is an ancient astronomical navigation instrument. I saw that on Nova," Kylie said. "But what's a stele?"

Marshall said, "A stele is an upright stone or slab of stone. Usually, they're inscribed or carved with symbols or writing, like a monument."

"Like the Chaka Stones," Stavero said.

Iruno continued, "There is a primitive planisphere that overlaps the time wheel—Starry Stele—which will help set the astrolabe."

"I can't say I understand the math, or the concept behind it, if it's understandable, but I don't see how the Chaka Stones can get me back to a specific point in time," Marshall said. "That's what I'm struggling with."

"The anchor," Kylie said. "The third point of the triangle." She pointed at the drawing that still lay on the table before Marshall.

Marshall nodded.

"What is it then?" Stavero said.

"The final piece is you," Iruno said. "You create the anchor."

Marshall said nothing because he didn't know what to ask.

"Your memory, the moment you crossed, provides an anchor in time for the Chaka Stones, as long as Woodhenge is set correctly."

Pain knotted Marshall's stomach. "The moment?"

"The memory of the instant you crossed the plains of existence, rode the sinuous strings of time and space. You recall how you came to be here, yes?" Iruno said.

Marshall rubbed his chin and looked around at his companions. Lester stared at Iruno in disbelief, Stavero focused all his attention on the triangle drawn on the back of the map, and Kylie and Mary Pat exchanged glances before looking to Marshall for guidance he couldn't provide. He recalled a memory…that flash of light, just as the final glare of the dying day drained from Hicks Dome, a spark of light, like a tiny dying flame, appeared within the broken circle of pink stones. Was that the memory?

"Woodhenge and the Chaka Stones create the time path, but you must find the clearing at its end," Iruno said.

Lester laughed, not chuckled, a full-throated onslaught of skepticism. "This all sounds ridiculous."

"Don't believe me?" Iruno asked.

Lester looked around for support, found none, and said nothing.

Marshall understood where the guy was coming from, but after spending a couple of weeks in the dinosaur domain his definition of impossible had changed.

"Time itself is connected to your perception of it, every event. So what you believe happened, your memory if you will, marks each event as a literal point in time, a rock in a stream, a frozen point amidst a crawling swarm."

"What if my memory is wrong?" asked Mary Pat.

"Try, try, try, and try again," Iruno said. "You've got plenty of time to search your memory, but the anchor must be exact."

"That means we can't go back until the summer solstice?" Mary Pat said.

At first, Marshall didn't understand, but his memory was definitely seasonal-specific; warm breeze, no ice, and no snow.

Iruno shook his head. "No. But others might be able to, and there is always the possibility others may arrive. I will be there observing, as always."

"No trip to the future this time?" Kylie said.

"Not this time," Iruno said. "I rarely travel anymore…" He stared wistfully at the triangle on the back of the map as if it might speak to him. "The risk of getting stuck in your world, regardless of the age…"

What else needed to be said? For the first time, Marshall considered the idea that perhaps staying in the dinosaur domain wasn't so crazy.

"Wait," Kylie said. "You have to start over every time you come back from the future? Like you were never here before?"

Iruno smiled. "No, I simply create new anchors as I experience the new transfer points."

The group said nothing.

"Don't worry," Iruno said. "Coming up with your anchor is the least of your problems."

"Has anyone's anchor ever sent them to the wrong place?" Kylie asked.

Iruno frowned. "Unknown. I myself have never experienced such a phenomenon."

Lester emerged from his silence and said, "Too bad. We could have traveled to the future."

"I believe this is another failsafe the creators of the portals put in place," Iruno said.

"Creators? Who..." stammered Stavero. "Where did all this come from and why?"

Iruno hiked his shoulders. "There's no way I would have figured all this out on my own. What I've told you so far represents several lifetimes of study and struggle and is far from complete. You can find clues to the answers to your questions at the Toro ki' Temple, though not having the lexicon for their writings and symbols makes understanding the temple nearly impossible. There are Egyptian hieroglyphics like those found on temples in Egypt—I checked once. The formulas and physics are all well beyond most folk's comprehension, but not all. Though I can't claim to understand what I read, I was able to tie in several portions of the time wheel formula with known physics. The gap, the unknown, the dark matter, of course, is the anchor."

"That borders on the paranormal," Stavero said.

"Yes and no," Iruno said. "We humans are primitive beasts. Nothing more than bags of skin and bone and chemicals that have more developed brains than the other beasts around us. Does this make us intelligent? No. All seeing? No. There are things our primitive senses can't register—things that perhaps the Toro ki' could see and sense."

"You're saying the Toro ki' weren't human?" Marshall asked.

Iruno hiked his shoulders in that annoying way that jumped on Marshall's last nerve. "What I'm saying is the Toro ki', whatever or whoever they were, may have had different, or more advanced sensory perception and intelligence that allowed them to experience and mold things beyond our understanding. See things we can't see."

"Like how we can't see certain bands on the light spectrum," Stavero said.

"Yes," Iruno said.

Marshall felt the excitement drain from the room.

"If you're anything like me, you're feeling overwhelmed right now," Iruno said. "Had I not been instructed, taught, and given that..." Iruno pointed to a notebook sitting on a table beside a primitive cot, "I don't know where I'd be."

"At least you know how to work the portal," Marshall said.

"Soon so shall you," Iruno said. "There are steps in the notebook that detail how to get the Woodhenge reading from the time wheel. We'll put the formula in your phone, and you should be O.K."

"Is Woodhenge still set based on this past summer?" Marshall asked.

Iruno nodded. "It's a simple task to reset the poles. Sometimes the local fauna messes with them, but there are straight evergreens all around and new poles can be constructed if need be."

"How far is the temple from here?" Kylie asked.

"Three or four days to the south," Iruno said. "It won't shorten your way home, but it won't lengthen it, either."

"Is there a path?" Marshall asked.

"No, but I can add the route to your map, and you must follow the Shokra," Iruno said. "They are markers that lead to the Toro ki' Temple."

Marshall recalled the timeworn stone statue on the hillside of Hicks Dome where he'd met Iruno. "That statue, where you and I met… Was that… Is that a Shokra?"

Iruno nodded and smiled.

"You're not coming with us to the temple, Iruno?" Kylie asked.

Iruno shook his head no. "But if all goes well, I'll see you at the winter solstice."

The distant screams of a Pterosaur leaked into the mountain.

Iruno performed a perfectly exaggerated yawn that brought the conversation to a close. "Rest my friends. We can talk again tomorrow," he said.

The party laid out their woven straw bedrolls on the cave floor as their host climbed onto his vine-woven cot. The camp light winked out and blackness filled the cave.

As Marshall lay staring into the darkness, he should have felt encouraged. He'd found answers, but his muscles ached with the knowledge that he had a long way to go. The winter solstice was coming, but it appeared that his field at the end of the path bloomed with summer flowers.

18

The fellowship rested and studied up at Mount Sight for two days, listening to Iruno's stories and advice. Marshall planned to depart at daybreak on the third day, and the party awoke to find Iruno gone. There was no note, no breakfast was laid out, but there was a care package containing a small gourd-flask of Jack Daniels, the Bowie knife Iruno claimed to have found on a skeleton in the jungle, and some dried meat wrapped in what looked like plastic wrap from the future.

As the wind whistled through the caves Marshall felt a deep sense of loss. Iruno had agreed to meet at the Chaka Stones for the winter solstice, but that was months away, and in the dinosaur domain that was a lifetime.

At the same time, Iruno had placed great trust in him and his companions. When they left Iruno's sanctuary, its location would be made clear to them.

"Do you think he didn't want to say goodbye?" Kylie asked.

"Maybe he went to drain the main vein," Lester said.

"Nice," Mary Pat said.

As the group gathered themselves to leave, Marshall appraised his team, minus Leeri, and he marveled at how much they'd changed since their arrival in the Cretaceous. It wasn't just their attitudes or their newfound connection to their environment, but their physical appearances had deteriorated to a state beyond what was normal in civilized societies.

Lester looked the worse for wear. His sneakers were mud black, his jeans ripped, and what was once a colorful Hawaiian shirt was now a gray flowered rag with a gaping hole on its right side and missing half its collar. His cloth sack containing his meager possessions, which amounted to basically nothing, was slung over his shoulder. The man had made no effort on their travels to enhance his weapon skills, so he still carried the pointed club, which he had yet to use.

Kylie wore her black leather shoes, her uniform pants and utility belt, gun in its holster, but her blue shirt and badge were packed away. She wore her white t-shirt, her hair pulled back, and she looked like she'd just left the gym.

Stavero, well, was Stavero. Rather than change to normal clothes, which he'd been offered several times by Iruno, he was still attired in tattered, yellow robes as if members of Destinies Shrine had taken a vow of poverty. He carried his bow, arrows, spear, and whatever was hidden in the folds of his robes.

Mary Pat had somehow gone unbruised, and her clothes seemed cleaner than everyone else's. Her major change had occurred in her facial expressions, which had gone from jovial and positive to sullen and wary. She carried more than her share; weapons, food, water, not only for her, but for the party.

Marshall considered backtracking to see what could be found of Leeri, and more importantly, as horrible as it was, his possessions. The dead man had items that would provide valuable currency in the months ahead, but when last seen most of Leeri was getting pulled down a giant snake hole. It wasn't worth risking life and limb for an Army canteen, ripped clothes, a purse, a pocketknife, and a finely tuned sling that was accurate from fifty yards.

It was worrisome how fast Leeri had been forgotten, wiped clean from the party's collective memory as if he'd never existed. That was the problem with trauma relationships. It was somewhat like a video game. You had X number of lives and when you used one, oh well, you had more.

Marshall stuffed the map in his backpack and slung the bag over his shoulder as he grabbed his pike. The prior night the entire party had watched as Marshall, using sheets of notebook paper smuggled to the dinosaur domain, transcribed the appropriate passages and Iruno's instructions for the time wheel.

Iruno claimed the notebook never left the cave, and that it never would. If they ever needed it again, and should he no longer be around, the companions knew where it could be found.

In another display of trust, Iruno agreed to provide his guidance under one condition. He insisted that Marshall be the sole owner of the new pages and updated map and that they were not to be passed on to anyone else. Ever. Without Iruno's approval. The last thing the old man wanted was a worn path to his doorstep because that defeated the purpose of the location of the doorstep.

Marshall wandered through the maze of lava caves one last time, hoping Iruno would return from taking care of morning necessities. But the old man didn't appear, and as the sun rose over the mountain and dusk spread over the wastelands it was time to move on from Mount Sight.

Some things never change, regardless of what point in time one is currently living in. Gravity was gravity, and going down was always easier than going up. Something about the necessary expenditure of energy.

Climbing down the mountain proved uneventful and quick. A thick blanket of clouds hid the sky, and shrieks and cries came from within. Nothing could be seen moving on the open plain. The party made good time as they trekked southeast in single file, cutting diagonally across the plain and avoiding the large patch of devil grass. The snake didn't show itself, but there were slashes all over the hardpan that marked its passing.

By midday, the fellowship reached the edge of the wastelands where the jungle crept tentatively onto the hardened lava and dirt. Vines snaked over the ground, and tall weeds fought their way toward light, reclaiming their territory inch by inch.

A thin path led into the jungle, but it soon disappeared, and Marshall was pressed into service using the compass. Following a heading was next to impossible, and the party was constantly forced to shift direction to move around holes, boulders, thickets of vegetation, and great rents in the landscape that represented the remains of the upheaval of a world.

In the tight jungle, the party didn't see many of the domain's larger beasts, but they heard them. Braying and moaning and clicking and screeching filled the forest at all times, and smaller creatures, both of the mammal and lizard variety, fought and frolicked in the coolness beneath the thick tree canopy.

The map showed a huge lake to the east of their course, but throughout the day the party strayed too far east, and they emerged from the thick rainforest at the edge of the vast lake.

Marshall estimated on average the lake was two miles across and four miles long. The westerly route was the quickest way around, but not in the dark, so Marshall called a halt for the night. Judging by the map, the fellowship had traveled a third of the way to the temple.

The lake didn't have a firm shoreline to speak of. Thick patches of reeds surrounded the water, and in several spots, the reeds had been flattened and broken by something's passage. Even with his limited dinosaur knowledge, Marshall knew that in the dinosaur domain, the creatures of the deep were just as ferocious as those that crawled on land.

"Let's move back into the jungle," Marshall said. "I don't like being so close to the lake. The surface is—"

A plop resounded over the water and a tiny tsunami rippled outward from a point twenty feet out on the lake where a stone had just knifed into the water.

Marshall wheeled. "Who the hell did that?"

All eyes fell on Lester who stared sheepishly at the vine-covered ground.

Out on the lake, the circles grew larger as they spread out over the smooth water.

Marshall reined in his anger and frustration and said, "Do you think drawing attention is smart? Do you!" Marshall's voice went up four notches with the last two words.

"No, sorry," Lester said. "I wasn't thinking."

"Do you ever?" said Mary Pat.

Marshall marched back into the jungle without another word. There was a tall tree with thick spreading branches about fifty paces in, and he picked a spot about ten feet from the ground and proclaimed it as the perfect spot to build a platform because of the many crisscrossing branches.

The party gathered wood and vegetation and within an hour the fellowship had built themselves a sturdy perch hidden within the cover of the tree.

On the ground, at the base of the tree, Kylie started a fire, and the companions ate a meal of smoked dinosaur meat, mushrooms, and salad. The greens were from a tree that appeared everywhere in the domain, and the huge leaves tasted like basil. A citrus dressing made from an odd pink fruit called 'a bitter' finished off the meal, and the group drank their fill of fresh water from the lake, which was so clear Marshall saw the tall tendrils of water plants reaching up from unknown depths in the moonlight.

There wasn't much conversation. Everything that had to be said was said out on the trail, and as the party's eyelids drooped, Marshall suggested they all climb up onto the platform while they still could.

The platform was only ten feet by ten feet, so the group pretended like they liked each other and packed in tight, the edges of the roost boxed in by the tree's thick plumage.

As the party dropped off to sleep Marshall tried to see starlight through the thick void that filled in the gaps between the tangle of tree branches. With the fire out, and his eyes adjusting to the impenetrable darkness, Marshall saw glowing pinpricks of light in the blackness above.

He jerked to a sitting position and woke Kylie.

"What? What?" she said as she drew her gun.

"Ssh," Marshall said as he pointed up.

The field of eyes had grown brighter. Among the shadows, the unmistakable outline of nocturnal hunters could be seen, their keen eyes glowing within the maze of branches and leaves.

"Let's wake the others. Carefully," Marshall said. "I don't want anyone—"

A knot of churning legs and claws surged through the tree canopy, a haze of movement that came into focus as it drew nearer. The creatures were the size of a house cat and covered in brown and white feathers. Their heads were elongated and narrow, and they had pointed snouts with sharp beaks containing leaf-shaped teeth that glowed white in the blackness.

Lester screamed upon waking, tried to press to his feet, and knocked Stavero off the platform.

Stavero woke as he fell, and his scream was cut off when he hit the ground with a thud.

Branches snapped and leaves fell as the beasts tore through the tree canopy, screeching and hollering, the field of eyes growing as it got closer. The beasts barked and whistled as they came on. They were incredibly fast and agile, and the swarm would be upon the party in seconds.

Kylie fired twice into the field of eyes and the creatures slowed as two of their mates fell dead, the corpses bouncing off branches as they fell.

But the creatures didn't stop.

Lester was climbing slowly down the tree, but as Marshall started his way down, he drove the man down with his feet and Lester jumped to the ground.

Kylie used a branch for leverage and swung to the ground, and Mary Pat followed in her wake.

"Stay close to the shoreline," Marshall yelled. "I don't want us getting separated in the jungle."

Lester picked himself up and darted into the greenery, but Mary Pat cut off his escape route. The woman's face was red with sleep and anger, and she gripped Lester by the arm and said, "Help me."

Marshall had forgotten about Stavero, but Mary Pat hadn't. Reluctantly, Lester helped Mary Pat lift Stavero and drag the groggy man into the jungle. Stavero was moving and moaning, so he was alive. Not surprising. He'd only fallen ten feet.

With everyone on the ground safely, Marshall turned the flashlight on the creatures and the crowd of tiny dinosaurs came to a halt. Leaves fell and branches creaked and cracked as he waved the light around, covering it with his hand to create a strobing effect.

The rest of the party fled, except Kylie who had Marshall's back, the Glock at the ready.

As the beasts got used to the light, one by one they surged back into motion. The creatures bounced and climbed using their two rear legs, which were twice the size of their forward appendages, and ended in three-toed feet equipped with sharp claws. At four feet from snout to tail tip, the creatures looked to weigh about thirty pounds, and their bodies were slender with long necks and heads that bore triangular crests.

Marshall backed away, light out before him like a weapon, and as he and Kylie slipped into the jungle the knot in his stomach loosened.

"Kylie! Marshall!" The panicked scream came from the jungle in the direction of the lake.

As if some cosmic primeval warning had been sent out over the dinosaur telegraph, the swarm of bird-like dinosaurs stopped advancing, their long necks gyrating. Then they turned tail and the entire group climbed back up the tree as if the hounds of hell were chasing them.

"Come on," Marshall said, as he headed toward the panicked screams of Mary Pat.

19

Marshall arrived to find Mary Pat tending to Stavero, who was awake, and thrashing and yelling about being lied to. Lester was nowhere in sight.

Moonlight shimmered off the lake and angled into the jungle, and along the lake's shoreline water reeds bent and snapped as a gigantic creature stirred. The silvery lake surged into the water reeds as a behemoth emerged—a twenty-five-foot monster that looked to be the bastard child of an alligator and a monitor lizard.

Orbs of glowing onyx peered through the dense foliage, and as the beast came forward water surged and splashed, and the earth trembled. The jungle fell silent, and with a sinuous grace that defied its size, the titan slipped from the reeds into the jungle.

Marshall turned the light on the beast, but it wasn't deterred. Fiona's paper she'd written for Nature Magazine came rushing back; Deinosuchus was one of the largest crocodilians to have ever existed. But despite its immense size, with estimated lengths ranging upwards of forty feet, Deinosuchus was not a true dinosaur, but rather a relative of modern crocodiles.

The creature was all scales and sinew, its hide rough, each scale the size of a dinner plate. The scutes overlapped, creating a natural armor, and a ridge of thick, bony plates ran down the length of its back. Jagged spikes protruded from its powerful tail, which swung lazily as it flattened vegetation.

An ominous deep-throated growl carried over the water, and the air was thick with the scent of moss, damp earth, and the beast's primal musk, which smelled like rotten eggs stuffed in a dirty sock. Vines and creepers parted before the monster, and trees bent and branches cracked.

"Can Stavero stand?" Marshall asked.

"He has to," Mary Pat said.

"We all can't outrun it. We need to split…" Her voice fell dead as her gaze strayed from the monster to a patch of darkness to her left.

Marshall squinted as he tried to see what she was looking at, his heart racing as the ground trembled and the 'terrible crocodile' bore down on the party.

Lester, having learned nothing from Leeri's ill-advised attempt to hide from the Titanoboa, had taken shelter behind a thick tree. The impressive specimen looked like an oak and may have been a distant relative, though its leaves were twice the size, and they glowed yellow in the gloom.

The Deinosuchus turned its long, narrow head, and its legs churned faster as Lester became prey.

No matter how big and tough you think you are, there is always someone... or something, stronger than you. Few things throughout time were as consistent.

Snapping water reeds and the gurgle of a surging knot of whitewater rolling into the jungle brought the giant croc to a halt. It swung its flat head, its wet eyes searching for the source of the ruckus.

Marshall, caught in the moment, trained the flashlight on the commotion.

A huge brown sail, ribbed with dark lines, like a giant striped dorsal fin, rose from the lake.

The king croc screamed, and its jaws flexed open, revealing large, conical teeth.

A massive shadow surged from the lake, a blur of movement that streaked over the water reeds like smoke, a rolling wave of debris and lake water clearing its path.

Spinosaurus was a leviathan of water and land. The sail-like form on its back cast a long shadow through the jungle, and its powerful rear legs flattened vegetation as the beast pushed into the jungle. Its head was long and flat, and it ended in a broad snout that tapered to a pointed tip with elongated jaws filled with teeth.

In the cloud of LED light that filled the forest, the Spinosaurus's basketball-sized eyes shined with menace, but the alpha only had eyes for the other titan, which, like Lester, had decided it was time to make like a tree and leave.

Lester left cover and wove his way through the vegetation away from the upcoming heavyweight bout, and the beasts didn't appear to notice.

With a sudden surge of motion, its teeth gleaming, the Spinosaurus closed the distance between itself and the giant croc with terrifying speed.

The Deinosuchus lashed out with its powerful jaws, snapping at the air in a futile attempt to defend itself. Its tail swung in a wide arc, but it missed its mark and hit a tree. A loud crack, and then the shriek and pop of splintering wood carried over the chaos.

With a cry that sounded like all the paper ever produced was getting shredded, the Spinosaurus lunged. Its muscular rear legs pounded through the underbrush, its mouth gaping wide as the monster's jaws clamped down on the Deinosuchus's armored hide with bone-crushing force and lifted it aloft like a toy.

The crocodilian beast roared as it thrashed, its powerful tail lashing out in a desperate bid for freedom.

But the Spinosaurus held fast, its razor-sharp teeth sinking deeper into flesh as blood splattered the vegetation.

A thunderous crack, like a bolt of lightning, pierced the night, and the tree the Deinosuchus had smacked with its tail gave up the ghost. Splinters flew as the giant tree fell, but the death of the tree wasn't what turned Marshall's stomach into a roiling flesh-bag of maggots.

Under the harsh LED light, Lester fled before the falling tree. He threw himself forward, trying to out race gravity, but there was too far to go, and not enough time.

Marshall wanted to yell, to tell the guy to make a hard turn, but the words died on his tongue. The tree had many large branches that protruded from the trunk in every direction, and making a sudden turn might make things worse.

With a final, desperate effort, the Deinosuchus unleashed a flurry of blows as it thrashed, striking out with its tail, the claws at the ends of its four appendages raking at the Spinosaurus.

But the giant croc was no match for the sheer power of the Spinosaurus, whose grip only tightened with each passing moment.

The falling tree tore through the shorter trees and plants, branches breaking, leaves falling like rain as it crashed to the jungle floor. The ground shook, and a scream that would forever give Marshall nightmares rose above all other sounds.

It was Lester, and he was yelling, crying, and wailing as if the weight of the entire tree had landed on him. But that couldn't be. The man would already be dead.

The Deinosuchus's struggles weakened as its lifeblood ebbed away, leaving it gasping for breath as its strength faded. Blood leaked from its mouth and from where the Spinosaurus's teeth punctured the giant croc's armored hide.

A sickening *crunch* echoed through the jungle as jaws closed and the Deinosuchus fell still, its corpse hanging from the giant's mouth.

For a moment, the only sound was Lester's crying and screams for help.

Lake water lapped into the jungle as the Spinosaurus hoisted its prey aloft, a grisly trophy silhouetted against the greenery in the moonlight. The monster turned and stalked through the jungle, then charged back into the lake like Godzilla disappearing back into the sea after a victory. Whitewater surged and the last thing to sink into the silvery depths was the beast's dorsal fin-like sail.

Crying and whimpering filled the forest as Marshall and the others gaped at the lake in silence.

Stavero had passed out and missed all the action, and Mary Pat held his head in her hands.

Marshall still held the flashlight, and he shifted its beam in an attempt to find Lester.

Kylie gasped, the Glock held at her side.

"Shit," Marshall said as he surged into motion, then stopped and turned back to Mary Pat. "Stay with Stavero and do what you can."

Mary Pat nodded, her eyes trained on Lester.

Marshall and Kylie worked their way through the devastation along the fallen tree trunk. Branches crisscrossed the jungle, and when Marshall reached Lester, all hope fled.

Lester's arm was pinned beneath a thick branch. "I can't get it free!" Lester whined.

Marshall handed the flashlight to Kylie and bent to examine the area where Lester's arm met the unyielding tree branch. Blood leaked onto the wood, and he could see that Lester's right forearm and hand were crushed. The branch pinning the hand hadn't broken away from the tree trunk, and it held some of the fallen tree's weight, which pressed the branch against a stone, Lester's arm in between.

"It hurts, Marshall, baaa..." Lester started to fade out as he gritted his teeth.

Marshall shook him. "Stay with me," he said. Then he turned to Kylie. "Go get..." He couldn't believe he was going to say it. "Get that knife Iruno gave us. And whatever is left of the Jack Daniels."

"What?" stammered Lester. "What do you need a knife for?"

"Then get a small fire going," Marshall said. "I'm going to need a red-hot piece of wood." He left unsaid what he would need it for.

Kylie nodded, her eyes shifting to Lester before finding the ground as she left Lester and Marshall alone.

"What do you need a hot piece of wood for?" Lester wailed.

Marshall understood the denial, but there was no time for it, and he ripped off the band-aid. "The wood needs to be hot enough to cauterize a stump."

"A... stump?"

Marshall waited and let the realization dawn before saying, "There is no way we can move this tree, or cut you free without an axe or saw, and your hand... It's already lost, Lester. I'm sorry."

Lester's eyes grew glassy, and he wept.

"There are no other options. You can't stay here, and there's no way you're leaving here with your hand, and the longer we wait, the more blood you're going to lose," Marshall said as he grimaced and looked away. He didn't particularly like the guy, but he didn't know if it was fair that he was literally being forced to give a pound of flesh.

As if to put a period on the discussion a roar echoed through the jungle.

A fire sprouted in the darkness, its glow knifing through the forest.

Lester wailed, but he no longer protested.

The next ten minutes played out like a slow-moving nightmare as Lester slipped in and out of consciousness and Marshall tried to summon his bravery. Lester had no choice, but did he have it in him to sever another man's hand?

Kylie returned with the half-empty gourd of whiskey and a knife, the twelve-inch Bowie that Iruno left for them. It had a deer antler handle, but the metal was finely worked, and heavy, and he thought it would do the job, but could he? If it meant saving Lester's life, he thought he could.

Marshall's nerves danced just beneath his skin, and a ringing started to build in his head. He dropped his pack and dug for the pieces of the shredded t-shirt the party had used as blindfolds. When he had them all he twisted them together to make a tourniquet.

Lester's eyes grew wider, spittle leaking from his mouth, his face a deep shade of pink.

"You know what I need to do with this, right?" Marshall asked.

Lester nodded, but his sobs became louder and more frantic.

Kylie put her hand on Marshall's shoulder and said, "Let me know when you need me." She wandered off toward the fire to tend the bat-sized limb she had stuck in the embers.

"O.K.," he said, then turned his attention to Lester. "Are you ready?"

Lester looked away, but said nothing.

"Here." Marshall handed Lester a stick to bite down on. "Your forearm is crushed, so hopefully it won't take all that much to get through the bones." He took a deep breath, closed his eyes, and gathered his courage. Once he started, he couldn't stop.

With Lester staring at the jungle and trying to pretend what was about to happen didn't concern him, Marshall tied the tourniquet tightly around Lester's arm, leaving enough space for the blade to cut. "Ready, Kylie?"

"Yes."

Marshall splashed the remainder of the whiskey on Lester's arm just above where it was pinned under the tree. "Bring me the burning wood!" he yelled.

He focused on the spot where Lester's arm disappeared under the tree trunk and paused, the horror of it all hitting him like a brick. Do it now! Now! Marshall raised the knife over his head, sweat dripping into his eyes, and he felt the heat of his companion's stares on his back.

With a screech from Lester, Marshall brought the blade down, a vicious strike that cracked bone. Lester wailed and Marshall pulled the knife free and struck again.

But still, the blade didn't cut through, and he swung again, and again, harder and harder, Lester's screaming blending with the ringing that filled Marshall's head.

There was a lot of blood, and on his sixth strike the blade hit wood, but the tendons were still holding. Marshall sawed back and forth with the blade, his vision going red.

A *pop* resounded through the jungle as Lester's hand was severed. The barely conscious man flopped free of the branch's grip as blood geysered from the purple, sponge-like stump. Marshall dropped the knife, gripped what remained of the arm to steady it, and accepted the red-hot torch from Kylie.

Blood sprayed Marshall as he pressed the scorching hot end of the wood onto the stump, and the alcohol caught. Flames licked the darkness as the wound burned and sizzled and puckered.

The scent of burning flesh filled Marshall's nostrils and black smoke clogged the air as Lester writhed and screamed.

Marshall slapped the flames with his free hand until they sputtered out, but he kept the tip of the burning wood pressed to the wound.

Then Lester's eyes rolled back in his head, he stopped fighting the inevitable and passed out.

20

Lester's stump had been burned black and shiny, and it was coated with tar and sludge. The jungle had settled down to a constant high-pitched buzz, but Marshall's heart still hammered in his chest and Lester's blood was still hot on his face.

Marshall stubbed out the burning torch, dropped it to the ground, and fell back onto his ass, suddenly exhausted, his muscles like bags of sand.

Kylie and Mary Pat moved in to help, and they laid Lester on his side and made sure he hadn't swallowed his tongue.

"You alright?" Kylie asked.

Marshall licked his lips. He didn't know.

Mary Pat placed the empty gourd flask that had held the whiskey under Lester's nose, and the man moaned and came awake. He looked up into Marshall's eyes and said, "Thank you."

The party cleaned up and hunkered down for the night. Stavero came around, and though his left side ached and would be purple-black by morning, he didn't appear to have any lasting injuries. His urine was free of blood, all his appendages worked, and he had no other pains other than his headache and the throb of the entire left side of his body.

Kylie, Marshall, and Mary Pat took turns keeping watch, but other than having to chase away some smaller beasts, the darkness passed into dusk without further incident.

The next morning Stavero kept an eye on a sleeping Lester as the rest of the group foraged for food. Water was easy as the lake was right there, though they stayed away from the lake's shoreline as much as possible.

Lester was weak and couldn't walk, so the group made a better camp within a tangle of pricker bushes hidden on the leeward side of a large boulder covered in moss. There was nothing for it. Lester had to regain some of his strength before the party could continue.

Marshall and Mary Pat made Lester a sling, and two days after having his uncomfortable date with the tree, and the knife, the fellowship worked their way around the western edge of the lake and got themselves back on course.

The Fellowship was sullen as they left the western edge of the lake behind and headed southwest toward a spot on the map called Tall Woodland. Iruno had explained that he'd named the forest because conifers towered a hundred feet above the ground, and beneath their canopy, a world of perpetual dusk provided a home for different types of prehistoric beasts.

Iruno said the forest stretched for hundreds of miles to the east and west, but was a narrow stretch from north to south. Beyond the thin band of woodland to the south, the map showed a jungle that spilled down to a river that led to the group's first real marker.

"How are you doing today, Lester?" asked Mary Pat, who had become the de facto nurse.

"Better," Lester said. "But I still feel hot and cold at the same time." The stump had been burned thoroughly so it hadn't festered. It was red around the edges where pink skin met the charred black, but it wasn't swollen. With no topical cream, no painkillers, not so much as an aspirin, Lester endured the torture, which he described as a steady throbbing that sent shards of pain through all his extremities.

With no drugs and no way to give Lester blood, the only way to bring him back to full health was for him to eat and rest, which would let his body reproduce the fluids it had lost.

But in the dinosaur domain staying in one spot was never a good idea and Lester had made tremendous progress in two days. He got a triple food ration and twice the water, and at one point proclaimed himself full. The color was returning to his face and his step was quickening. The pain in his stump had morphed into an intense itching that Lester said was worse than pain, but he was getting by. Marshall had no doubts that eventually Lester would be back to some semblance of himself. Minus his hand.

Marshall wished he could have done more to help the man, maybe try to ease his pain, but there was nothing any of them could do but walk.

When the fellowship reached the edge of the thick forest, the sun was racing toward the horizon, and Marshall didn't want to spend the night in the middle of the ominous woods. Though the forest was narrow, the map wasn't to scale, and he didn't want to take the unnecessary risk. Plus, Stavero and Lester were shot, so he called a halt and the companions made camp along the edge of the forest, deep enough in for cover, but close enough to the wood's edge should escape be necessary.

As he stood watch, Marshall stared at the map in the faint light of the dying fire. They were getting close to the area where a Shokra should guide them on the final steps to the temple, but before that, the party needed to make a major navigational shift at the Arrow.

Though unimaginative, the name represented the actual marker. Iruno had taken the time to chisel an arrow into a huge stone at a particularly confusing junction in the road, so he, and others who followed him, wouldn't get lost. The marker stone was along a stream labeled Rant's Run that meandered across the land and cut not too far southeast of New Holland.

There was no path through the Tall Woodlands, but that proved to be a good thing. Though it was slow going, the tight confines and bronze needle-covered hardpan kept away the larger creatures. So it was that the party saw no dinosaurs in the woods, but when they emerged from the trees, a river gurgling through a spattering of tropical vegetation, a flock of Ankylosaurus bathed and frolicked in the tranquil river.

Eight behemoths were armored in thick, bony plates and equipped with formidable club tails. The group gathered along the water's edge, their rough, scaly hides shimmering in the early morning sun. Towering trees swayed gently in the breeze, casting dappled shadows upon the mumbling river, while the distant calls of unseen creatures carried from the Tall Woodlands.

The Ankylosaurus, with their low-slung bodies and sturdy limbs, moved with a deliberate grace as they splashed and drank. Each step sent waves rolling over the river's surface, breaking the reflection of the surrounding trees into a mesmerizing mosaic of light and shadow.

Marshall consulted the map and determined the party needed to follow the river west, but he decided to take a break, rest up, and wait for the Ankylosaurus herd to move on. The creatures might prefer salad, but the clubs at the end of their tails would knock a human into the next world and the last thing he wanted to do was spook the beasts. Plus, what did Fiona and her colleagues really know for sure? For all he knew, these gentle plant eaters might prefer an occasional taste of flesh.

As they waded deeper into the river, the Ankylosaurus lowered their massive heads to drink, their long, slender necks bending as they lapped up the water. Their beady eyes, set deep within their broad skulls, constantly scanned their surroundings, ever vigilant for signs of danger. Like the other massive beasts in the dinosaur domain, despite their formidable size, the creatures always appeared skittish and wary, which Marshall felt was understandable.

One of the Ankylosaurus paused and shook its head, and with each movement, the bony club at the end of its tail swayed, a silent reminder of the power that lay dormant.

The giant beasts gleamed like polished stone as they dipped beneath the river's surface, and the light refraction in the water highlighted the intricate patterns of their scales. Along their backs ran rows of thick, knobby plates, overlapping like the tiles of an ancient fortress wall, and beneath these armored plates, their bodies rippled with muscles.

Two hours slipped away as the fellowship rested beneath the spreading boughs of a tree with huge green leaves and small clusters of nuts. Most of the Ankylosaurus continued on their way, and two smaller members of the tribe lounged on the far shore. It was time for the party to make a final push.

Trekking along the riverbank was slow going. The river ran from east to west, but it constantly twisted and turned, and the fellowship was forced to climb across huge piles of boulders or retreat into the jungle which took the party far from the river. Several times, had it not been for the static of the river's rapids, Marshall may have lost his way.

Based on the map, Marshall figured if he had his kayak, he could paddle all the way to the inland sea that separated the two halves of what would become the United States.

But he had no kayak, and with his current luck, there would be a waterfall. He chuckled to himself. All he would need was Will and Holly.

The companions found the marker at midday where the river split into three forks. A huge, flat, standing stone blocked the main flow of the river, splitting its path into three tributaries.

Beyond the rock to the west, the land rose and was covered in tropical vegetation. Its northern edge was packed with the conifers of Tall Woodlands, and sparse jungle filled the southern shoreline, but the forest looked thin and gave way to a vast savanna beyond.

A huge, angled arrow, the image still white from being freshly chiseled, cut across the face of the stone pointing directly at the southernmost tributary of the river. Marshall marveled at the arrow's size and wondered how many days of labor it had taken to create. All Iruno had said about the marker was he'd created it because he was tired of falling for the land's deceptions, and nothing frustrated him more than getting lost, especially when he supposedly knew where he was going.

The fellowship followed the southerly tributary of the river until it bent hard left and ran due south. Here the map said to continue straight on a southwest heading of 312 degrees, which would bring them to what was labeled on the map as "anomaly." From there it was a short hike to the Shokra, which would guide them to the Toro ki' Temple.

The anomaly, which Iruno had described as not of this world, was a rock formation that looked to have been constructed by dripping stone. Tall spires of sharp red rock clawed at the sky, and there were hundreds of these odd spires spread across a relatively small area. It looked as though the ground had boiled and spat lava and stones, but there hadn't been enough pressure to create a volcano.

Pterosaurs circled overhead, their faint cries reminding Marshall that the party was always being watched, always being weighed and measured.

When the group reached the section of the jungle where the Shokra's location had been marked on the map, Marshall called a halt. Stavero and Lester ate and rested as Marshall, Kylie, and Mary Pat searched the area. The trio split up and performed a simple grid search, and as the sun started its curtain call for the day, Mary Pat found the statue and called the rest of the party to her side.

The Shokra didn't look much like the one he'd seen at Hicks Dome. The area wasn't overrun with vines, and though there was no sign of anyone tending the statue or the surrounding area, nothing encroached on the monument.

Despite its lack of arms, the Shokra emanated strength and resilience through its thick, sturdy legs which were firmly planted in the ground, as if tied to the roots of the Earth. The surface of the statuette was smooth yet weathered, bearing the marks of time in the form of subtle fissures and gentle indentations. Each chisel mark defined the monument's features, and the pristine white hue of the rock contrasted starkly against the surrounding landscape.

Like the Hicks Dome specimen, atop the apex of the statue's head rested a crown of glistening quartz stones, arranged in a circular pattern. The stones caught the light and cast a dazzling array of reflections that danced over the statue's face, which was adorned with distinct features. Deep-set eyes gazed out into the jungle with a rigid intensity that seemed to pierce through the veil of time, hinting at knowledge and wisdom. The nose was wide and prominent, exuding a sense of authority, and lips curved upwards in a serene smile that conveyed a sense of inner peace.

"Not like the one at Hicks Dome at all," Marshall said. "But I can see it... You know, like when a person gets fat, but you can still see the thin person within."

Nobody spoke. The group was exhausted.

"Any objection to pushing on?" Marshall said. The statue was facing due south, and according to the map, the temple was very close.

Mumbles, moans, but the party shuffled forward, the ground rising steadily, Kylie at their head, Glock at the ready.

As expected, the fellowship didn't have to march far. Atop a hill with a commanding view of the surrounding area, the party reached their destination.

Unlike New Holland, the temple was barren of all greenery as if weed killer had been sprayed perpetually across the ground, or some other unknown force had kept the jungle at bay. There was a twenty-foot band of brown hardpan separating the jungle from the temple, and not a single creeper trailed across the barren strip that ended at a wall of intricately fitted stones.

Kylie led the group along the wall, and when they reached the entrance the temple gates stood open. As the party entered the compound, Marshall saw there were no gates.

The entry archway was decorated with symbols, both common and uncommon. There were petroglyphs, pictographs, and numbers, and a vast mathematical formula sprawled over the curved portion of the arch.

With his heart racing, Marshall flipped the map over, and there, within the triangle he'd drawn, was the same formula.

21

The fellowship walked beneath the entry arch, and they were greeted by a monument stone. The tall, black, pylon-shaped stele had no symbols on it, no numbers, or formulas. What appeared to be eight letters in an unknown tongue ran down each side of the monolith and formed what he believed to be the word Toro Ki'.

Marshall was able to venture a guess because he had heard of the name from Iruno, and he'd seen the description in the notebook and copied it onto his pages. How Iruno or those who came before him came up with the translation, Marshall didn't know. He sort of saw the T at the beginning, and the K, and maybe the Os, but all he was certain of was the letters weren't English.

Equally as mysterious as the pylon was the pile of possessions at its base. There was a wedding ring, a pink stone polished so bright it looked like a gem, a sneaker, a child's rattle, and an old black-and-white picture of an elderly woman sitting in a rocking chair and staring at an empty fireplace.

"He told me about this," Kylie said. "Iruno, I mean. What shall we leave as an offering?"

Marshall wasn't carrying anything that he could go without except… He put up a finger to stall the onslaught of questions as he dropped his pack and pulled out the plastic bag of power bar wrappers he had saved from the bars the group had eaten when they'd first arrived in the dinosaur domain.

There were three wrappers, and he ripped them apart and passed out the shreds.

"I hope our success isn't tied to the quality of our offerings," Mary Pat said.

Marshall and his companions weren't the first ones to think of leaving garbage at the gate of the shrine. There was an ancient Coke can, a silver bottle top, a piece of metal, its purpose no longer discernible, and other handmade items; dolls, broken weapons, and a carving depicting an octopus-like beast.

As dusk crept over the land, the party left their offerings and delved deeper into the Toro Ki' shrine.

A circular six-foot wall surrounded the complex. There were few structures, all made of stone and brick and weathered by time. There were no creeping vines, no weeds sprouting from cracks, but whatever force kept the jungle at bay couldn't keep away the sand, dust, and grit.

Most of the stonework looked like poured concrete, or it had been chiseled from the land itself and smoothed by some miraculous method that seemed impossible given the time period. The whitewashed stone was gray and streaked with black in spots, and it reminded Marshall of old stadiums and old tombstones.

Marshall could see how the complex could easily be lost in the fabric of the land—the entire temple grounds covered maybe an acre. Without a drone, one would have to stumble upon the place, and without the pages in his pocket, the temple would be nothing more than a fantastical monument to what he believed had to be an alien race, or a race of people who lived on Earth long before the Cretaceous, though that idea would send most modern scientists into anaphylactic shock.

Beyond the Toro Ki' marker, there were two huge statues that appeared to be large Shokras. The tall figures stared down at the party as they threaded between them, and Marshall felt their ancient stone eyes following him.

Beyond the Shokras there was a field of stone heads, the octopus head from the statue Marshall had come across in the jungle among them. There were animal heads, dinosaurs, bastardizations of human heads, and a few that were unrecognizable.

Stavero whistled. "How the hell did they get that head all the way here?"

Marshall hiked his shoulders. Judging by the map, the head had been transported at least fifty miles. "It's actually not that odd. I mean, collecting the heads of statues is odd, but primitive races have been moving heavy objects since the beginning of time. The Egyptians and their massive obelisks come to mind."

"The real question is why?" Kylie said.

The fellowship threaded through the heads and at the heart of the architectural wonder there was a circular courtyard, a vast expanse of weathered stone that stretched outward like a celestial canvas. Etched into the courtyard floor there were celestial maps and intricate patterns, which revealed the cosmos and a myriad of unknown wonders. Symbols of stars, planets, and constellations intertwined with geometric motifs, creating a tapestry of knowledge that spoke to the temple's cosmic purpose.

Encircling the courtyard there were a series of towering stone steles, each rectangle of stone adorned with intricate carvings and inscriptions. Marshall looked on in wonder as the sun touched the western horizon and the steles directed columns of celestial light onto the decorated stone circle.

The courtyard was a colossal astrolabe, its intricate mechanism spanning the entirety of the circular arena. Crafted from stone and adorned with celestial symbols, the giant instrument was the centerpiece of the temple, the conduit through which the mysteries of the cosmos would be revealed. At least that was what Iruno claimed, and as Marshall looked upon the spectacle, some of his doubts fell away.

Within the main circle of the astrolabe, there were concentric rings of polished stone, each inscribed with celestial markings and mathematical equations. Marshall was drawn to these rings as he traced the intricate patterns, his mind spinning backward to Iruno's lectures and the pages in his pocket. He felt a profound sense of awe as if the fellowship was standing at the threshold of infinite knowledge.

Beyond the courtyard, the temple's architecture unfolded in a series of smooth geometric shapes and flowing lines. There were towering spires, their tips disappearing into the gray haze that filtered over the temple, and sparks of light danced between the steles. Each spire was adorned with intricate carvings and symbols, and the containment walls that surrounded the astrolabe were adorned with friezes and reliefs that depicted unknown scenes Marshall assumed comprised the mythology of the temple's creators.

As day turned to night the temple underwent a breathtaking transformation, as if awakening from a slumber to greet the stars above. Ghostly lights flickered to life along the surface of the astrolabe, casting an otherworldly glow across the courtyard. The glyphs and symbols carved into the stone steles shimmered with an iridescent luminescence as the stars twinkled overhead, their light reflected in the surfaces of the steles.

Kylie snapped on her flashlight and the companions strolled across the circular plaza, examining the markings on the stone floor. There were rings of numbers, and an odd series of symbols ran around the outer edge of the circular courtyard like numbers on a clock.

Marshall said, "Let's call it a day. We can get up before daybreak and observe the sunrise. That will give us all day to make our adjustments and prepare for the next morning." Because Marshall and the others had crossed over at sunset, they needed to return at sunrise. When Marshall had asked about this, Iruno had provided a detailed explanation that Marshall didn't fully understand, though he knew it had something to do with the balancing of the solstice and equinox.

There were several stone mausoleum-like structures, and none of them had doors. For the most part, the structures were empty other than the rubble of what appeared to be the remains of a community that had disappeared long ago.

Marshall picked the building Iruno used when he came to the temple, and he and Kylie trekked back out to the jungle to collect dead branches for firewood as Mary Pat tended to Lester's wound and Stavero rested and ate.

Chores completed, the fellowship settled in for the night. Shadows danced on the stone walls and the fire cracked and popped, tiny embers shooting from the flames. Marshall wasn't hungry, but he forced himself to eat a strip of jerky and drink some water. His stomach was a mess of possibilities, fears, and doubts. But everything Iruno had told him about the temple was true. Now all he needed to do was make the damn thing work.

"Did any of you guys see the brooms Iruno mentioned?" Marshall asked. There was a layer of grit on everything, and any fine grooves or intricate mechanisms would have to be cleaned.

"I did," Kylie said. "They were leaning against the wall that ran along the pathway that went down to the astrolabe."

"We're gonna have to do some sweeping before we even attempt to move the rete," Marshall said.

"Move the what?" Lester said.

Marshall wanted to scold the man for not paying attention to Iruno's instructions, but he had to admit he didn't remember everything himself. Before Iruno's lecture, he knew what an astrolabe was, but someone could have offered him a million dollars to explain what it did or how to use it and he would've been down a million bucks. The paper pages crinkled as he pulled them from his pocket and spread them across his lap.

He cleared his throat for effect and began to read. "An astrolabe operates on geometric principles. The temple's courtyard disk represents the celestial sphere, and it's marked with stars and celestial objects. This is called the mater. What we need to move—rotate, is the rete at the center. The rete's skeletal framework represents the celestial sphere, Earth, with pointers for stars and other celestial objects.

"By aligning the astrolabe with a star and measuring its altitude above the horizon, a mathematical formula determines its position in the sky. Tying this to a point in time involves aligning the rete with the Sun or Polaris, which uses angular measurements to calculate time. By doing this one can predict celestial positions and events like sunrise and sunset." Marshall paused to let that sink in.

"I'm not clear how the astrolabe will give us the setting for Woodhenge," Kylie said. "Sorry, I've read those notes ten times. Math was never my thing."

"Nor mine," said Mary Pat.

"It doesn't matter," Marshall said. "The base formula, which I have in my phone, converts the traditional, modern date of travel into a code of three numbers and a symbol."

"I get it," Stavero said. "We adjust the rete so the astrolabe—the time compass, is set to match the symbol and two numbers the formula will give us."

"That's it," Marshall said. "When the sun rises, and the first light of day falls on the astrolabe, if it's set right, we'll get our measurements in the form of shadows falling over the appropriate numbers on the mater."

"How do you think the... Toro Ki' came up with all this?" Lester asked.

To that, nobody had an answer.

"I'll take the first watch," said Lester. He had been steadily getting better and was now only getting double food rations. The stump still itched with an aggressive intensity, and tentacles of pain randomly spidered over the missing hand. Marshall didn't have the heart to tell the man that phantom limb syndrome was very common, and feeling pain and itching in his invisible hand would be something he would have to deal with for the rest of his life, whether he escaped the dinosaur domain or not.

Stavero said, "I'll wake you and take over." The man who had fallen ten feet from the sleeping platform was bruised as a peach that had been used as a softball, but he was walking normally, and the pain had lessened considerably.

It was good to see both men getting back into the game. Marshall would need them, even if in the real world both men would be backups.

The fire grew low and sputtered out, and the room was filled with a dull orange glow.

Marshall felt a sense of accomplishment as he settled down to sleep. His mind was racing, and he would have paid a thousand dollars for a hit of whiskey. He'd been in the dinosaur domain less than a month, and it had taken Iruno years, but Marshall felt confident that he at least knew enough to attempt to get home next summer solstice. In the meantime, he could help others try on the winter solstice, which would provide invaluable experience and knowledge that could help him with his own attempt.

He closed his eyes, the snores of his mates gentle and comforting.

A clicking, like a chain being pulled over metal, carried into the stone building, followed by scraping, like talons raking over a rock, and then a low gurgling growl.

Marshall pushed up onto his elbows and peered at the dark maw of the entryway.

Two wet eyes stared back at him.

22

"What should I do?" Lester asked. He sat next to the entrance keeping watch.

"Don't move," said Kylie.

Marshall glanced to his right and in the faint glow of the fire's dying embers, he saw Kylie's dark form raise the Glock. "Wait," he hissed. "We're in a stone box. Ricochets, and the sound—"

A low growl and the eyes came forward.

The gunshots were deafening in the enclosed space, the muzzle flash like a shooting star.

Marshall fell onto his back as if the sound had physically hit him, and intense ringing split his head. He covered his ears, sure he was going to find drips of blood, but there was no blood, only pain.

The eyes surging from the blackness crossed, then fell forward as their owner died.

Stavero, Mary Pat, and Lester came awake, all of them screaming and yelling various admonishments of distress and frustration.

Kylie turned on her flashlight and its beam cut through the gun smoke haze.

The dead beast was all teeth, half its head composed of narrow jaws filled with needles. It looked to be in the raptor class of dinosaurs, but the creature had no feathers, and its forward arms were larger and more muscular than was typical for Utahraptors and their ilk. Blood leaked from bullet holes in the monster's chest, and the scent of waste filled the room as the corpse deflated and the dead monster emptied its bowels.

When they were done throwing up dino-jerky, Marshall and Stavero dragged the dead beast out of the building as the others did their best to clean the place up and get rid of the smell. No luck, and with the stars staring down at them the party moved to another building.

Marshall was first up the next morning, and he found Mary Pat asleep at her lookout post. As the eastern horizon slowly faded from black to gray, he began rousing his companions. So it was that as the sun crept over the rim of the world, its rays angling through the Starry Stele, arcs of light fell across the numbers arranged on the mater of the massive astrolabe.

The cosmic compass needed to be cleaned before it could be used because a thick layer of dust and grit filled every crack.

Like the hands of a clock, shadows inched across the Toro Ki' Temple as the sunrise slowly painted the land in shadowy dusk.

Phones were turned on, pictures were taken, and the exact time was recorded. At the moment of sunrise, when the sun itself was released from the eastern horizon's grasp, two strong beams of light arced from holes atop two of the tall steles. Marshall hadn't noticed the holes before.

The light arrows speared two numbers. There could be no doubt, the identifications were unmistakable, and the beams settled on the numbers for ten heartbeats. As the sun shifted ever so slightly, so did the angle of the light, and the holes in the steles darkened and the beams of light faded and blinked out.

"You all saw that, right?" Stavero said.

Murmurs of yup, and nods.

"I'll do the math later when we're resting," Marshall said.

"Better you than me," Kylie said.

The race known simply as the Toro Ki' didn't use feet or inches or meters or cubits or arm lengths or strides or astronomical units or fathoms or chains or leagues or hands or furlongs. Through many years of observation and trial and error a conversion chart had been created, which Marshall had meticulously copied into his notes. With that, the numbers generated by the Starry Stele could be converted to feet.

The fellowship ate a light breakfast and got to work. There were three brooms made from sturdy tree branches with dried straw bound at their ends. Marshall noted that the tools didn't look much different than the ones his grandmother had used when he was a boy. A steady buzz rode a scent-wave of rot that carried over the temple. The decaying dead beast from the night before was already being consumed by the larva that kept life moving no matter the age.

"Anyone else feel like they were in Raiders of the Lost Ark this morning?" Lester asked. He was standing to the side, not sweeping because, well, old-school whisk brooms didn't work too well if their user only had one hand.

Marshall threw the man a sympathetic laugh. His brief physical and mental improvements had subsided, and the sullen man had returned. "It was kind of like that, wasn't it?" Marshall said.

"What I don't get is doesn't all that change?" Kylie said. "Positions of stuff on the Earth, the stars, the sun, the angles, the tilt of the Earth, all that shifts and changes. No?"

Everybody looked at her and nobody spoke.

"'Nova," she said. "Since I was a little girl."

"Yes, everything is always in motion and changing," Marshall said. "The continents are moving, remember? Even in our time. But that's part of what the astrolabe does, that's why the planetary settings are part of it. The settings adjust to the current sky and align time."

It sounded even crazier when spoken out loud, and the companions swept on in silence.

The main portion of the astrolabe was essentially crack-free, but it was large. What was more difficult to sweep was the grooves that allowed the rete and the planisphere to be adjusted. These markers all sat in grooves that guided their movements, and they were mounted on stone pins which allowed the rete and planisphere to spin freely when pushed by two people.

By lunch, the giant astrolabe was cleaned and ready for business. For safety and shade, the party retreated to their domicile to take a break before attempting to set the cosmic compass.

With Stavero at his side, Marshall tried to work the formula in reverse, using the numbers from the morning's sunrise.

Stavero said, "I took a look at the main Starry Stele stones very closely today. There are two holes bored at different angles at the top of each."

"To be expected. No?" Marshall said. "Sunup and sundown. To the future and from the future."

"It's a little odd how we didn't see them the prior day," Kylie said.

"I don't know," Marshall said. "It was dusk, we were tired." What he left unsaid was that Marshall didn't think the holes were meant to be seen. "O.K.," Marshall said as he sat back. "I think I've got some good news here." He looked up from the phone and met the hesitant and confused stares of his teammates.

"As you would imagine, as the sun moves the adjustment from today isn't all that much," he said. "Even though we're a day off, logic dictates that tomorrow morning's numbers shouldn't be that much different when it comes to the celestial cycle."

"What have we got?" Kylie asked. "Based on this morning's data."

"When translated the reading for 2022 relative to the current celestial sky is 179 and 36, if broken down into the Woodhenge settings."

Lester said. "And that's for an entire year? Last I checked there were three hundred and sixty-five days in a year."

"And a quarter," Stavero said.

"And there are twenty-four hours in a day, 1440 minutes, and... a lot of seconds!" Lester said.

"But there is only one summer solstice and one winter solstice," Marshall said.

"And on those two days you must find your anchor," Kylie said.

There was nothing left to say, and Marshall went over his calculations one last time as the group rested, and he prepared to adjust the astrolabe. If his companions were like him, they were all thinking about how their theory of the universe being random and chaotic was wrong. The Toro Ki' time compass proved the cosmos are orderly, mathematical, and predictable.

Even though Marshall knew the sunset numbers would be different, he set the astrolabe for the sunrise. He and Mary Pat pushed the rete, and the sound of stone scraping on stone echoed through the temple as the stele and planisphere shifted.

The adjustment didn't take long, and Marshall and Mary Pat only had to pause twice to allow Stavero and Kylie to clean clogged tracks. He set the rete at the translated year of 2022, which meant the setting was 102 and 27, and a corresponding symbol along the outer edge that looked like an elongated H was marked on the mater.

Iruno had explained that the numbers provided by the astrolabe at sunrise, once converted, corresponded to the distance the Woodhenge poles needed to be from the Chaka Stones and the distance between each pole. A simple check and balance of these numbers would occur when the actual wooden poles were adjusted. Like a puzzle where all the pieces must fit, if the poles couldn't be arranged using the distances given something was wrong.

The sun went down, beams of light marked their spots, and the party hunkered down for another night of waiting.

Kylie took the first watch.

As Marshall dozed off his mind wandered. He was surprised that the party hadn't encountered any local fauna during their day's activities. It was as if the dinosaurs wanted no part of the ancient temple.

The party woke in the predawn hours and prepared to observe the sunrise as they drank the last of their water and ate the remaining dino-jerky.

"I had a crazy thought last night," Stavero said. "We all came... through, at relatively the same time. What about others who might want to go back? Won't they need their own Woodhenge settings?"

"I thought of that also," Mary Pat said. "That means only one attempt can be made per solstice cycle."

Iruno had mentioned that to Marshall, but he didn't think it was worth repeating until he got back to New Holland, if then. That was a problem for Ida. Or was it? In that instant, Marshall realized how much power he and his fellow travelers had, and spilling everything to the folks at New Holland might not be the smartest play. Marshall recalled

Leeri and his purpose. He made a mental note to talk with the group on the long trek back to New Holland, so they'd be prepared.

As the sun came up the group stood mesmerized, the spectacle just as spectacular as the prior day. The symbols along the mater glowed with bioluminescence that didn't seem possible given there was no moss—nothing covering the stone, but Marshall figured it had something to do with the composition of the rock.

Beams of light arced through the Starry Stele, and the numbers 181 and thirty-eight were illuminated on the courtyard floor.

Marshall put the numbers into his phone, hit calculate, and waited. "That translates to 113 and eighteen... hang on while I check that..."

The sun started its climb across the sky and the beams of light cutting over the temple blinked out.

"Iruno said there were ten poles, right?" Marshall asked, but he didn't wait for an answer. "If we have a circle with a radius of eighteen feet and the poles are 113 feet apart... The formula to calculate the circumference of a circle is $2\pi r$, where r is the radius of the circle and π is a mathematical constant approximately equal to 3.14159. That gives us..." Marshall smiled and nodded. "It's not exact, but 9.9998 looks like ten poles to me. We're good to go to 2022."

"Set each pole eighteen feet from the Chaka Stones and space them 113 feet apart?" Kylie questioned.

"So says the Starry Stele," Stavero said.

"How are we going to walk the curved line so exactly?" Lester asked.

"You should have listened to Iruno more," Marshall said.

"Or your fifth grade math teacher," Kylie said. "It's easy. We make a compass using rope and a center pin."

With the reading taken, there wasn't much left to do. Stavero asked if it made sense to rest another day and check their calculations the next morning, but the companions were ready to move on and Marshall was as convinced as he could be that he'd done everything right. The numbers jived with the prior day, and he was confident.

As the party packed up and set out, the question that had been bouncing around inside Marshall's head was voiced by Stavero. "Should we tell Ida and the others... everything? I mean... I'm not sure what I mean."

"I do," Marshall said. "The information we have is... well, probably more valuable than anything in the dinosaur domain. There are sure to be people in New Holland that will want to try and get home based on the new information we have, but how will the order be decided?"

"Who goes first?" Lester said.

Marshall said, "Well, there's four of us going to the same place, so…" He knew that meant very little and would mean less if Ida and Ringo and the folks of New Holland wanted to change the batting order.

"And don't forget why Leeri came with us," Lester pushed.

Marshall nodded. "We've got a few days to think on it and get our story straight, whatever the story ends up being."

The fellowship left the Toro Ki' Temple behind, but Marshall's gut told him he'd be back.

23

Though the shortest distance between two points is a straight line, there was no path from the temple to New Holland. The group considered following the trail to the Chaka Stones, and then traveling the beaten path east to New Holland, but without Rib and Bone that path was essentially unknown territory to the party, so what was the point of taking the longer route?

Marshall led the fellowship southeast, and as the companions descended the elevated plateau and put the temple at their backs, a wide expanse of virgin forest stretched into the distance. A light mist hung just above the greenery, and in the foggy thermals, dark shapes swooped and squawked. The riot leaking from the jungle scratched at Marshall's last nerve, but there was nothing for it. There was never more than a moment's silence in the dinosaur domain. Ever.

Avoiding a T-rex squabble knocked the party off course, and they were forced to traverse a thick patch of spike-covered bushes and progress slowed to a crawl. It was in this tangle, where most beasts were too large and smart to tread, that the fellowship discovered the skeleton.

The knight was a soldier of the medieval Christian military order known as the Knights Templar. Renowned for their martial prowess, religious devotion, and strict code of conduct, the Templar knights emerged during the Crusades and were tasked with protecting pilgrims journeying to the Holy Land. Marshall knew from his many history classes that the Templar knights took vows of poverty, chastity, and obedience, living a life of discipline and sacrifice as they traveled Earth doing God's bidding. The knights were among the most prominent legends, if not the greatest enigma, in human history.

Vines, weeds, and years of dirt, silt, and sand covered most of the remains, and had it not been for the sun sparkling off the conical-shaped helmet sticking from the ground the party would've walked right by the forlorn soldier.

With Lester and Stavero watching, Kylie, Mary Pat, and Marshall set about clearing the dirt and debris from the remains. Nobody protested because everyone understood Marshall's interest in the knight was more than curiosity. Objects were currency in the dinosaur domain and it was possible the old soldier had a sword on his person or something else of value.

Once most of the loose dirt and debris had been cleared away, Marshall was surprised to find that the knight's clothing was still relatively intact, which meant the Templar knight had come through the time portal recently.

The knight's white mantle, a long cloak adorned with the distinctive red cross, was dirty and marred with holes, but the potent symbolism still relayed the lost soldier's commitment to God. Beneath this, chainmail hung over dirty bones, and as a soldier of God, the knight was arrayed for battle.

Upon the soldier's skull, which was covered in brown leathery skin and topped with dirty-blonde hair, sat a distinctive conical-shaped helmet with a nasal guard. His shield bore the iconic Templar cross, and there was a broadsword lying next to the skeleton. If the knight had a bag or other personal belongings, he had left them in the future.

Marshall made the sign of the cross, though he wasn't a religious man—the opposite, really, but he felt a reverence for the fallen soldier as myths and tall tales coalesced into reality.

Kylie had the gun, and Marshall had seen the helmet, so he claimed the sword and the dry-rotted leather belt and scabbard.

Mary Pat claimed the shield, though it was heavy. The party scavenged the helmet, and rotted boots, and as Marshall searched the bones, he found a finger metacarpal with a signet ring still wrapped around it.

The ring boasted a striking design featuring a raised depiction of the order's iconic red cross set against a field of gleaming silver. Encircling the emblem were intricate engravings, depicting sacred symbols, invoking the order's legacy of piety and fighting prowess.

Marshall slipped the ring on his finger and a bolt of static electricity raced through his extremities and stung the tips of his fingers and toes. He held out the ring like a newlywed staring at their wedding ring, and he thought of where and when the ring was made. The signet ring was thousands of years old and wouldn't be made for millions of years.

"What do you think he was doing over in the Americas?" Kylie said. "He sure was a long way from home."

There were so many myths surrounding the knights he didn't know where to begin. Marshall hiked his shoulders.

Stavero said, "They were sent on a quest to find the holy grail, for one."

"That is one of the more popular myths, but there is little proof," Marshall said.

"Look down," Lester said. "That looks like proof."

"Not really," Marshall said. "What isn't in dispute, I don't think, is the fact that the knights traveled the known world in service of their lord."

To that, nobody had anything to say.

When the bones were picked clean, Marshall felt dirty. So the group spent half an hour moving dirt and covering the old knight's bones. There was no prayer. No soliloquy, and as the group marched on a great sense of loss settled on Marshall. He knew that could be him. Today. A beast could jump out of the foliage right now and end his time in the dinosaur domain—and end his time everywhere.

That night the party made camp atop a hillock at the edge of a wide savanna that stretched to a series of hills in the north and a land of jagged cracks to the south. Using the map for reference from his elevated position, Marshall identified Rant's Run, the river that ran southwest of New Holland and cut directly across the proposed trail.

Mary Pat went hunting and came back with two of the furry little mammal-like creatures that tasted like fatty bison when butchered properly and charred over an open flame. Kylie cooked as the party drank water and told stories of their travels in the domain, but no one mentioned the time before. It was as if the fellowship's prior lives had been washed away, and Marshall wondered if his team was thinking what he was; maybe I should stay in the dinosaur domain.

Then Marshall thought of Fiona and his stomach soured. That would be abandonment, pure and simple, and she didn't deserve that. If their time together was limited, he needed to tell her. He couldn't leave her hanging. Now, if he couldn't get home… What was an appropriate amount of time to wait? He glanced at Kylie. Marshall didn't know how long was long enough, but he did know that merely thinking about the question was a problem.

At key portions in the trail, as Marshall marked the map, he used the knife, which had been cleaned of Lester's blood, to mark Xs on trees. The party also built piles of stones, and in one case the companions took the time to construct a bridge from a fallen tree over a tributary of Rant's Run.

Marshall transcribed all these markers onto the map, and as he sat by the stream, gazing east, Marshall thought he recognized the terrain. The party was nearing the spot where their path should cross the eastern path that led from the Chaka Stones to New Holland. If all went according to plan, they'd have a shelter to sleep in.

All didn't go according to plan.

Kylie was on point, picking her way through huge elephant ear leaves, the sound of snapping branches and tearing leaves carrying through the jungle.

Three Utahraptors appeared from the foliage; one blocking the party's forward progress, one to their right and one to the left. The creatures could hardly be seen, their brown and green leathery skin blending into the jungle like advanced heat-changing camouflage. Standing at seven feet tall, they slithered through the dense undergrowth like snakes with legs.

The alpha surged forward, a blur of teeth and rippling muscles.

Kylie, Glock perpetually in hand, brought the gun up and fired, but she was off balance and the shots smacked into a tree.

The crack of the gunshots brought the alpha to a halt, head bobbing, teeth glinting as its head swayed side to side as if telling its mates to take the lead. If the other two raptors understood, they didn't let on, because they stayed entrenched within the underbrush.

Marshall's ears rang as he unsheathed his new sword and swung it in a wide arc.

The alpha shrieked and inched forward.

Kylie held the Glock in a doublehanded grip, aimed at the lead raptor, and fired... one, two, three, four shots that hit the alpha in the head and chest.

At such close range, the 9 MM bullets tore through the creature's tough exterior and blew out the back of its head, blood, brain, and bone spraying the greenery.

Marshall stood holding his sword like a statue, and the others looked on as Kylie shifted her aim right and fired three more times.

The remaining raptor squawked, but the sound was weak.

Before her second target hit the ground, Kylie aimed and squeezed the trigger until the hollow click of metal striking metal reverberated through the forest.

All the shots thumped home, and the final raptor joined its posse.

Kylie let the gun fall to her side and she sagged against a tree trunk as her adrenaline fled. She pulled the empty magazine from the gun and replaced it with a fresh one before jacking a bullet into the firing chamber.

It didn't go unnoticed that now Kylie only had forty bullets left. Twenty in the magazine she'd just loaded, and twenty in the second spare she had in a black leather pouch on her utility belt.

The stench of blood and earth filled the forest as the companions left the corpses behind. Luck had been with them since they'd left the temple, but if there was one certainty in the dinosaur domain it was that luck, if you had any at all, was fleeting.

At midday, Lester and Stavero recognized an outcropping of stone that jutted from the jungle like an afterthought. Both men recalled the odd formation from their first trip to New Holland.

"If my memory serves, there's a lean-to not far away, and if we push we might make it by nightfall," Stavero said.

The fellowship didn't make it by nightfall, and the dejected, dried-out, and bruised travelers spent the evening under the stars at the center of a small clearing as each member of the party took a turn keeping watch.

Lester, who had become wallpaper over the last few days, constantly bitched and complained about the itching of his invisible hand. Marshall felt for the guy—he did, but he'd had just about enough.

The next day the party reached Rant's Run and Marshall called a halt along its banks.

A flock of ostrich-like dinosaurs with huge glassy eyes and long spindly legs waded in the rushing water, their muscular necks bent as the beasts drank. The river was fifty feet across, and downstream it bent hard right on a pile of boulders as it poured its way west toward the inland sea.

Kylie drew her Glock.

If the dinosaurs noticed, they made no sign.

"I don't think you're going to need that," Marshall said.

"No?"

"No." Marshall lifted a stone from the riverbank and tossed it into the water. It hit the river with a *plop*.

The crowd of beasts all swung their heads toward the source of the noise. For a moment everything fell still as the creatures appraised the newcomers and the jungle buzzed. Then the dinosaurs yipped and screamed and bitched as they fled into the forest, irritated, but not willing to fight.

Marshall's eyes locked on the gun in Kylie's hand, and then his gaze fell to his pike and sword.

"Yeah," Kylie said when she noticed him staring at the Glock. "I've been thinking about that also. Do we hide it again? If not, what?"

Marshall took a long pull of water and felt the group watching him. They'd all agreed to keep their cards close to the vest, but the pistol was a big card. He rolled his shoulders and said, "Nothing. We do nothing."

The party exchanged glances.

"My thinking is, we're in control of our information, and with the gun we have a say in things," Marshall said.

"Look, I'm not opposed to—" Kylie paused when Marshall put up a hand.

"I'm not asking you to do anything tawdry," Marshall said. "We can keep our secrets until the time is right, but the gun will douse any… stupid ideas that might involve us or our freedom."

"Yeah," Lester said.

That made Marshall's stomach crawl, but he said, "We tell them the truth. We hid it before because we were afraid, blah blah blah, and we didn't know if we could trust you. Now we know we can."

"Then there's Leeri," Stavero said.

"He didn't seem well-liked," Lester said.

"Regardless..." Kylie rolled her shoulders and licked her lips. "They might be upset with us because he's dead. Blame us, even."

Marshall nodded, lifted his sword, and motioned toward Mary Pat's shield. "Our newly found weapons fall into the same category."

The fellowship trekked two more days, not rushing, but not taking it slow, as they avoided the local fauna. With a suddenness that almost made Kylie shoot the lead watcher, four New Holland citizens emerged from their hiding places as the party approached the town.

The leader of the team sent a guard to notify Ida, and as he broke free of the jungle Marshall couldn't stop a smile from spreading over his face.

New Holland rose from nature's embrace as if part of the forest, a perfect blend of organic beauty and rustic craftsmanship. Fires burned in earthen basins atop the crude battlements, and the large gates stood closed, their rough wooden surfaces scarred with tales of storms and claws.

The fellowship was home.

Mary Pat hailed the gate guard and gaining admittance into New Holland was much easier than Marshall's first time. Everyone in the party were well-known commodities, and they were expected.

New Holland was aglow with torchlight and bonfires, and the chatter, laughs, and rumble of the town's inhabitants echoed down the dirt streets that wandered through the shanties. The moon glared down like a winking eye, and within the flicker of firelight, Marshall saw the dazzled faces of the townsfolk watching the fellowship walk through town.

Marshall could tell from some of those looks that he hadn't been expected back. Hell, Marshall was still a little surprised he'd made it.

Ida met Marshall and the others on the road, and though he was weary beyond words, he knew his night was just beginning.

24

The wind carried a slight chill and Marshall's mind wandered to winter and home. Back in 2022, it was mid-December, and if history was any indicator of future events snow and freezing temperatures dominated much of North America. In the dinosaur domain, the climate was warm and humid, and with little to no polar ice caps, sea levels were high, resulting in the creation of the inland sea and the ocean's encroachment deep into once-dry lands.

Marshall rubbed his eyes. Clouds of dust and grit filled the air as the path plunged into a shallow dell devoid of vegetation. A scree pile of red stones of various sizes spilled into the shallow bowl that Marshall estimated to be half a mile across. It was clear something had struck the Earth here, and as the party made their way through the shattered rocks, he saw a hollowed-out section where the stone had been quarried. The color and composition of the rock was different than that used to construct the Toro Ki' Temple, so it wasn't the location of the mythical meteorite crater Iruno had told him about.

Rib and Bone said Marshall and the others didn't recognize the spot because they hadn't taken this path on their first trip to New Holland. Communication with the guides was difficult, but they'd both insisted on leading the winter solstice party to the Chaka Stones as it was one of the pair's main jobs. From what Marshall could gather the slightly different route was an uphill, downhill thing, and Rib and Bone had chosen the less strenuous trail. The winter solstice wasn't for twelve days, so they had plenty of time.

The crater's stones were superheated by the intense sunlight, and the temperature went up ten degrees as the party walked the well-trodden trail through the depression. Though only two people were returning to the future, and Marshall had argued extensively about how the smaller the group the better, nine people were on the trip to the Chaka Stones.

When the group climbed from the depression Rib called a water break.

Marshall was no longer the guide, and he was thankful for that. Though he did keep a close eye on the trail this time around so he wouldn't need Rib and Bone should they be forced to sit out the summer solstice trip.

Devon and Anna Hemply, a middle-aged couple from 1979 who had been in the dinosaur domain for seven years, were going to attempt to get home. They'd come through on a winter's eve after a moon dance ceremony, just like Marshall. They'd won Ida's lottery, had accepted the first slot, and Marshall and Kylie had traveled with the couple to the Toro Ki' Temple to assist them in getting their Woodhenge settings.

The decision to tell the folks at New Holland about the one setting per solstice issue had been necessary. Though the group had decided to keep that piece of information as their last bargaining chip, when nitty met gritty Marshall had to throw cold water on New Holland's excitement.

Not everyone was pleased with the new information, and Ida, Ringo, and those like them who had invested their lives in New Holland and the dinosaur domain saw their fortunes falling.

Marshall took a long pull of water and Kylie settled in beside him. Having her at his side, or better yet, watching his back, had been a welcome surprise. Lester and Stavero had decided to sit out the winter trip, but at last check, both men intended to travel home with him and Kylie next summer.

Unlike the lottery, Marshall and the others had bartered for first rights as they told the tale of Mount Sight from first to last. The entire community had looked on as the math was explained, and charts drawn, but in the end, it was hope that sold the day. Hope based on facts. If one believed Iruno had traveled the paths of time—and everyone believed Marshall's story that he'd met the man in the future—there could be little doubt.

A Pterosaur shrieked in the clouds above and Kylie's hand fell to the Glock.

Ida had been skeptical about much of what Marshall and the others said, but the sword and other artifacts were evidence that couldn't be denied. The gun—that fib hadn't gone over well, and Ringo had almost knocked things off the rails with an outburst that not only got him admonishment from Ida but got him assigned as security chief for the winter solstice mission.

In the early moments of Marshall telling the fellowship's story, it was clear to him that the residents of New Holland were buying what he was selling. There had been numerous volunteers for the winter mission, and there was no debate as to if a mission should occur. Ida and the others—even Ringo—accepted the solstice mission as a foregone conclusion. Not a huge surprise since Rib and Bone made the trip twice yearly to collect any who might wander through the portal unknowingly. Then there was the fact that if recent discoveries did ultimately kill New Holland, it was going to take a very long time.

That had raised a great debate. The key to the time compass, its location, and its purpose, had dramatically changed the outlook of those in the dinosaur domain, and new citizens would face an entirely different reality. One where they would be forced to wait their turn to get home, and as they waited, serve as farmers to stay alive.

Mary Pat, who had become a de facto member of the family, had shaken off the idea that she couldn't return to the future with her teammates. Her lottery spot put her three years down on the list, but she had volunteered to assist with every return mission until her time came.

That left the man everyone called Marmaduke because he was big, had a long head with droopy eyes and large ears, and occasionally barked at people. To his face, he was called Mar, and the man was obsessed with changing the future because he was from 2042. He rarely spoke, citing the butterfly effect and saying he didn't want to be the man that ended existence as we know it by farting. He was an observer on this mission, but he was up the summer after Marshall and the others unless he changed his mind.

Rib grunted and the party pushed to their feet and lifted themselves off stones. They had two days to go, and Marshall's back already ached like he'd run a marathon.

A sparse woodland of evergreens filled the western horizon, and it grew thicker as the party trekked deeper into the shade beneath the tree canopy.

Marshall jumped when a tiny snake crossed his path, and Kylie chuckled, her laugh like music. They'd become good friends and had come close to the romantic line, but never crossed it.

The snake made Marshall think of Leeri. The man's death had been accepted with shrugs and murmurs. Ida's style was such that her number two was the bad guy—kind of like how schools ran. The principal never levied student punishment. Nobody spoke up when Leeri's death was communicated, and as Marshall told the story nobody asked any questions or shed a single tear at his sparsely attended memorial, where his stone was added to the town's small cemetery. That made Marshall feel like shit. Not only could it have been him who died, the guy was on a mission for the community, and nobody seemed to give a turd.

There was one piece of information that only the members of the Mount Sight fellowship knew about. It hadn't been planned, but somehow throughout the lengthy discussion as the fellowship recounted its trip, they'd forgotten to mention that Iruno—Coeus himself, would be present at the winter solstice. When the oversight was noticed by Lester, the group decided to keep the information to themselves for fear of Ida, and perhaps many others, insisting on making the trip for the winter solstice.

A gleam caught his eye and Marshall looked down to find his signet ring sending daggers of light into the perpetual gloom. The brazen cross stood out as if lifting from the metal. He stared at the ring, its history pulling his focus from his surroundings.

That's why he didn't hear Rib call a halt and he bumped into Mar.

A huge ant hill blocked the path, its steepled termite-like spires rising five feet from the pine needle-encrusted hardpan. The nest was a monument to nature's ingenuity, and it looked to have many intricate tunnels and chambers. At the mound's peak, there was a flurry of activity as a legion of red ants the size of a thumbnail each carried fragments of a massive leaf.

The ants, tiny compared to their burden, exhibited remarkable coordination as they maneuvered the shredded leaf through a labyrinth of rocks, sticks, and drifts of pine needles. A gentle hum carried over the forest as the ants scurried about, their trails crisscrossing in a symphony of motion. Despite their size, the ants carried burdens many times heavier than themselves. Marshall recalled that ants are among the strongest creatures on Earth, relative to the weight they can lift.

As the leaf disappeared into the depths of the ant hill, Rib yelled for the group to get moving again.

The forest grew dense, the humidity stifling despite the tree cover, and the rumblings began for an early end to the day's march, but Rib and Bone wouldn't have it. Both natives seemed ill at ease, and Bone's eyes darted around more than normal.

Marshall's thoughts drifted to Fiona, the rhythmic thump of his pike—walking stick—tapping the ground as he walked. With each passing day, it was getting harder to see his wife's face in his mind's eye. Her striking blue eyes had lost their luster, and the definition in her cheekbones had diminished. She was becoming faceless to him, and he made an effort every day to picture her likeness and hold it as if taking a mental picture, but that wasn't stopping her from fading.

The forest became less dense and gave way to the jungle-covered hills that separated the party from their journey's end. Here Rib did call a halt for the night. There were many fields and bare patches in the hills ahead, and that made for good hunting grounds for the larger creatures and would best be traversed in the daylight.

It seemed as though the universe wouldn't give the companions a moment's peace. The next day, while the group was replenishing their water supply at the edge of a narrow, meandering stream, Marshall spotted what he believed were Troodons.

Rib grunted loudly and the disheveled travelers stopped what they were doing and stared.

The bird-like Troodons stood three feet tall and looked to weigh fifty pounds. The beasts were sleek and emaciated, but they also appeared agile, their physiques reminiscent of modern birds. Long, slender legs suggested swift movement, and the dinosaurs' bodies were covered in shiny white feathers. The heads of the Troodons were large, which suggested a braincase relative to its body size, hinting at high intelligence. A field of large, forward-facing eyes, indicative of binocular vision and keen depth perception, were locked on the party.

Marshall knew the creatures were carnivorous predators, and that their sharp, serrated teeth, set within narrow snouts, were adapted for tearing flesh.

The horde of Troodons came together, a dense circle forming around their communal nest, tails up, their slender bodies poised for any sign of danger.

At the center of the nest, nestled amidst ferns and undergrowth, lay a clutch of eggs—small, delicate orbs that held the future of their species. The Troodons, with their keen senses, stood guard, their amber eyes always scanning their surroundings.

Some of the beasts advanced on the party, their tails twitching with anticipation, while others paced the perimeter of the nest, emitting low, rumbling calls to communicate their readiness. Their slender claws flexed and dug into the ground, and the plumage atop their heads shifted and swayed as the beasts' heads cycled around.

Mary Pat stepped back, intending to slip behind a tree trunk for cover, and stepped on a twig.

A snap reverberated through the forest and the Troodons at the edge of the pack squawked as they advanced, feathers standing on end.

Kylie fired once into the sky, and everything froze for a heartbeat as if the cosmic pause button had been pressed.

It's said mothers of all species will do anything to protect their young. Well, not Troodons. In a cloud of churning feathers, claws, and teeth the creatures surged into motion as one and scattered into the jungle, leaving the nest and eggs unprotected.

The party moved on but was soon forced to stop and hide from a flock of creatures that looked like bears but had no fur, but saggy white skin, narrow yellow eyes, and long walrus tusks that hung almost to the ground. Marshall had seen pictures of the beasts but couldn't recall the name of the species.

Two days later the companions climbed a small rise, following the well-worn path to a series of natural stone steps that led to the top of the hill.

The sun sat like a fried egg on the purple-orange horizon, and in the foreground, atop what would someday be called Hicks Dome, was the Chaka Stones.

25

Marshall trailed the tips of his fingers across the pink stones as he walked through the circle—the portal at the eastern end of the Chaka Stones. The triangle of tall standing stones towered over him, glimmering walls of white filling the gaps between them.

There were fourteen standing stones arranged in the shape of an equilateral triangle, and though they were weathered the stones didn't show much wear, and petroglyphs and pictographs could be seen all along the standing stones' smooth surfaces. Within the triangle of monolithic stones, four piles of rocks placed in a square filled the center of the stones where the ceremonial fire would've been in the future. The mounds of rocks were unique to the dinosaur domain Chaka Stones, and Marshall scoured his memory yet again, and recalled the fire on Hicks Dome, the people chanting... But there were no piles of stones.

Beyond the ancient monument, Woodhenge stood like an upset parent. Early sunlight streamed through the tall poles casting long, narrow, clock hand-like shadows across the Chaka Stones.

The sun was charging towards noon, and there wasn't a cloud in the sky, and a giddy joyfulness ran through the party as they made camp. For some members of the group just finishing the long trip from New Holland was an accomplishment.

Devon and Anna hadn't seen the stones since they'd been collected seven years prior, and Mary Pat had only been back to the spot once. Rib and Bone were old experts, and Ringo knew much about the area, despite only having been there four times himself, the first time being when he'd arrived in the dinosaur domain.

Still, given his ability to communicate better than Rib and Bone, Ringo led the search of the area. Smaller beasts were chased away, and the land was surveyed, measurements taken, but of Iruno there was no sign.

Bone chose a campsite he'd used before under the wide boughs of a broad oak-like tree that was six feet round and climbed a hundred feet into the sky. The behemoth provided total shade and was surrounded by others of its kind, which protected the party from the encroachment of anything larger than a raptor. The Pterosaur wing tarp was spread in the trees, and multiple fire pits were dug and circled with stones to secure the perimeter of the camp. By lunchtime the company was sitting at ease, eating roasted meat and leaf greens, and drinking fresh water.

Marshall's hand trembled and his throat burned with the imaginary flow of whiskey. If he did decide to stay in the dinosaur domain, Marshall would have to travel back at least once a year for one thing at least. Booze. The thought of living without whiskey, or a martini, made his stomach grumble and his head hurt from a phantom hangover.

But again, like many of the things he'd considered during this perpetual internal debate, wasn't drinking alcohol a bad thing? Everyone knew the stuff slowly killed you piece by piece, organ by organ, brain cell by brain cell. Yet he continued to drink... the feeling of the burn and subsequent mental fog was more important than years of potential suffering. And it wasn't only alcohol. He hadn't had his cellphone on in days, and he hadn't thought about T.V., restaurants, concerts, sports, travel, vacation—all these things he held so dear back in 2022 that he'd shed like so much dead skin. It felt good, and he wondered how he'd feel when all those unnecessary possessions, expenses, and worries were heaped on him once more.

The bigheads say it's better to have never loved than to have loved and lost—the saying also had been applied to money, but in Marshall's case, he'd been forced to leave comfort for the rough and raw dinosaur domain, yet... He felt less stressed, and beasts were trying to kill him constantly, so what did that say about the people back home that he felt more comfortable with apex predators than he did with his own kind?

It proved there is no animal, no apex predator, no killer more dangerous than humans.

"You in there?" Mary Pat asked as she seated herself beside him.

Marshall looked up at her, the words not registering.

"Do you have a minute?" asked Mary Pat. Kylie stood over her shoulder.

"Of course."

"Kylie and I took a look at Woodhenge, and it's exactly how Iruno and the others described it. The poles sit in holes that are about a foot deep, and there are more than one for each pole, but none at eighteen feet from the standing stones."

"So we have to dig ten holes," Marshall said.

Kylie and Mary Pat nodded. "It's a shame the celestial sky has shifted, or we could have left the things set the way Iruno left them."

"Wouldn't have needed to go to the temple either," Marshall said. "What of the poles?"

"They're roughly the size of a telephone pole, though some are a little thinner, some thicker," Kylie said. "The poles are held in place with ropes and vines attached to the pole about five feet below its top and secured to the ground via stakes."

"What about moving them?" Marshall had been skeptical when Iruno explained the plan, and he was still concerned after the man had drawn a diagram. "Is the plan going to work?"

To that the two people Marshall counted on most in the dinosaur domain had no answer.

Marshall had learned during his six months in New Holland that not much was known about Woodhenge, which had appeared prior to any of the current residents of New Holland arriving. Though folks were aware of the poles, they knew nothing of their purpose or that they could be moved until Marshall and the others filled them in. Rib and Bone were the only ones who made the trip twice yearly, and rarely did any other New Holland citizens travel with them. Rib and Bone's communication skills being what they were, most of the information they found on the trail—like seeing Woodhenge—didn't get passed on, not even to Ida.

None of this slipped by Ringo, who wore a scowl on his face twenty-three hours of the day, and maybe twenty-four—Marshall didn't see the man for an hour every morning when he wandered off to take care of personal hygiene.

To give Devon and Anna the best chance of success, the couple planned to try and crossover not only on the solstice day, but the day before, and if need be the next day. It was possible the day count was off, or that Marshall had made an error in his calculations, or some small unaccounted-for deviation caused the numbers to be off by a day, which had sunk more than one expedition throughout time.

It was eight days until the winter solstice, so seven days to the party's first attempt, which Marshall felt was more than enough time to adjust the ten poles, even if each took longer than anticipated.

The companions lounged for the rest of the day and turned in early. They all woke in the hour before dawn and the nine members of the new fellowship watched eagerly as the sunrise played off Woodhenge, tall shadows falling over the Chaka Stones. Nothing unusual was observed; the sun was neither in the right position nor at the correct angle.

Breakfast was eaten and water was consumed as Marshall gave out the team's assignments.

Moving the tall poles, which Marshall estimated weighed in excess of seven hundred pounds each, involved an intricate system of ropes and pulleys that would require the help of all nine team members.

Ringo set the pulleys, which were made of scrap metal and wood and were held together with rope and steel that had been pounded into nails. He also supervised the laying out of the ropes as the group prepared to move the southernmost pole five feet forward to its new position, where the rest of the team was digging a hole with their hands and the bark from trees.

Meanwhile, Kylie and Mary Pat constructed a basic compass using a rope and a stake. With the wooden stake planted at the circumcenter of the triangle that made up the standing stones, Mary Pat walked off the eighteen feet of rope. Marking the new locations for the poles took extra time, because the standing stones were in the way, and after each new hole was marked, the rope had to be recoiled, and the process began again.

Overhead Pterosaurs circled, and several small dinosaurs ventured up the hillside to investigate what was happening, but Kylie scared them off by firing into the sky as Mary Pat pounded her Templar shield with a stone. The companions had gotten very adept at avoiding the larger beasts, and thus far none of the big alphas had taken the time to climb the steep slope to the standing stones.

The next day, the party was still exhausted, their faces sagging, muscles protesting, and it took the entire day to move one pole. Given the time constraints this was concerning, and suddenly everyone was worried they weren't going to be ready in time for Devon and Anna's attempt.

But over the following three days, the team improved, and the team shifted five poles, leaving four to be moved over the next three days.

The day of Devon and Anna's first attempt arrived, and there had still been no sign of Iruno. This was deeply troubling, and Marshall found himself gazing at the northern horizon hoping... expecting to see the old Native American strolling up the hillside. But he didn't arrive, and Marshall and the others were forced to proceed on their own.

Perhaps that had been Iruno's plan all along? He'd passed on the critical information needed to travel the paths of time, and with that burden lifted, maybe he'd decided to... retire? To do what? And why lie about coming this winter? None of it made sense and Marshall's mind had no problem conjuring a series of possible explanations, and none of them were good.

The day before the solstice the team assembled before dawn, though there was nothing for them to do. Woodhenge was set, and as Devon and Anna stood hand-in-hand within the circle of pink stones at the eastern end of the Chaka Stones, Marshall felt tremendous pride mixed with these uncertainties and fears. He and his team accomplished something that had taken others years to achieve, and they'd managed to do it while keeping all their fingers and toes—except for Leeri... and Lester.

Marshall's stomach grew hot. How could he have forgotten about the man whose hand he'd severed was beyond him, and yet it was further proof that Marshall's mind was no longer preoccupied with the past, or the future, but was firmly focused on the present.

The sun inched over the eastern horizon as the group waited, the excitement palpable, a static electricity filling the air like just before a storm. Beams of sunlight angled over the hilltop, and Woodhenge cast long shadows over the standing stones.

Nothing happened. Devon and Anna didn't blink out of existence or fade away as if erased from time.

When the shadows passed the stones Marshall declared failure, but the party was still upbeat. All records and calculations pointed to the following day being the shortest of the year, and Marshall was confident.

That night nobody arrived from the future, at least not anyone the party saw.

The next day the sun rose, shadows fell, and the pink stone portal glowed with a pale light.

When the moment of sunrise had passed, Devon and Anna still stood within the circle of pink stone.

This failure was taken much more to heart, and when no time travelers emerged from the Chaka Stones that night dinner was a solemn affair.

Things didn't get better the next morning, and as dawn passed into day Devon and Anna were still in the dinosaur domain.

No explanation was given or asked for, and the party was left to marinate in their doubts and fears. There had been no new arrivals, which further sowed the seeds of skepticism. Had the entire quest to Mount Sight, and the subsequent trip to the Toro Ki' Temple all been for nothing?

It was suggested that while the party had the people and momentum of the learning curve, Woodhenge should be set for the summer solstice. Marshall discarded this idea, citing the local fauna. "We were lucky none of the poles were knocked over when we got here, and it wouldn't be a surprise if we returned this summer to find a couple of the poles on the ground," Marshall said. Raising a pole required a sailboat mast step-like process that took much longer than inching the poles across the hardpan into their new notches.

Marshall kept his skepticism about his calculations to himself. Could it be that they made some mistakes at the Toro Ki' Temple? And was there any reason he shouldn't travel there again before heading to the Chaka Stones for the summer solstice? At a minimum, such a trip would reconfirm his numbers, or... He made a mental note to discuss it with Kylie and Mary Pat.

The party left the standing stones with their tails between their legs, and the failure raised so many questions Marshall didn't know where to begin. The measurements and positioning of the Woodhenge? Or, had the memories of Devon and Anna, which were seven years old, failed to provide a satisfactory anchor? Whatever the cause, the failure would do nothing to ease the concerns of Ida, Ringo, and those like them.

Doubt crept through Marshall as the party started the long trek back to New Holland.

Iruno sat in a cluster of trees to the south of the Chaka Stones, his binoculars pressed to his eyes.

Sunrise had come and gone, and for the third day in a row, Marshall and the others had failed. Disappointing, but not unexpected. It had taken him three tries to perfect his anchor, which was why he hadn't joined Marshall and the others as he'd told them he would.

In the months following the visitors from New Holland, Iruno questioned the speed and ease with which he'd provided years of hard-earned information. Knowledge obtained without sacrifice is rarely respected, and he couldn't help but wonder if he'd made a mistake pushing things along so quickly.

These concerns were the reason for his absence. Had he been with Marshall and the others, he would have been pressed for explanations, and answers to questions he didn't have.

As he watched the New Holland party disappear into the jungle, he thought, perhaps, this was his last trip to the Chaka Stones.

26

It was a winter of discontent.

Marshall wandered through the graveyard, the tall grass at the edge of the field hissing in the breeze. Whoever had selected the site had done a good job. The field, which was roughly five acres in size, was surrounded by tall hardwoods with thick trunks, and they filled the forest like soldiers. Only smaller beasts found their way to the green and thus the area between the tombstones was perpetually mowed by the local fauna. The only consistent pests were the forest rats and the scourge from the sky.

He counted seventy-one stones, each chiseled with a name. Some had dates of birth, but because the specific date was unknown in the dinosaur domain, the number of days in the domain was used as the end date or was the only date identification. New Holland measured its time in days until the next solstice, and it was someone's job to maintain the record, which went back forty-two years. The count was started by a woman named Grace, and the number on her tombstone said she'd been in the dinosaur domain 16,298 days.

Ida had explained that the graveyard contained a fraction of those from the future who died in the dinosaur domain, because many folks disappeared out on the trail, never to be heard of again, or never made it to New Holland. Devon and Anna were the exceptions. It was rare that family members or spouses came to the dinosaur domain together, but there were a couple of cases where significant others had pushed for a stone, despite the lack of a body.

The wind brought the scent of smoke and baking bread. Nestled not far from the southeast corner of New Holland, the graveyard was one of New Holland's few community projects. There were flowers on some of the graves, and the stones were all different colors and oddly shaped. The place was eerie, yet soothing and comforting. As a history professor, Marshall spent a good deal of time in graveyards, searching for the past and taking impressions of tombstones. He'd always found it calming, the voices on the wind, the ghosts of those who refused to move on following him around. He felt them. He felt them here.

Marshall gave in to the urge to turn on his cellphone. The power percentage in the upper right-hand corner read thirty-six percent, but he had to connect with Fiona. He swiped until her final two text messages were displayed in the blue bubble. The initial message was sent on June

20th at 5:44 PM. It said, "Where are you? Gary just shared the funniest story. Hurry up, or we'll run out of wine." Then, at 5:48 PM, "???"

Picturing his wife's face was getting harder and harder, and the invisible connection that had allowed them to finish each other's sentences had been severed. Could it be repaired? Did he want it to?

A low-power message streamed across the screen, and he saw the battery percentage had plunged to less than ten percent, and the numbers and percent symbol had turned red.

Panic surged through him. The count, the dates, his old life... How would he maintain the connections that might help him get home?

With a flash, the phone went dark.

Anger superheated his stomach and sweat dripped down his forehead and back. His rage eased as the realization hit him: he didn't need the phone any longer. The days to the next solstice weren't in question, and he could still check the numbers at the Toro Ki' Temple should he choose to do so. The loss of the phone's calculator and the preprogrammed formula wasn't an issue anymore, and Kylie's phone still had power. He had to assume the formula was correct, which wasn't much of a leap given he knew Iruno had used it.

Marshall cocked his arm, intending to hurl the device into the forest, but something held him back. Everything in the dinosaur domain had value, even useless pieces of electronics. He slipped the device in a pocket.

He continued, passing the stones marking lost lives, and when he came to Leeri's stone he made the sign of the cross. The gesture meant very little to him, but it was the only way he knew how to show respect for the dead.

The gleam of the Templar ring caught his eye, the cross screaming for him to say something, voice a word of thanks to some God who, if one existed, owed humanity a big explanation for their lack of intervention. Instead, Marshall said nothing. He hadn't known Leeri well and hadn't trusted the man, but the guy certainly didn't deserve to die in the dinosaur domain. They'd slogged through the shit together, saved each other's bacon, and like a guy you shared a foxhole with, but whom you hated and wouldn't share a beer with in the real world, Marshall felt sorrow for his fallen mate. He wished he'd done something to help on that fateful day, the shadow of Mount Sight watching over him—but what? It had all happened so fast.

He had overheard Leeri telling Lester about the woman he loved, who had shunned him for better options. Where he was from in China there were many more men than women and finding a partner was a challenge. Money often played a huge role, of which he'd had little, which was why he'd come to the United States in search of a fortune and a bride.

"Mary Pat told me you were out here." Kylie's voice carried over the graveyard. The dinosaur domain agreed with her. Her white freckled face was tanned, her blonde hair bleached white, and she'd grown it out and her long locks were pulled back in a long ponytail. She wore a blue button-up blouse that she'd bartered for, but she still wore her blue uniform pants and black leather shoes. On this day, she wore her gun belt. She'd taken to not wearing it while within the protective wall of New Holland, but she strapped it on whenever she left town.

Their relationship had cooled as the possibility of going home set in. Or not going home. The prospect of staying in the domain was weighing on both of them, and they both agreed it was no time to start a relationship.

Especially since Marshall was already in one.

An awkward silence followed as Marshall started back to the gates.

Kylie fell in beside him but still said nothing. Though they'd drifted apart, he still knew her pretty well and something was bothering her. "What's up? You didn't come out here to commune with the spirits."

She chuckled. Kylie's skepticism of organized religion was one of the many things they saw eye to eye on. It was amazing what you learned about a person when you were trapped on the trail with nothing to do except chat about the mundane. "The number of people that think this entire getting home thing is a farce, or at a minimum wrong, is growing."

"Fueled by Ida, no doubt."

Kylie shook her head no. "I don't think so. Ringo was there, and he told everyone of the non-event at the Chaka Stones. Devon and Anna have shared their disappointment as well. I think people are comfortable here, and maybe... just maybe, they're looking for excuses to stay and don't want to admit it to themselves."

"They might not even know themselves," he said.

"Yeah."

Kylie was considering staying in the dinosaur domain and he'd done nothing to assuage her concerns. "Still struggling with your decision?"

She said nothing.

"What's really bothering you?"

Kylie sighed. "Do you think... I mean, do you think there's a real possibility of... ending up in the wrong time? Or, nowhere at all?"

Marshall had considered the ultimate prison of the void, but he was reassured by the knowledge that whoever... whatever made the Chaka Stones, understood the universe on an entirely different level. He said,

"The Toro Ki' must have had the ability to time travel. There's no other way the Chaka Stones, and what they do, makes sense."

"I'm not following."

"The Toro Ki' knew what the celestial sky would look like in the future, the cycles of the Earth's formation. The existence of the Chaka Stones proves it."

Still, Kylie said nothing.

"The Toro Ki' chose a location for the Chaka Stones, and the monument has remained for millions of years through a complete upheaval of Earth. That can't be by chance."

"They knew the spot would be around…" Kylie nodded.

"That doesn't mean we haven't made errors," he said. "It still amazes me that the information we were given was even discovered. How many people before Iruno—"

Horns blasted and the ring of metal being beaten carried over the graveyard.

"Great," Kylie said as she drew her Glock.

Marshall and Kylie broke into a run, heading for the gates. The sounding of the alarm could mean only one thing; New Holland was under attack.

The duo arrived at the gates to find chaos. A cart filled with fresh produce from the fields was wedged between the open gates, and three dinosaurs Marshall could only describe as baby T-rexes attacked from three sides.

Men fired arrows from above, spears were thrown, and two men and a woman held pikes that jabbed at the creatures as they closed in.

The mini-T-rexes stood fifteen feet tall, and though their heads and snouts were much narrower than a Tyrannosaur's, their teeth were bigger, and two long fangs curved over red gums. Red bulbous eyes were locked on the open gates, their tails swaying, heads bobbing erratically.

With a sickening realization, Marshall knew the beasts didn't want the produce or its growers. They wanted to get into New Holland. Waiting until the gate was open showed advanced intelligence, and Marshall knew from Fiona and her friends that there was an ongoing debate within the dino-geek community about dinosaurs being more intelligent than originally believed. And more interesting, what mental heights would they have achieved had they not been wiped from the Earth?

The alpha shrieked and Marshall skidded to a halt. He had his sword, so he drew it from its sheath, but what good would it do against three apex predators that seemed angry to be alive?

Nor did it matter.

Upon seeing Marshall, and more importantly Kylie, the three people defending the food cart turned tail and bolted through the open gates into town.

Kylie planted her feet, aimed, and fired. One, two, three fast shots that hit the lead dino in the head, back, and right upper thigh.

The wounded beast's thick muscular legs churned, and the creature swung around, its eyes finding Kylie, its tiny arms reaching out, claws raking the air. With a surge of rippling muscles, the dinosaur lunged forward but only took two steps before faceplanting onto the hardpan.

Cheering from atop the wall as more arrows rained down.

Kylie shifted her aim and squeezed off two more shots, which took down a second monster.

The third mini-T-rex's head cycled around, as if the beast was looking for help, or cover, and then with a squawk of derision the creature fled into the jungle.

Dust clouds settled over the gates, the bitter stench of gun smoke filling the air.

The men atop the wall began to clap and cheer, and Marshall was disappointed to see the smile spread over Kylie's face. She was a hero here. An important and respected person, but... He hadn't had the heart to tell her, and he didn't know if he ever would, that once the bullets ran out...

The food cart jerked into motion and the gate guard called out to Marshall and Kylie.

"Coming," Marshall yelled. He didn't want to hang around and get caught up in the disposal of the dinosaur corpses.

The streets were lined with people, and they all waved, nodded—and some bowed, bowed! –as Kylie strolled through town like a returning warrior. Marshall saw the appeal, and he asked himself the same question he'd been asking himself for months: Fiona aside, was he better off in 2022 or the dinosaur domain? Every time he got close to an answer he pushed it away, because regardless of whether or not he wanted to stay, he had to go home, no matter the price.

27

Marshall wore a canvas hat with a torn brim that was stained with rain, dirt, and time. He'd traded his useless cellphone for the lid, but not before pulling the SIM card and destroying it with a stone. A piece of him was still worried the entire quest would go tits up, so extra precautions were taken.

The party had been on the trail for five days, taking it slow, being extra careful. Marshall had argued, and there had been no debate, that the company needed to leave far in advance of the solstice. So it was that the group of seven set out twenty-five days before Marshall and Lester were going to make their attempt.

Taking things slowly made a lot of sense, and after moving the poles over the winter, and seeing how difficult it would be to stand the poles up should they be knocked over, Marshall wanted to give the group more than enough time. Pressure bred mistakes, which caused injury, which, in the dinosaur domain, meant death.

What Marshall didn't tell his mates was the conflict raging inside him. The thought of spending another year in the dinosaur domain, at first, had been a strong motivator, but now, not so much. Once he'd gotten through the winter of discontent, Marshall settled into a routine that had him smiling and laughing most days, worries of getting home far from his mind as he lost himself in field work and enjoyed the company of the people who seemed to have found a second life in the domain. There were those in town who called it Heaven, and some had started to question if they were, in fact, still alive.

A beast roared in the distance, and it carried through the jungle and silenced the endless buzz of insects. Slowly the creatures of the forest came back online, the ringing starting low and then building like a tuning orchestra. Marshall was reminded of the dangers that lurked in every shadow and behind every stone. But he'd already done those mental gymnastics. Many times. Were the dangers of the domain any different than back in 2022? Hell, depending on where you lived, one could argue 2022 was worse.

The companions reached one of Marshall's marker stones and the group turned southwest and followed the faint grumble of the river. Kylie was on point, Glock at the ready as the party shuffled single file through a gap in a thicket of saw-palmetto-like trees, their fronds tough, sharp, and pointed. Marshall's number one had decided she was going to stay in the dinosaur domain, and it hadn't been a huge surprise to

Marshall. What did she have back in 2022? In the dinosaur domain, she was akin to Wyatt Earp. But her decision hadn't been made without taking precautions. There were twelve bullets in the magazine currently in the Glock, and a spare magazine was filled with twenty 9 MM rounds. Her final leverage should she need any.

As preparations for the summer trip were being made, Marshall was certain that the composition of the party would be of great debate, but in the end, it wasn't. With Marshall and Lester, Kylie, Mary Pat, Rib, Bone, and Ringo would make the trip.

Kylie insisted on seeing Marshall and Lester off, and the party needed the gun. She would return to New Holland along with Rib, Bone, and Ringo, and they would relay the events at the Chaka Stones to Ida and the others. Marshall had tried to persuade Kylie not to come on the trip because it was an unnecessary risk, but she'd answered that if she was going to live in the domain, she wasn't going to let it control her life. What she hadn't said, but Marshall suspected, was that there was no conceivable scenario where she would loan out her gun.

Stavero had also decided to stay in the domain, and his decision had been no surprise to Marshall.

There was much curiosity and over the six months between the winter and the summer solstices, many townsfolk considered making the trek to watch and see for themselves if what Marshall was preaching was true. There had been a great flurry of names put on the list and the priority order set, but after the winter failure, excitement and eagerness had cooled.

Marmaduke was scheduled for the following summer, and because of Devon and Anna's failure, who should make an attempt this winter had been hotly debated. Whether Devon and Anna should get another chance, an opportunity to build on their unsuccessful attempt, or should the next person in line get their chance was complicated and the ultimate decision fell to Ida. She decided that each team or individual would get two tries, and if unsuccessful, they would have to go to the back of the line.

Marshall figured if a successful crossover wasn't observed soon, it wouldn't matter and people would be able to try as much as they wanted, though he didn't see how that would work.

The group made fast work of the odd depression filled with stones they'd passed through on the winter trip. Marshall paused briefly to examine the quarried section of the hole. Many tall stones had been removed, though how they'd been hauled out of the pit was unknown, as was their final destination and who had done the herculean work. Whatever road or mechanism had been used was long gone.

Marshall and his companions spent a day and a night at a lean-to atop a hill with a good view. The jungle covering the hills that rolled into the distance was blanketed with a thick layer of mist that stretched to the western horizon. At top speed, the group had two more days to go. At their current pace, four. Rant's Run wove through the hills to the south and by lunch the next day the party would reach its banks.

Extra time had been spent mapping the river and Marshall had suggested that the waterway should be considered as a form of travel to assist in getting back and forth to the Chaka Stones, and if necessary to the Toro Ki' Temple, though a considerable amount of hiking would still be necessary. The idea was initially met with enthusiasm until an old man named Jasper described the monster he'd seen just below the surface of the clear water.

"It was a sea serpent, a demon, I say," the old guy had said. "Its body was sinuous and snake-like, and it stretched impossibly long as it undulated and slithered through the river. Scales, iridescent and shimmering, covered its hide and reflected the light, each scale the size of Mary Pat's shield."

The old man had paused and shaken his head. "There were large ridges and crests, like a crown, atop its head, and its eyes..." Another shake of the head as his eyes shifted to the ground. "I felt it appraising me? You know what I mean? Then there were the teeth. So many teeth."

That had been enough for Marshall, and his sails had gone slack as he recalled the giant croc mutant, the appearance of which had led to Lester losing his hand. With no support for building a communal boat—and there was nobody in New Holland who felt they could supervise such a task—the idea was scrapped.

The static of rapids leaked through the forest and the team arrived at a bend in Rant's Run. Though he couldn't see it, Marshall heard a waterfall that wasn't on the map. He drank his fill and grabbed some dried dino-jerky and a piece of the delicious flatbread that Marshall had taken to calling Lembas because of its restorative powers. Kylie said the baker put a bunch of unknown herbs in the stuff, and it was great.

Marshall planted himself in the shade under the boughs of a conifer and let his mind wander. He thought of Back to the Future and the sports almanac Biff used to get rich. Was there a play like that to be made? Certainly, there was nothing of value in the dinosaur domain—except beasts—and bringing valuable things from the future to the domain might make you popular, but it wouldn't make you rich. Or could it?

The need for an anchor closed the loophole. Yet another use for the Toro Ki' failsafe. Marshall closed his eyes and took a deep breath, sucking in the fresh air. The musky stink of a wet animal carried on the wind, and he sat up.

A beast eased from the cover of the forest and waded out into the river, its narrow head rotating as its eyes locked on Marshall.

Another first in the dinosaur domain, he believed. The beast looked to be a type of Kaprosuchus, though something in the back of his memory said those beasts weren't from around these parts—or it could just mean no fossils had been found in the area. Either way, the beast was an enigma even amongst its own kind. Marshall knew the fearsome predator belonged to the family of crocodylomorphs, distant relatives of modern crocodiles, but its appearance was a striking departure from a croc.

The creature inched forward through the shallows as it alternated between quadrupedal and bipedal stances. It rose onto two legs as it navigated boulders but slipped back onto all fours when wading through the water. Unlike its contemporary counterparts, the monster's most distinctive trait was its elongated, pig-like snout, which earned it the epithet "boar-crocodile", which was why Marshall remembered the beast. The snout was adorned with numerous sharp teeth that were perfectly adapted for seizing and tearing apart prey, which was why Fiona and her colleagues believed the beast to be a carnivore.

A growl followed by deep clicks carried down the river as the beast advanced.

Marshall pushed to his feet as he searched for Kylie, who he didn't see.

Measuring approximately sixteen feet in length from snout to tail, the Kaprosuchus possessed a muscular build, its body covered in a thick scaly hide. The coloration of its skin made the creature look like an orca, the black broken occasionally by large patches of white. The beast's forelimbs were muscular, its rear legs twice the size, suggesting a high degree of terrestrial mobility.

Marshall knew the beast ambushed unsuspecting prey with lightning-fast strikes, so he put the tree he'd been leaning on between himself and the beast.

The creature's head bobbed and weaved as it watched Marshall.

Mary Pat, Rib, and Bone had taken up positions behind a boulder, and Ringo had fled into the woods. That left Lester standing alone, knee-deep in the flowing river as he wrung out the t-shirt he'd just washed.

The dinosaur paused and reared back when Kylie strode from the forest, whistling, a varmint slung over her shoulder. "Shit," she said as she dropped dinner and drew down.

With a squeal, the beast charged forward on all fours, water splashing and obscuring the beast from view.

Kylie fired at the creature, but it moved too quickly, darting through the raging water and zigzagging like alligators do.

Lester ran for the forest, and the Kaprosuchus darted past him, the creature's gaze locked on Marshall. Water splashed as Lester fought through the river, just ten feet from the edge of the forest, when the dinosaur's powerful tail—tapered to a point and lined with bony osteoderms—swung and struck him with a bone-cracking force.

A hollow thud echoed over the churning river as Kylie fired.

Lester sailed through the air, his wail like tearing paper, and he hit the ground in a tangle, the sound of crunching bone running through Marshall.

Kylie fired and missed again, but then she rolled back her right shoulder, reset her aim, and pulled the trigger. Three fast shots... tap, tap, tap...

The Kaprosuchus slowed, stood still, then gazed skyward as it toppled over with a whimper thirty feet from Marshall.

The river settled, raucous noise once again leaked from the jungle, and Marshall let out the breath he hadn't known he was holding.

28

Lester's wailing spurred everyone into motion, and that's when Ringo bit the donut.

Another Kaprosuchus burst from the jungle engulfed in a cloud of leaves.

Ringo appeared a second later as he stumbled from the jungle, creepers and leaves clinging to his deerskin tunic. Within the dense tangle of undergrowth in the forest, the pursuing Kaprosuchus had overtaken and passed its prey.

The dinosaur cried out, a stuttering yelp that ended with a hiss, and when the creature saw Ringo lying on the hardpan, its head jerked back, and its jaws flexed open as it surged forward.

Ringo, dazed, dirt and blood smeared over his face, saw the approaching menace, and at the last instant rolled.

The beast's jaws snapped shut, and its claws slashed through the air as it skidded to a stop. Pivoting on its muscular hind legs, the creature almost stood upright.

Kylie aimed and fired, but she was fifty yards away and the Kaprosuchus was ducking and weaving like a heavyweight champ.

With a crack, the beast's muscular tail smacked a tree, and the sound of splintering wood brought back bad memories.

Lester's screaming carried over the chaos, the man no doubt reliving the worst ten seconds of his life. Well, maybe not the worst ten seconds.

The monster's tail whipped as Ringo crab-walked backward, trying to put as much space between himself and the monster as possible. The river loomed behind him, and for a heartbeat, Marshall thought the flow of the river might help the man.

But the Kaprosuchus was too fast, too vicious, and its body had been built for one purpose, the goal of its entire existence—to track and kill prey.

Ringo pressed to his feet, but his movements were sluggish and awkward when compared to the Kaprosuchus.

The dinosaur's footwork was like a boxer, and the animal bobbed, its forelimbs reaching out, three-inch claws gleaming. Jaws snapped as the animal used its greatest weapon—its head—to attack.

Ringo backed away, searching for something to fend the beast off with.

Kylie let loose with a frustrated wail as she ran forward, Glock out as she tried to sight the dinosaur, but Ringo was too close, and both the figures were moving.

A sickening crunch echoed over the river, and Ringo screamed, but then fell still as he gargled blood.

When the dust cleared the Kaprosuchus was standing over Ringo. The creature didn't have the man in its jaws, but the two claw slashes across his chest had been the man's undoing. Entrails leaked onto the ground, and there was blood. So much blood the stink of it drove out the fresh perfume of the river mist.

Marshall stood stunned, mind spinning with fear. Would the sound bring an alpha?

The Kaprosuchus clamped down on one of Ringo's legs with its jaws and began dragging the man toward the jungle.

"Help... Help me," pleaded Ringo. His head hung at a right angle, his clothes were covered in blood, and what looked like purple lobster meat bursting from its shell seeped from the gaping hole in his stomach.

Kylie ran forward until she was twenty yards from the monster, stopped, planted her feet, and fired.

The beast squealed as the first shot hit its chest, but it didn't stop trying to secure its prey. A second bullet tore off the side of Ringo's face and put the man out of his misery.

Kylie held her fire as a long stream of air, like a balloon deflating, rose above the sound of arguing water.

The creature collapsed atop Ringo's destroyed body.

Water gurgled, a gentle breeze blew, and Lester's whimpering pushed the group onto their next nightmare.

Lester was alive, but his leg was badly broken.

With Ringo's death still replaying across his mental canvas, Marshall trailed after Kylie as she ran to Lester's side. The rest of the group stood around as they searched for more of the deadly creatures, but the dinosaur domain had done enough damage on this day.

Kylie had medical experience as part of her police officer training, so she took the lead on setting the leg and splinting it. That was a painful process... for Lester, during which he passed out, which allowed the party to have an honest discussion about how to move forward.

Lester's journey was over, at least for now, and no debate on that was necessary.

Rib, Bone, and Mary Pat joined the group. Mary Pat held one of her throwing stars. She'd carried her gifts throughout the dinosaur domain, but unlike her bow, which she used to hunt, she hadn't even practiced with the stars in months. "I guess we have to ask the question, who has to go on?" said Mary Pat. "I don't."

"Nor I," Kylie admitted. Her tone was sullen, and she couldn't meet Marshall's eye.

Rib and Bone said nothing. They were needed on the trail.

"What are you suggesting?" Marshall asked.

Now Kylie did look up and meet Marshall's eye. "We wait," Kylie said.

The words hit Marshall like a rock to the jaw. Those two words had so many meanings. None of which he understood or was prepared to deal with.

"Come back here," said Rib.

All eyes turned in the woman's direction, her slender form casting a needle shadow across a nearby boulder.

Water gurgled and popped as the river sang.

Marshall nodded slowly. That was the longest sentence he'd ever heard the woman speak, but he guessed hanging around the time travelers for so long, something had to rub off.

"I'll stay with him," Mary Pat said. "All I ask is that you set us up with a fortification, and we'll wait it out until Kylie, Rib, and Bone get back." She looked at the ground. "I'll need a supply of food, also, because all I've got is those." She pointed at her bow, quiver of arrows, and her shield.

And there it was. As it always was. The gun and its importance within the societal structure of the dinosaur domain.

Lester climbed from sleep, and asked, "You would do that for me, Mary Pat?"

"We haven't sunk so low that we can leave you out here to be…" Mary Pat's voice trailed off as everyone's eyes strayed to the pile of blood, bones, and decaying muscle that had once been Ringo and a Kaprosuchus.

With that settled, preparations were made.

There was a tall pile of stones at the bend in the river, and Marshall and Mary Pat carried Lester into its tight cradle. The man winced and moaned with each movement, but to his credit, he didn't scream, though he couldn't stop the tears from leaking down his face. Marshall had never gotten used to the blackened stump, but it had fully healed.

If the group were comprised of different types of individuals, Lester would have most likely been left for dead. Regardless of how the following days played out, Lester was going to be a tremendous burden on New Holland and those who called it home. He was an amputee who was looking at being off his feet for months, unable to help with chores as others took care of him. This would create a tremendous debt, and Lester might not be attempting to go home anytime soon.

That was if his leg didn't get infected. In the future antibiotics would have been administered, and tetanus shots verified, but out here, before recorded time, there was nothing to do except let the various herbal concoctions available do what they could and hope the leg healed right.

The party left Mary Pat with enough food for two people for thirty days, which was basically the group of seven's entire stock. Mary Pat and Rib stripped meat from the dead Kaprosuchus before it spoiled as Kylie and Marshall built a small fireplace and covered the den of stones with a simple roof of leafy branches.

With that done, Ringo's remains were buried under a mound of stones, everyone in the group working to make it happen except Lester, who was hidden within his new stone fortress, where he would spend the next couple of weeks in Mary Pat's care.

Saying goodbye to Mary Pat was hard, though his gut said he was going to see her again. The feeling unsettled his nerves because that meant he was going to fail. He turned and looked at Kylie.

She stared at the ground and didn't look up.

The remainder of the trek was uneventful. Marshall and Kylie knew the trail well enough that Rib and Bone had taken to scouting ahead, which helped the group avoid the local fauna.

Ringo's loss stung, because the man hunted, helped around camp, and could be trusted to keep watch. Ida was sure to be upset, though she'd replaced Leeri without shedding a single tear. He thought that maybe the woman had no sympathy left and all the tears had been used up.

The Templar signet ring gleamed as he walked, its cross a constant reminder of the burden he bore. If he was successful and got home, what would he tell Fiona? Would she—would anyone, believe him? Was she capable of belief? There were days when even Marshall thought he might be living in a dream.

He would cross that bridge when he came to it if it was still standing.

The western Shokra was marked on the map and a brief halt was called when they reached it. Everyone was tired and hungry, but there wasn't much farther to go. They drank water and ate their last rations. With Kylie a member of the party, hunting was a standard affair because of the gun, and at dusk, a fire could be started, and meat roasted and smoked.

Clouds rolled in overhead, but they were white as snow and carried no rain. As he got the group moving again a silence settled over the jungle that made Marshall nervous. Usually when the jungle band stopped playing an apex trombonist was looking for a solo, but he'd heard no cracking branches, no rustling leaves, none of the telltale signs of a large beast moving through the vegetation.

Whether it had been some inbred instinct, or some extra special sensory perception he'd developed by paying such close attention to his environment over the last year, a feeling that something was very wrong filled him with dread. Marshall's breath caught in his throat like a fish bone as he came over a rise and the Chaka Stones could be seen atop what would someday be called Hicks Dome.

Marshall dropped his pack and pulled out his binoculars.

Kylie gasped.

Bone grunted, but Rib made no sound.

Woodhenge no longer surrounded the tall standing stones. Each pole had been knocked from its position, lines cut, and all ten poles lay flat on the ground.

Marshall's head pounded as he fell back onto his ass, the ringing in his head so loud it drove out all other sounds. What beast… No… His eye sockets hurt as he pressed the lenses of the binoculars to his eyes.

The ropes and vines holding up the Woodhenge poles had been cut, that was clear. And all the poles? He could see the local fauna taking down a pole or two, but all of them? That was just too large of a coincidence to swallow. No, rippers had done this. Had Marshall and the others been observed during the winter visit?

Suddenly he felt exposed, and Marshall pushed to his feet, eyes searching for anything that might tell him what had happened. But there was nothing except the cajoling winds, the Chaka Stones, and a suffocating sense of helplessness and anxiety that threatened to take him down.

"We've got sixteen days until the day before the first attempt," Kylie said.

"Yes. Yes," encouraged Bone.

The group had the tackle, the rope, and more vines could easily be found in the jungle. Maybe Kylie was right, but again the tiny piece of him that hid in the dark corner in the back of his brain asked again if that was really what he wanted. Was the universe telling him something? Giving him one of those signs everyone was always looking for, but that never seemed to materialize?

That was up to the universe. All he could do was try, which was exactly what he intended to do. If he failed, then he failed, and with another year in the dinosaur domain perhaps something would change. To that the logical side of his brain countered, if you changed any more than you already have Fiona won't recognize you. Regardless of whether he was successful in getting home or not, he feared that shoe had already dropped.

29

It only took the team eight days to reset Woodhenge.

As it turned out, using a series of stakes and pully tackle, it wasn't difficult righting the poles, and when they were set straight the team made sure they were in their new locations per the Starry Stele. This allowed Marshall and crew to skip the arduous task of inching the upright poles over the hardpan to their new holes. In some cases, the poles had rolled, but some were in better positions than others, and the power of the pulley saved the day. When the team hit their stride, they completed three in one day.

That left the companions eight days to sit around, stand guard, and marinate in their worries, fears, and doubts.

Rib and Bone spent most of their time gathering firewood and shoring up the lean-to that had been built on the permanent campsite. It was decided that since more New Hollanders would be traveling to the Chaka Stones, it made sense to invest in a bit of dinosaur domain infrastructure.

Kylie kept to herself most of the time, and she'd taken to cataloging the flora around the standing stones. There were flowers, broadleaf variegated Hosta-like plants, and a few weeds that Marshall hadn't seen anywhere else in the dinosaur domain. It was as if the seeds of the future had traveled the winds of time through the portal, and perhaps that was exactly what had happened.

Marshall thought of Marmaduke as he wandered around the outskirts of Woodhenge, and kept watch. Mar was due to travel home in one year... if Marshall made it home. Mar was always concerned about small things changing the future. In 2022 corporations were creating non-germinating seeds that they owned the rights to so only they could grow said fruit or vegetable. Research had shown that wind was pollinating nearby fields and rendering their seeds sterile. What would happen in the dinosaur domain if such a thing happened? It would be—

He stopped short, and beer sloshed over the rim of his cup.

In the southeastern sky, high above the dark peaks of the mountains, a dot of light stood out much brighter than the rest.

Marshall's mind spun back to Iruno—who was still a no-show—and he recalled all the man's talk about the asteroid that almost wiped all living things off the genetic map. He was married to a dinosaur nerd, so he knew more than he cared to admit about the space rock that was believed to have caused the extinction of the dinosaurs. That asteroid, approximately six miles in diameter, struck Earth around sixty-six million years ago, and its impact crater was buried beneath the Yucatán Peninsula in Mexico. The date of the impact coincided with the K–Pg boundary and the mass extinction of seventy-five percent of all plant and animal species on Earth, including all non-avian dinosaurs.

Was he looking at the infamous rock that ended the age of the dinosaurs? The dot appeared brighter than the North Star, and had it been there yesterday? Many factors needed to be considered as an asteroid approached Earth, and its visibility depended on its size, distance from Earth, and the rock's trajectory.

But then he remembered the documentary… The Last Day, or was it When It All Ended? He couldn't recall, but he did remember a scientist's response to the question, "Could the dinosaurs have seen the asteroid approaching?"

The professor had answered, "It's likely that the asteroid that caused the extinction event would have been visible in the sky for a short period before impact, possibly days, no more than a couple of weeks."

Marshall stared at the light in the sky, and he saw no movement. The stars were so bright without light pollution. He was going to miss seeing the galaxy with its clothes off. He considered waking Kylie but decided against it. If it was the famous asteroid, there was nothing he could do about it. It would be here in days, and there was no way he could get back to New Holland in time, and even if he could, what would they do? Hide in the bunker? The destruction would be widespread and catastrophic, yet the Chaka Stones had survived. He decided to say nothing until he knew more.

The days dripped away, and the light in the sky grew, but no one else noticed.

As the sun rose above the rim of the world the day before the summer solstice, Marshall stood beneath the Chaka Stones, eyes closed as he thought back to that night a year ago. He'd visualized the scene many times; smelled the scent of smoke and the sharp tang of evergreens, and he listened for the rumble of cars on the interstate, looked through his mind's eye for the glow of artificial light.

Woodhenge cast long finger-like shadows over the Chaka Stones, and Marshall rolled his shoulders, keeping his anchor firmly planted in his mind.

A Pterosaur crowed, the insects in the jungle buzzed, and he felt a cool mist on his face.

When Marshall opened his eyes, his companions were still standing before him.

"O.K.," Marshall said. "Let's prepare for our last supper together."

That night the rippers made their play, and a weak play it was. Motivation and ultimate goal aside, one would think that people who lived in the dinosaur domain and spent their lives hiding from apex predators would be more cunning and stealthy.

The attack on the camp turned out to be a diversion.

With screams of bloody rage, a man and a woman dressed in rags and carrying spears surged into camp.

Kylie reached for her gun, but before she could bring it to bear on the intruders, Rib and Bone beat her to the punch.

Rib wrapped the man up and lifted him off the ground as she drove forward with her skinny, muscle-corded legs. The guy hit the ground with a thud, and Rib held him in place by his neck.

Bone simply stuck out a foot, and the woman tripped, went sailing through the air, and landed at Marshall's feet.

Marshall looked down at the woman as he put his foot on her chest and displayed the Bowie knife.

Kylie chuckled and the team was feeling good about themselves until the twang and pop of lines being cut, and the thud of a pole hitting the ground carried over the hilltop.

"Watch them!" Kylie said to Rib and Bone as she darted into the darkness, Glock at the ready.

"Wait? It could be a trap!" yelled Marshall, but Kylie was gone, and there was nothing to do but chase after her.

"Stop that! Now. Or I'll shoot!" yelled Kylie. She grunted as she fired once into the sky.

Shadowy figures ran into the darkness as a second pole fell to the hardpan with a crash.

Marshall arrived at Kylie's side. She stood next to a fallen pole, her gun trained on the darkness. "Can't waste ammo," she hissed. "If I—"

A primal roar thundered over the hilltop, its echo bouncing around inside the Chaka Stones like a megaphone.

Yelling and screaming as Rib and Bone tried restraining their prisoners, but Marshall yelled for them to let the primitives go. He was more concerned with the alpha that had been drawn to the commotion and had taken an interest in the festivities.

A T-rex head rose above the foliage on the southern side of the slope that led up to the Chaka Stones. Its baseball-sized eyes glowed in the darkness as it ranged its head around, moonlight glinting off the creature's thick teeth.

Kylie aimed the Glock at the monster and asked, "Fire?"

The question was more complicated than it appeared. Based on a year of experience, single bullets tended to irritate the creatures more than hurt them and often incited violence. Hiding was usually the best option. "No," Marshall said. "Stay still."

Rib and Bone had disappeared like smoke on the wind along with their prisoners, and the apex predator hadn't moved as it waited to ambush its prey.

This stalemate stretched out to three minutes before the T-rex grumbled and disappeared back into the jungle, leaving the sounds of snapping branches and the crackle of vegetation being crushed in its wake.

With Kylie standing guard with the gun, the party worked through the night to get the two poles righted and in position.

"Why would they do that?" Kylie asked. "Do they have any idea what they're doing?"

Under the harsh glare of Kylie's flashlight, Marshall hiked his shoulders as he tied the tackle off onto a stake. "Pull!" he yelled, and slowly, after twenty-eight jerks of the rope, pole number one lifted back into position.

Marshall was preparing to raise the second knocked-over pole when Kylie's flashlight gave up the ghost and the work site fell into shadowy darkness. The companions waited for their eyes to adjust, and with the stars and moon glaring down at them they got back to work, the darkness pressing in around them, the summer solstice dawn hours away.

The team finished two hours before sunrise, though there was no rest for the weary. Marshall feared another ripper attack, so the four companions patrolled the outside of Woodhenge like they were protecting a pile of gold.

Kylie walked with Marshall, whose gaze kept straying to the southeastern sky. The asteroid had grown to the size of a golf ball in the heavens, and though he couldn't be sure, to Marshall it looked like stardust trailed behind the light.

Still, Kylie hadn't noticed, but now that there was no doubt, he felt obligated to tell her. Marshall stopped walking and stared up at the heavens.

"What is it?" Kylie said as she ranged the Glock around, searching for targets.

Marshall stared at the bright light.

"What the hell are you lo—" Then she saw it and the Glock fell to her side. "Is that… is that what I think it is?"

"I believe so," he said. "Does that change your decision?"

"We have to go back. We have to warn them. We have to..." Kylie's face twisted. "How long have you known?"

"A couple of days, but I wasn't sure until tonight."

"And there's not enough time?"

He shook his head no.

"It could take months.... Couldn't it?" she pleaded.

Marshall said nothing.

"Maybe it's just a shooting star or a comet or something that will come nowhere near Earth. The extinction could still be millions of years off."

"Is that what you believe?" Marshall said.

It was Kylie's turn to say nothing.

"Besides," Marshall said. "What could we possibly do? What would we say? 'See that light in the sky? It's going to kill you all so follow me.' Where?"

"O.K.," she said. "I'll come with you."

Before daybreak Marshall and Kylie left Rib and Bone to guard Woodhenge and went into the jungle. The pair found a spot next to a huge boulder to hide the gun, sword, Bowie knife, map, and compass. Those treasures were for Mary Pat if she wanted them. Marshall wrote the woman a note and gave it to Rib and Bone to give to her as he was certain neither of them could read, at least not common English. If she wanted the stuff, she knew where to find it.

The eastern horizon blurred from black to gray. Goodbyes were said, though with the communication gap Marshall couldn't tell if Rib and Bone were sad to see him and Kylie go, or if they were happy to be rid of the pair. To the east, along Rant's Run, Mary Pat and Lester waited, and he hoped they would survive the coming storm.

Even in the gray dusk of sunrise, the white ball of approaching death could be seen, but Rib and Bone had yet to notice, so Marshall pointed it out to the pair and received shrugs in return. After much frustration, R&B understood they needed to point the light out for Ida when they got back to New Holland, though Marshall feared that would be too late.

The Chaka Stones seemed to glow in the growing light as Marshall and Kylie stood within the standing circle of pink stone.

Rib and Bone patrolled the outskirts of Woodhenge, and to Marshall's dismay, the rippers reappeared as the sun inched over the lip of the world.

Kylie surged forward. "We have to help them."

Marshall gripped her arm. "This might be our only chance."

Woodhenge cast tall shadows over the Chaka Stones as the sun was released by the horizon. Shadows flitted around the Woodhenge poles, and the yelling and the sound of snapping rope carried over the hilltop.

Marshall pictured his anchor, the instant he passed over.

A roar pierced the morning as the first rays of the rising day fell across Woodhenge, and a spark of light, like a growing flame, appeared within the circle of pink stones.

30

Drums beat in rhythm with his heart as Marshall opened his eyes and looked over at Kylie, but she no longer stood beside him. The grayness had faded in the blink of an eye and oppressive sunlight glared down at him.

Marshall covered his eyes, and said, "Kylie?"

There was no answer.

The morning ceremony had been completed, and thin tendrils of smoke rose from the dying ceremonial fire. Marshall looked down at his hand and the Templar ring was still there. It hadn't been a dream.

Few people milled about—but they wore normal clothes... clothes! No one appeared to notice him, and suddenly he felt very alone. He hadn't expected a ticker tape parade, but something would have been nice. There was no Fiona... No Kylie. He called out again and a woman looked in his direction, but there was no reply.

Kylie had failed to cross over.

There was no asteroid in the sky, and Marshall felt sick to his stomach as he wandered through the Merlin Stones, the broken ring of pink stones behind him. It hit him then that he must look like a homeless person. His pants were threadbare, his shirt was torn and had been transformed into an earthly camouflage of dirt and grime, and the soles of his shoes had holes.

He had no money, but if he couldn't contact Fiona he could—

"Marshall?"

He turned to find Mary Pat standing between two tall standing stones.

She had aged considerably since he'd last seen her. The years in the domain plus the years she'd been back in her own time. He recalled her saying she'd been in the dinosaur domain eight years, so her anchor would have taken her back to her origin point eight years before Marshall's. Her hair, which had formally been streaked with gray, had gone full gray, but Marshall still recognized the woman he'd known under the wrinkled skin and liver spots. And her blue eyes—they still radiated strength and vigor.

"How?" was all Marshall could manage.

"Same as you."

"But the asteroid? How did you all survive? Get the settings and set Woodhenge?" Marshall's mind was spinning, the Chaka Stones dancing in his peripheral vision.

"It must have been a shooting star, or a comet, or who the hell knows what," Mary Pat said. "It got bigger then passed us by."

Marshall laughed. "And Kylie?"

"She was still safe in New Holland when I left," Mary Pat said.

That didn't mean she wouldn't come through in the future.

A chill breeze carried over Hicks Dome as the sun arced toward midday.

Mary Pat and Marshall embraced then, and the scent of her perfume drove out the question that was stuck in his throat. "Fiona? Did you check up on her?"

She nodded. "The first time it was a little weird because you were with her... but when you disappeared to the domain, she wouldn't give up searching, and still hasn't. You're listed missing, not pronounced dead. There was no funeral, nothing..."

"That's good, I guess."

Mary Pat had brought a bag of clothes for Marshall, and some money, food, and water. The stuff was in her car and the pair hiked down the side of Hicks Dome in silence. Marshall couldn't keep his gaze from straying toward the woods where he knew a Shokra waited.

As the pair got into Mary Pat's car, she asked, "So what's the plan, Captain?"

Marshall couldn't tell her to take him home because he was no longer certain where home was. He asked, "Does Fiona still live in our old place?"

"She moved to St. Louis to spearhead the search for you," Mary Pat said. "She was at the dome this morning."

Marshall's head jerked back like he'd been punched. "How long have I been gone?"

Mary Pat chuckled. "Just the year."

On the way to the gas station, so Marshall could clean up and get changed, he used Mary Pat's phone to call his wife. Fiona was suspicious, but after Marshall described a particular night in Chicago that only he and his wife knew about, she agreed to meet him in a public place and Terry Park in St. Louis was selected.

Saying goodbye to Mary Pat a second time was much easier. He thanked her profusely, and the duo agreed to get together as soon as Marshall was feeling up to it.

"It's not easy being back here," Mary Pat said as she pulled to the curb. "Call me when you feel yourself getting overwhelmed."

"Like a dinosaur domain sponsor?"

"Yeah, like that."

Mary Pat dropped Marshall up the road from Terry Park. He and Mary Pat had agreed that it was probably best, at least for now, that she not meet Fiona.

As Mary Pat drove off the reality of his situation hit him, and he began to sweat. The noise—car horns, yelling, thumps, bangs, and the constant bitching and complaining of humanity, all circled in his head like a tornado.

What was he going to tell his wife about where he'd been for the last year?

Marshall was no F. Paul Wilson, and the stories he came up with were bad at best. He considered amnesia. He'd hit his head, had just escaped the hospital, and he doesn't remember the hospital's location. Neat, unverifiable, but smelling so strong of bullshit even those with the smallest noses wouldn't buy it.

He considered kidnapping as a cause for his absence but determined that Fiona would never let that go. There would be a police investigation, facts would be gathered, and his story would come out as false which would put him in a worse position than he was currently in.

That left him with the truth or a version of the truth. A version that allowed for a generous sprinkling of bullshit or the strategic leaving out of facts. He decided it was a game-time decision.

Fiona was standing in the park's parking lot, leaning against her car, and chewing on her nails. When she saw him, she took two hesitant steps forward, her hands falling to her sides. Then she rushed toward him, leaped into the air, and threw her arms around him as Marshall caught her.

The couple stood in the parking lot for a long time, holding each other, cars streaming by, the smell of exhaust irritating Marshall's eyes and the back of his throat. His eyes... He was crying.

Marshall didn't remember getting in the car, and his head rang as Fiona told Marshall about how the last year had been for her, how she thought he was dead and gone forever, how she didn't know what to do. Through it all Marshall couldn't hear himself think. The noise of humanity was deafening.

The time had come for Marshall to tell his tale, though Fiona didn't ask. It was one of those questions that didn't need to be voiced. He was wearing new clothes she'd never seen, and though he'd rubbed off much of the grime, his hair was different and the thick lines creasing his face couldn't be ignored. He hadn't been frozen for 365 days. If she noticed the coincidence of him returning one year to the day, she didn't let on.

They went to a restaurant and Marshall ate and ate and ate. Still, Fiona asked nothing of him, and he appreciated that.

After two vodka martinis, a huge bowl of pasta and shrimp, a big dessert, and three cups of coffee, he spilled it. All of it. From the time he wandered to the top of the hill to the moment he found himself hugging her in a parking lot.

Fiona listened in silence, her gaze shifting from her plate to him, tears welling in her eyes.

Marshall saw her struggle to believe as the lines of her face thinned, her eyes narrowed, and her lips twisted. She didn't say it—maybe she couldn't or didn't know it herself, but she didn't believe him.

"Oh, my God," she finally uttered when he was done. "That's unbe—fantastic." She chuckled, but it wasn't a mirthful sound. "Ironic also. The history professor gets to go to the Cretaceous and the paleontologist doesn't."

"You're jealous?" He hadn't seen that one coming.

"No... No... It's just..."

"Hard to believe?"

She said nothing.

Marshall couldn't blame his wife for doubting him. Not at all. He needed to give her time to measure it all out and think about why he would lie. But the question that he kept asking himself clogged his mind. Would he believe if the roles were reversed?

31

Marshall's life only got worse.

Fiona said she believed, but Marshall had to agree, that with no proof—he'd traded away his phone and the Templar ring didn't prove time travel—that a better story needed to be developed. The couple decided that until said story was available and supported, it was best if, at least on paper, Marshall remained lost. He continually got the feeling that she'd expected... hoped even, that some end-game scenario would free her of her guilt, which Marshall felt was the only thing holding their marriage together.

It burned him that underneath it all was the hard fact that Fiona didn't believe his tale, though she never voiced that opinion.

The result was a dull month, during which Fiona went back to work and Marshall stayed in the background, trying to figure out a way to reenter society without being put in an asylum.

Proof. He'd taken pictures for that very reason, but as the days in the domain dragged out it had exited his priority list. Fighting for survival will do that.

He called Mary Pat regularly and he visited the Chaka Stones often.

Two months later Marshall and Fiona were ensconced in a trial separation that was only a trial in the name of the law.

In his search to settle his future, Marshall turned to the past. He checked up on Devon and Anna Hemply, the middle-aged couple from 1979 who had been in the dinosaur domain for seven years. Though Marshall had watched them fail, he hadn't been around to see their second attempt.

Marshall's search for the couple led him to a news article on the internet that described the couple as missing, how there were no leads, and that the pair was last seen at Hicks Dome. There was nothing after that, but as he dug deeper, he discovered a MEME that had percolated through the Internet for years and appeared on several sites and therefore was undeletable, like an immortal thing. The MEME read simply, "Marshall we got back. Thank you. Devon and Anna." That was proof positive that the couple had chosen to leave their old lives behind and start anew. That was easier to do when your partner was on board.

Would Marmaduke be back? Who knew? What he did know was he was going to spend the rest of his life fighting the doldrums with the knowledge that a New Hollander could walk into his life at any moment.

He went for the winter solstice ceremony, and nobody showed. Not surprising. Mar would have gone deep into Marshall's future, and he wondered if the man had been observing him from afar. He doubted it. That might change his precious future.

Marshall saw Fiona less and less as he retreated further away from humanity and life. He hadn't gotten used to the noise, and the daily complication of what to eat and where was more stressful than hiding from a T-rex—O.K., maybe not a T-rex.

It was a cold day in early February when Marshall took the crowded bus to Chicago to meet Mary Pat. She'd found herself a new life, and though she was doing better than Marshall, and had eight years to adjust, every time he spoke to her, he sensed she was lost, just like him.

Lost in a world that was no longer his. He was a dinosaur, and when he finally realized what needed to be done, there was only one person he knew who would understand.

Mary Pat picked him up at the bus station and the pair settled in at a restaurant. They talked of old times in the dinosaur domain and speculated on how the others were doing, but they never strayed close to the question that was at the heart of their difficulties.

"You still wear the ring," Mary Pat said as she sipped wine.

Marshall held out his hand and displayed the Templar ring, the red cross rising from the gold.

Mary Pat's smile ran away from her face as Marshall leaned across the table and took her hands in his.

He'd decided, and whether she agreed or not his path was set. "Mary Pat, we need to go back," Marshall said.

The End

Other Severed Press novels by Edward J. McFadden III: Landfill Lizards, CRICS, Terror Lake, TRAGIC (#1 Amazon Bestseller Tag), Predators & Prey, Wolves of the Sea, Fortune's Cypher, Crimson Falls (#1 Amazon Bestseller Tag), Hell Creek, Barracuda Swarm, The Cryptid Club, Dinosaur Red, Drop Off (#1 Amazon Bestseller Tag), Jurassic Ark, Keepers of the Flame, Throwback, Sea Tremors, Primeval Valley, Shadow of the Abyss (#1 Amazon Bestseller Tag), Awake, and The Breach (#1 Amazon Bestseller Tag, Amazon #1 Hot New Audio Release Tag). His other novels include: Just Beneath the Skin, Terror Peak (#1 Amazon Bestseller Tag), the Theo Ramage Thriller series: Quick Sands, Sandbagged, and Too Much Grit, and Dogs Get Ten Lives, The Black Death of Babylon, and HOAXERS. Ed lives on Long Island with his wife Dawn, their daughter Samantha, and their cats Snoop and Skittles.

Check out other great

Dinosaur Thrillers!

Steve Metcalf

OBJEKT 221

Ruthless multi-national conglomerate Allied Genetics is under siege from a paramilitary force for hire. Allied calls in reinforcements and fortifies their crown-jewel property – an abandoned Soviet military facility in Crimea known during the Cold War as Objekt 221. Fortunately for the future of their research, O221 straddles a stretch of rocky landscape that hides a rift – a portal through time and space. Through this rift, Allied Genetics can travel, at will, to the Cretaceous – 100 million years into Earth's past – and bolster their genetic experiments with dinosaur DNA ... something their competitors want to stop at all costs."Objekt 221" is a story blending numerous science fiction elements such as repurposed military facilities, time travel, rogue corporate armies, dinosaurs and the hint of a super-ancient civilization.

Bestselling collection

PREHISTORIC: A DINOSAUR ANTHOLOGY

PREHISTORIC is an action packed collection of stories featuring terrifying creatures that once ruled the Earth. Lost worlds where T-Rex and Velociraptors still roam and man is now on the menu. Laboratories at the forefront of cloning technology experiment with dinosaurs they do not understand or are able to contain. The deepest parts of the ocean where Megalodon, the largest and most ferocious predator to have ever existed is stalking new prey. Plus many more thrillers filled with extinct prehistoric monsters written by some of the best creature feature authors this side of the Jurassic period.

CHECK OUT OTHER GREAT DINOSAUR BOOKS

PRIMORDIA
by **Greig Beck**

Ben Cartwright, former soldier, home to mourn the loss of his father stumbles upon cryptic letters from the past between the author, Arthur Conan Doyle and his great, great grandfather who vanished while exploring the Amazon jungle in 1908.

Amazingly, these letters lead Ben to believe that his ancestor's expedition was the basis for Doyle's fantastical tale of a lost world inhabited by long extinct creatures. As Ben digs some more he finds clues to the whereabouts of a lost notebook that might contain a map to a place that is home to creatures that would rewrite everything known about history, biology and evolution.

But other parties now know about the notebook, and will do anything to obtain it. For Ben and his friends, it becomes a race against time and against ruthless rivals.

In the remotest corners of Venezuela, along winding river trails known only to lost tribes, and through near impenetrable jungle, Ben and his novice team find a forbidden place more terrifying and dangerous than anything they could ever have imagined.

PANGAEA EXILES
by **Jeff Brackett**

Tried and convicted for his crimes, Sean Barrow is sent into temporal exile—banished to a time so far before recorded history that there is no chance that he, or any other criminal sent back, has any chance of altering history.

Now Sean must find a way to survive more than 200 million years in the past, in a world populated by monstrous creatures that would rend him limb from limb if they got the chance. And that's just his fellow prisoners.

The dinosaurs are almost as bad.

CHECK OUT OTHER GREAT DINOSAUR BOOKS

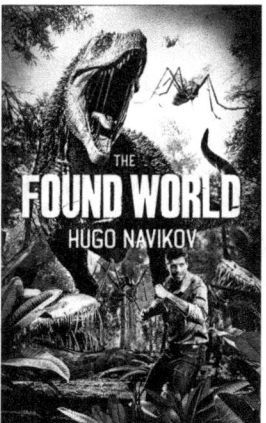

THE FOUND WORLD
by **Hugo Navikov**

A powerful global cabal wants adventurer Brett Russell to retrieve a superweapon stolen by the scientist who built it. To entice him to travel underneath one of the most dangerous volcanoes on Earth to find the scientist, this shadowy organization will pay him the only thing he cares about: information that will allow him to avenge his family's murder.

But before he can get paid, he and his team must enter an underground hellscape of killer plants, giant insects, terrifying dinosaurs, and an army of other predators never previously seen by man.

At the end of this journey awaits a revelation that could alter the fate of mankind ... if they can make it back from this horrifying found world.

HOUSE OF THE GODS
by **Davide Mana**

High above the steamy jungle of the Amazon basin, rise the flat plateaus known as the Tepui, the House of the Gods. Lost worlds of unknown beauty, a naturalistic wonder, each an ecology onto itself, shunned by the local tribes for centuries. The House of the Gods was not made for men.

But now, the crew and passengers of a small charter plane are about to find what was hidden for sixty million years.

Lost on an island in the clouds 10.000 feet above the jungle, surrounded by dinosaurs, hunted by mysterious mercenaries, the survivors of Sligo Air flight 001 will quickly learn the only rule of life on Earth: Extinction.